THE Three Keys

NMc Projects, a unit of A.A.R., Brooklyn, NY

Cover Design: Krystal Tibbs
Editing: Catherine Holecko
Book Design and Typesetting: Enchanted Ink Publishing

The text type was set in EB Garamond

ISBN: 979-8-9906358-3-8 (E-book)
ISBN: 979-8-9906358-2-1 (Paperback)

WWW.NELLOMCDANIEL.COM

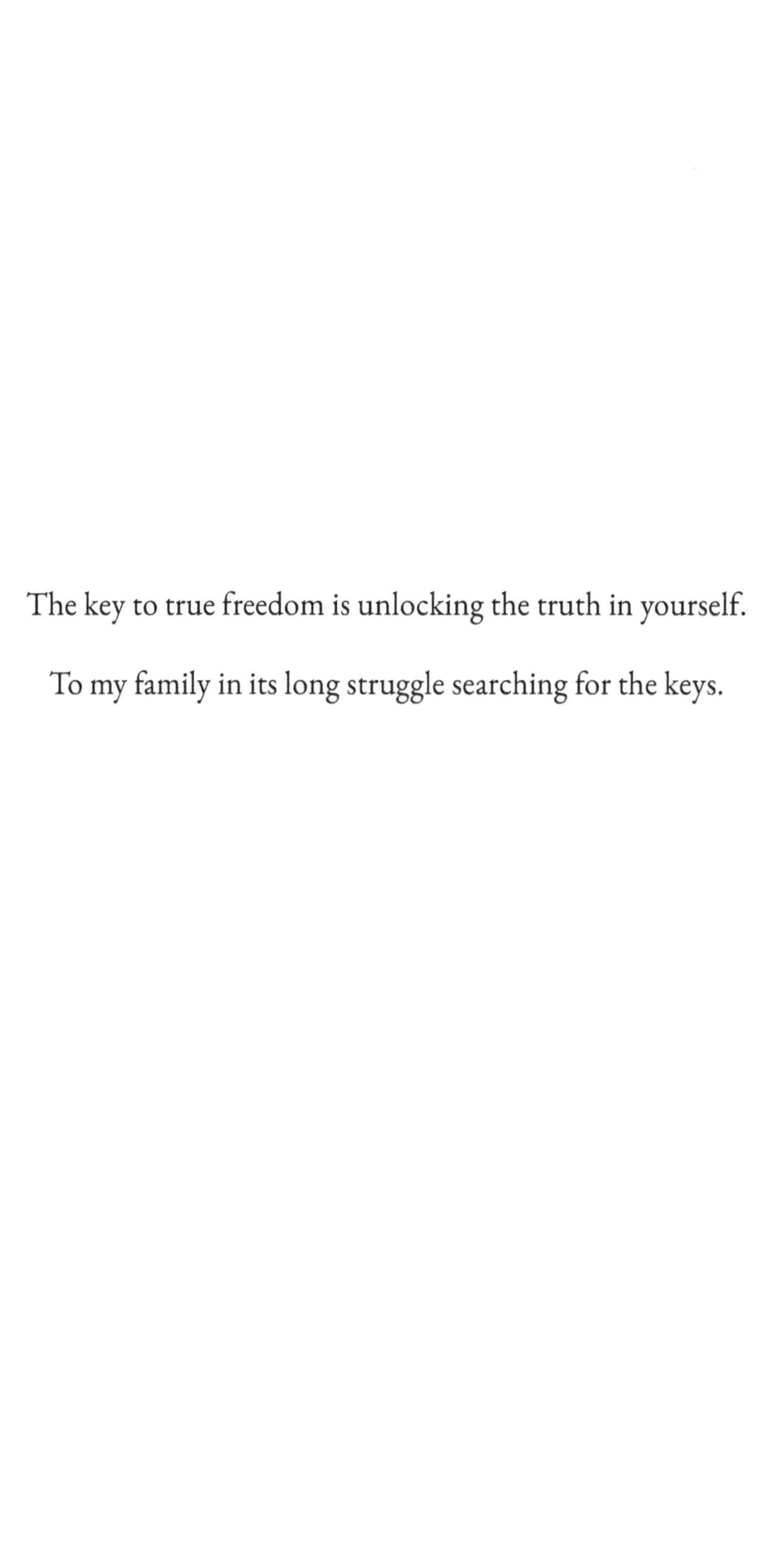

The key to true freedom is unlocking the truth in yourself.

To my family in its long struggle searching for the keys.

THE
Three Keys

Nello McDaniel

*Who would be free themselves must strike the
blow. Better even to die free than to live a slave.*

–Frederick Douglass

*Three things cannot long stay hidden:
the sun, the moon and the truth.*

–Buddha

PROLOGUE

Cloch County, Missouri, September 1856

THE DOGS ARE LOUDER THAN BEFORE AND NOW on both sides. She can feel them closing in. Closer and closer, relentless. Her lungs are aching and her legs shaking as she struggles to get up the sharp incline to the high point. She pulls the tattered blanket the old midwife gave her over the baby's head to protect her from the thicket. She can't stop, not for a second. She has to reach the high point. From there it's down to the river where she can complete her escape. The swaddled infant whimpers. "Shh, don't cry. Please don't cry, we're almost there," she whispers breathlessly. The dogs are so close. She struggles with one foot after the other in the loose dirt. Struggle, dear God, it's all she has ever known.

Luna was warned. Many times, she was warned. It's too soon to leave with so many runaways in the area, they said. Where there are runaways, there are bounty hunters and dogs, not just on the roads but scouring the hillsides and riverways. It's riskier still for a runaway escaping a county slaveholder.

The county police are looking for her too. And running with an infant only days old? Unimaginable. But all she can think about is getting herself and her baby out of Cloch County, out of Missouri, to freedom. She can't go back to that life. And she won't surrender her child to that life. It's the third time Luna has escaped, and she knows what awaits if she's caught again. Now, struggling to get to the high point, she's wishing she had listened to the warnings

Luna was just a child, only twelve years old, when she was torn away from her mother in Arkansas and brought to the Cloch County farm. She was set up in the master's house as a domestic worker. But she was also there for another purpose. The first night in the big house she was raped by the master. And she was raped and sodomized almost every night after that. The mistress worked her in the house with other house slaves from dawn into night, then left her to the cruel pleasures of her husband after that. After two weeks of this torturous existence Luna slipped away while fetching water. And she ran. But she didn't have her bearings and no means of support for such a flight. She was captured by the county police having run less than a mile. Returned to the big house, she was whipped and forced to wear ankle shackles when she worked and slept. The shackles were removed only while she was being raped.

A month shy of a year in the big house, she became pregnant. Her mistress ignored her ever-enlarging belly and the master was likewise oblivious to her condition. He was sodomizing her when her water broke and said nothing to his wife until he finished. The mistress ordered another house slave to take Luna to the midwife in the slave quarters. The midwife helped Luna deliver a small but loud baby girl. Luna received her name because she was born on a night with a full moon. This night there was no moon but many stars. Luna named her baby Starlet.

The morning after Starlet was born, the mistress, her house boy and another slave appeared at the door of the midwife's cabin and ordered Luna to return to the house. Barely outside, the house boy pulled the newborn from Luna's arms while the other held her. He handed Starlet to a woman sitting in a carriage. With Luna screaming for her baby, the carriage pulled away. The mistress had sold Luna's baby to another slaveholder on the other side of the county. Luna would not see Starlet again.

Luna had no time to heal from the birth. There was no respite in her workdays. The master continued to sodomize her. The only concession the mistress made was to allow Luna to work without the shackles. Within a couple of weeks, when she had regained much of her strength, the master came to her bed drunk – so drunk that he passed out before he could molest her. For a second time Luna seized the opportunity to run. This time she had better bearings and she was determined to find Starlet. She ran up the road in the direction that the carriage had taken her newborn. Once again, before she could get more than a couple of miles, a police militia spotted her and returned her to the estate.

Luna was punished again, more severely this time. She was whipped several times and again forced to wear ankle shackles. This time she was also forced to wear a neck shackle with spikes that made it nearly impossible for her to sleep. It kept her in a state of near exhaustion all the time. She wore the ankle and neck shackles for over a year. The estate mistress came to believe that Luna would no longer attempt an escape, given her punishments, so she had the shackles removed. But life remained the same for Luna, both day and night.

She again became pregnant and the cycle of pregnancy and delivery was much as before. In the privacy of the birthing room in the slaves' quarters, the old midwife discreetly shared with Luna some advice for runaways. Luna knew that, like the last time, she would not be allowed to keep her baby. If she wanted to keep and protect her child, she would have to run before the baby could be taken from her. The midwife and two of the other women spirited Luna into a wooded area, where she delivered a second baby girl out of earshot of the estate house. The midwife told the mistress that Luna was experiencing a longer labor and some difficulties. This bought two days for Luna to run and find her way to a temporary safe house.

These safe houses harboring runaway slaves had to be careful as to how long they allowed runaways to stay. Quakers, in particular, became adept at shuttling runaways from place to place and throwing bounty hunters and their dogs off the trail. But that can't go on endlessly. Even so Luna was told by the safe house people to wait. And now, with the bounty hunters and dogs nipping close at her heels, she regrets her impatience. Still the thought of freedom, keeping her baby and protecting her child from her own fate drives her to push harder to get away.

She finally reaches the high point. Her pursuers are closing in on her. She stops and takes the moment on the high point to hold her baby up. "See it? See there, Dawn. You're lookin' at freedom. We made it, baby girl. We're gon' be free."

ONE

Cloch County, Missouri, May 2016

"Yuck, Daddy, it's filthy," Amy grouses easing through the doorway. "And it stinks. We can't live here." She abruptly stops and starts moving backwards. But Lew is right behind and halts the retreat. He stands in place, scanning the room.

"Yeah, well, the old place has been neglected. Nobody has lived here for quite a while. But trust me, sweetie, it'll clean up. There's an old saying: 'The difference between a house and a home is TLC, Tender Loving Care.'"

Amy moves aside, arms crossed holding her stuffed cat. "And a crap sandwich tastes just like peanut butter if you believe in Mr. Peanut."

"Okay, enough of that kind of talk," Lew grumbles. "So what? So we have some cleaning to do. It'll be great, just you and me. We'll do this together. I mean, it's like our own reality show, *The Great Ozarks Survivors Race*. Big-city dad-daughter team takes on the wilds of Missouri. Can they beat the odds and make the old farmhouse their new home? Stay tuned."

"Oh, crap, crap and more crap! Maybe your new home but not mine!" she shrieks. "I have a home, and this isn't it. I want to go home!" She runs out, slamming the screen door behind her and gets back into their twenty-year old Toyota.

Get your belligerent ass back in here this minute . . . ! he screams in his head. That's what his mom would have said before breaking off a small limb from a tree, calling it a switch, and then thrashing his behind. But he knows better. Yelling always backfires. And both of them know he would never actually touch her in anger. He's getting smarter about letting her stew over things when she's like this. She's like a twelve-year-old version of her mother. Instead, Lew stands still and looks up at the ceiling. He shakes his head and talks himself down. *Ye gods, is it this age? Is it missing her mom? Is it ME? Is it possible for me to stop overthinking everything she does?*

Calmer, he refocuses, and again scans the room, left, right and back again. And he admits to himself what he can't admit to Amy: *She's right. The place is a fucking mess.* It smells of stale, musty air mixed with God knows what kind of mildews and molds, not to mention something not long dead. It's impossible distinguishing between the cobwebs and spiderwebs. But whether they ever manage to call it home or not, they have to live here. There's no place else to go now that Lew can't afford the rent on their apartment in St. Louis.

That's his official reason, at least. Unofficially, he can't stand to live in that place any longer. Or in St. Louis at all after Nora, his wife and Amy's mom, was killed in a police car chase. The guy the cops were chasing was going 110 miles per hour when he T-boned Nora's lightweight Prius at an intersection. Cops got their man. Lew lost his wife. She died instantly. For Lew, the shock and loss were also instant. For him it's like the five stages of grief are on a loop in his brain, but never quite arrives at *acceptance.* And Amy hasn't been herself at all.

Not being able to afford the rent is hardly a fiction. Nora was the family breadwinner. Lew lost his job as a writer at the *Globe-Dispatch* newspaper almost a year before she was killed. He tried picking up freelance writing and editing gigs with little success. But then, he enjoyed being a stay-at-home dad, spending time with Amy – maybe a little too much. He scolds himself now for becoming so reliant on Nora's salary alone. Not that it was a big salary. She was an attorney but chose the path of junior associate in the Public Defender's office. They barely managed to pay living expenses each month, especially since Nora was still paying off student loans. The two had very little savings, and her funeral and burial costs took a big bite. Nora's family wanted to pay for everything, but Lew rejected the offer out of hand. The Henderson family never approved of him. He remembers once overhearing Nora's mom telling her that she would be better off as a single parent. How ironic. The Henderson's grew even more hostile after Nora died. There were immediate threats of taking Amy from him since he had no means of support.

Making this move to the Ozarks means a small degree of financial relief, at least for a while. More than that, it's a new beginning, maybe a new life. A quieter and simpler life for him and Amy. New friends, new experiences and new memories to replace painful ones. No threats of being torn apart. But making the move is only half the equation. The challenge now is finding work before his meagre savings is completely gone.

Regardless of how bad it's been for Lew he feels the worst part of Nora's death is the effect he's seen it have on Amy. For the first period of time following her mom's funeral, she seemed in a state of shock. She didn't cry at the funeral or afterwards or speak to him or anyone for more than a week. She gradually became more communicative with Lew, but doesn't smile like before. It seems she doesn't express anything other than anger. She refuses to be around anyone but Lew and is constantly hugging Purry, the stuffed kitten that Lew gave her when she was a toddler. Lew's counting big on the change of surroundings to help Amy find her way back. Whatever it takes, whatever he has to do, he's determined to find a way to protect her. It's bad enough that Amy lost her mom; she's not going to be homeless too.

But for now, he has to figure out how to bring this house back to life. He has only ever been an apartment-dweller and while he knows all about oiling a squeaky door, or tightening a loose screw, he's never dealt with systems like gas, plumbing and electricity in a house. He steps over to the switch panel by the front door and flips a toggle. Nothing. A second one. Again, nothing. *Weird – the woman I talked to at Cloch Electric Co-op two days ago assured me that the power was never turned off. So, if the power's on, then there's either a bunch of light bulbs that need replacing or there's an electrical breaker box to be found somewhere. I'm guessing the breaker box is the place to start.*

When he, Nora and Amy visited here four years ago, they were in the house very little. Or as little as they had to be. Lew remembers the place better from when he visited for a few weeks one summer as a kid. The house and property came to Lew only a few months before Nora's accident, when his Uncle Sheldon died. He figured they would just sell it all. The house isn't worth much, but it sits on about fifty acres, and has a good-sized barn and a teetering tobacco shed too. And property values have risen a lot in Cloch County since the lake and hot springs resort areas were developed in the 1960s and '70s.

This was his mom's family homestead. They called it Free Haven. According to his mom, that was because the family originally homesteaded and got the land free. He didn't know much about the family. His mom talked about them very little. Mostly she described them as a bunch of ignorant hillbillies and Free Haven a place she escaped. To Lew the less his mom shared about the family in the Ozarks, the more he wanted to know, the more he craved a deeper connection to this family.

But for now, he had better figure out how to get productive or he and Amy will be camping out in the car for a night – or longer. Lew knows well what it is to live in a car. He and his mom were forced to do that twice when he was a kid. For that reason he's drawn hard lines that he's determined not to cross. *No daughter of mine will ever be homeless, or hungry. She won't dread her tomorrows because her yesterdays have been so dreadful. She will never experience the kind of dread that I did growing up. I swear this on my life.* But then, he also knows how close he's dancing along the lines he's drawn. Time is not cutting him any slack. Between this house and their dwindling finances, he has a lot to figure out and fast. It's actually a good time for Amy to be sulking in the car. He would rather stumble around trying to figure things out alone and not have his tween daughter observing.

THE HAND-HEWN CEDAR PLANK FRAME HOUSE, JUST a generation up from log cabins, is typical of other houses in the area built in the mid- and late nineteenth century. Lew's Uncle Sheldon lived here his entire life, most of those years alone. He was Lew's mother's last surviving sibling. Sheldon was three years younger than brother Dillard and four years older than Lew's mom, Christy. Sheldon nor his brother ever married or had children, at least as far as Lew knows.

Dillard died in a tractor accident in his forties. Lew's mom was the only sibling to leave home and the county. That makes Lew, the only child of his single mom, the sole remaining member of the family and therefore the obvious heir to Free Haven. He and Nora talked about making a trip to inspect the house and property a couple weeks before she was killed. He assumed they would deal with legal matters and figure out what to do with Free Haven then. Of course, that trip never happened. The place has been sitting unoccupied since Sheldon died.

The house is deceptively large. The living room spans the width of the house. The front door is exactly at center with windows on either side. From the circular driveway in front, it gives the impression of a face: The two windows are eyes, the front door a nose, the porch a mouth and the front stairs a gray beard. The windows on each side of the living room are nearly hidden behind ancient drapes that may predate Gran'mam herself. There's a freestanding wood-burning stove in the corner of the living room, likely the main heat source for most of the house. The dark wood floors, baseboards and yellowed walls would benefit from cleaning and painting. And a good dose of direct sunlight would go a long way toward making the house feel livable.

A double doorway leads from the living room into what Gran'mam called *the middle room*. It was kind of all-purpose, wide as the living room and half as deep. On the left entering the room is an almost vertical staircase leading up to three bedrooms on the second floor. Lew stayed in one of those rooms that summer years ago. Behind the staircase is a bolted door that likely goes to a crawl space or cellar below. Lew's happy to keep that door bolted for the time being. Opposite the staircase wall on the right side of the room is a bank of three windows looking down toward the river. There's a dining table by these windows with three chairs.

Stepping to the center of the middle room, Lew turns and notices that each side of the doorway wall to the living room is lined with bookshelves. The shelves on the left have a couple rows of old encyclopedias, a batch of journals – likely Gran'mam's gardening journals – and a mishmash of other bound books. The shelves on the right are full of small pieces of driftwood no doubt pulled from the banks of the river. He doesn't remember this at all from his childhood. But he does remember running down the stairs and out the front door as fast as he could to get down to the river. There are likely lots of things about this house he never noticed as a twelve-year-old.

At the rear of the middle room on the left side, a door leads into the main bedroom. To the right is the doorway into the kitchen. This Lew remembers well. The bathroom is attached to the back of the house with access from both the kitchen and main bedroom. It was likely built onto the house when indoor plumbing became available. It's a peculiar configuration by modern standards, but at the time, the miracle of indoor plumbing far outstripped any consideration of design aesthetics. As a reminder, the old brick and stone outhouse twenty feet from the back door still stands and is likely still functional. Hopefully he can avoid having to test that out.

The large kitchen has a breakfast nook still awash with late morning sunlight. Standing at the door of the kitchen, Lew remembers eating his Cheerios at the small breakfast table while Gran'mam had her coffee and chain-smoked unfiltered Chesterfield cigarettes. Grandad and the uncles were always out of the house working before Lew got up.

Lew scans the kitchen. *Odds are good the breaker box is in here somewhere. And it should be pretty obvious.* But it's not. *Maybe inside the cabinets above the sink.* He starts opening one after another. *Nope, not there, not that one, nope.* After number five he stops to reassess.

"I'm hungry!"

Lew jumps, turns and sees Amy at the kitchen door. "Whew, you startled me, sweetie. Hungry? Yeah, me too. We still have sandwiches in the car. Just give me a minute. I'm trying to find the breaker box to turn on the electricity. I'm sure it's around here somewhere." He steps to the corner of the room where there's small utility alcove. The hot water heater is in here. He reflexively pulls a dangling light chain in the closet to no effect and quickly reminds himself why. *Sorry Amy had to see that.*

Standing next to the breakfast table and staring out the window, Amy asks, "What's that metal box on the wall outside?"

Lew walks over and bends across the table. "Bingo! Good catch, sweetheart. That might be just what we're looking for."

He goes to the back door, opens it, flips the hook latch up on the screen door and is quickly down the back stairs and around the corner of the house to the partially rusted metal box on the side. He reaches up and pulls the lever on the right side of the box down. He feels a rush of gratification as the ceiling light above Amy's head goes on.

"YES!" he shouts, throwing a fist in the air. "One small step for Amy, one giant leap for our team." Amy shifts Purry from her right arm to her left, rolls her eyes and turns away from the window. Lew mumbles under his breath, "Screw it, a win's a win."

On his way back inside, Lew stops and looks to the opposite side of the back door and spots a large propane tank. *Aha, there's gas! If I can just figure out the water supply and get the gas going, then maybe hot showers and a real meal. That's a lot – but hot damn, maybe I'm on a roll.*

He turns and hops up the back stairs, through the back door and into the kitchen. Stepping into the middle room he stops mid-stride, stunned. Amy has gone into the middle room and is sitting at the bookshelf thumbing through one of the old books. Most stunning is that she has set Purry down by the chair. This is the first time he's seen her awake and not clutching the stuffed cat. This is big. He's tempted to ask what she's reading, but he knows better.

"I'm going to get the sandwiches and chips, sweetie. I assume you're having a root beer as usual?" Silence. "Okay, back in a jif."

After lunch, Lew cleans up using as little of their bottled water as possible. Their need for fresh water outweighs everything else. If worse comes to worst, there's a fresh underground stream that empties into the river not far down the hill from the house. Lew twists the cold handle on the kitchen faucet expecting nothing, and then, "Holy crap, the water is on! We actually have water, Amy! It's a little rusty from lack of use, but it's getting cleaner. I remember now – Uncle Sheldon said that the house water supply comes from a spring-fed well. It's probably that same spring that flows into the river. You know sweetie, it never occurred to me that the water is always on . . ." and turning he realizes he's talking to himself. Amy is back over at the bookshelf with another old book in hand.

With the help of the old *Reader's Digest Do It Yourself* book he got at a yard sale in St. Louis, Lew manages to get the gas tank turned on. He checks for leaks at all the connections with soapy water. He also gets the hot water heater filled and pilot light turned on. The hot water heater, maybe the oldest of the appliances, has a small water leak. But it's functioning for now and they have hot water, something he'll never take for granted again. And the refrigerator works pretty well. Umm, well enough.

Lew turns his attention to cleaning. He needs to stay a step ahead of Amy in finding dead critters. Mostly it's just shriveled field mice. But there is a questionable looking ball of fur upstairs that could have been a small squirrel, a large chipmunk, or a huge furball coughed up by a mountain lion. Fortunately, Amy continues focusing on the bookshelves. Lew sees her beginning to organize, rearrange and actually clean the books. Positive evidence that this may in fact be his natural daughter, not that there was ever any real doubt. Of course, Amy always favored her mom's looks more than Lew's. Except for his eyes and hair color, there's not much else he can lay claim to.

THE MAIN BEDROOM SEEMS THE LOGICAL PLACE FOR Lew to drop his things. The closet is still full of Sheldon's clothes, so he'll just live out of his suitcase for a while. He's not ready to tackle all of Sheldon's stuff and not at all sure what to do with it anyway – and there's a lot. Doesn't look like Sheldon threw anything away.

"Hey Amy, let's go have a look upstairs to see which bedroom you'd prefer. I've got a feeling you'll want the front bedroom. It's the biggest and it gets the most sunlight all day long." As he recalls, that was Uncle Dillard's room the summer he spent here.

"Nope. I like this middle room."

"But sweetie, this is not a bedroom. You'll be much more comfortable in one of the bedrooms, upstairs."

"Okay then, I'll just sleep in the car. That way I'll be ready when we leave this dump and go home. I want to go home."

Without another word, Lew climbs the stairs and begins taking apart the front bedroom bed to move down to the middle room. He drags the dining table across the middle room and pushes it against the side of the staircase. There's room now to set the bed up next to the bank of windows looking down toward the river. It is a nice location. Amy will get morning sunlight and have access to all the books all the time. Those old books. He keeps thinking that he needs to see what's there that she finds so captivating. But for now, it's great to have her focused on something other than leaving.

Lew is feeling pretty good about things. He has, in fact, been on a roll. It's late afternoon and the old house is humming with life. Amy has the bedroom she wants. At least for the last couple hours she hasn't been screaming about going home or locking herself in the car. Amazing how little it takes for a good day. And Lew has to give Sheldon credit. The old house was operating in pretty good shape when he died. The systems all work. The house is dirty, but it's been sitting unoccupied for a while so of course it's dirty. Everything in it is old, but works, so far. Maybe Uncle Sheldon wasn't the dysfunctional old codger Lew thought. He has acquired a new perspective on the old man.

TWO

MID-MAY AND THE FULL FLUSH OF SPRING IS the perfect time to experience Cloch County at its blossoming best. Wildflowers are running wild across the hills and valleys that haven't yet been claimed and leveled by kudzu. The dogwood and redbud trees play off of each other's colors and the light green leaves of the maple and slow-budding red and white oak trees paint splendid backgrounds. The trees are beautiful enough to almost overlook the vast amounts of pollen that they shed.

These mid-May days are warm but not yet sweltering. The nights are cool. The cacophony of bird sounds at pre-dawn is only the slightest indication of how many birds are nesting and warning off all others. What the human ear hears as songbirds singing is in fact nesting birds screaming. *"Warning, stay away! Keep your distance! Leave us alone!"* At first light, the bird battles begin in earnest, the screeching, accosting, chasing, nest violations, the bigger and stronger feeding off the smaller and weaker, bird families torn apart. It plays out every day.

Many believe that Cloch County was named for the rough and rocky terrain gouged out by eons of erosion inflicted on the Ozark Plateau. Cloch is the Gaelic word for *stone* and the first settlers in the area were from Ireland, their first language being Gaelic. That first wave of Irish who settled the area in the early 1800s did in fact name it Cloch County. But the name came from an area in Galway County, Ireland, called Cloch a'Leachta, from which those first settlers came to America. The green hills and rocky terrain of the area no doubt reminded them of their homeland. The second wave of Irish to arrive in the 1850s were from the southwestern part of Ireland that was hardest hit by the potato famine.

From the outset there have been myriad contradictions in the county, both in place and people. The countryside is green and beautiful, but the rolling, rocky terrain and red clay soil is far from ideal for farming. The frigid cold of winter and stifling heat of summer can be nearly unbearable. And while the two waves of Irish shared common heritage, they were as different as winter and summer. The first wave of settlers was Protestant and left Ireland to escape religious conflicts. The second wave was largely Catholic but left Ireland to escape starvation. The first wave embraced the American practice of slavery and indentured servitude. Many of the second wave rejected these practices and some fought actively against them.

The county sits close to the border between Missouri and Arkansas and while it officially aligned with the Union in the Civil War, it holds onto strong Confederate and Southern sensibilities to this day. It was one of the last areas in the state of Missouri to eliminate the sundown laws in its towns and villages. Sundown laws were a common feature of the Jim Crow South that told people of color, especially African-American, to be out of town by sundown or be arrested. It's common knowledge that the county retains an active chapter of the Ku Klux Klan.

Understandably, the cultural and religious differences of the original settlers resulted in years of conflicts in the county that echoed the conflicts in Ireland. These internecine tensions only began to fade when natural hot springs in the hills turned the area into a destination for tourists visiting spas and building vacation homes. The county is also adjacent to the Tablerock Lake area and the Branson entertainment scene. Cloch County quickly became a desirable place to live and vacation for many outside the county. Consequently, new conflicts arose between the deeply invested long-timers and the suddenly entitled new-comers. Desirable places naturally attract desirable people. But such places also have a way of attracting and harboring some shadier characters. Knowing the difference can confound even the most astute.

LEW WAS TWELVE, AMY'S AGE, THE SUMMER HE SPENT at Free Haven with his grandparents. His mom needed surgery and there was no one else to care for him while she convalesced. He remembers this being a lively farm, with chickens roaming the yard, some pigs, a couple dogs and several milk cows. He loved being outside, playing with local kids and spending time on the river that runs alongside the property about fifty yards down from the house. So much of the life of the farm that he remembers revolved around the River Saoirse, which the locals correctly pronounce *Seer-sha*. Visitors pronounce it all kinds of ways except correctly.

When he arrived that summer, his Uncle Dillard took him down to the river first thing. He showed Lew how to skip rocks. He identified the different river denizens, the tadpoles, frogs, crawdads and various minnows. He warned Lew about the snakes to watch for, especially the water moccasins that will sneak up behind you when you're swimming. He explained water currents and depths, warning Lew about the river right after big rainstorms. Lew remembers Uncle Dillard as a big, kind man who always smelled like hay and had a chewing tobacco stain down one or both sides of his mouth. It's sad that he died so young. It was Sheldon who never left home and cared for the farm and his parents until their passing. Back then Lew kept his distance from Uncle Sheldon, who seemed a little strange. He was quiet and reserved and paid little attention to Lew.

THREE YEARS BEFORE SHELDON DIED, LEW AND NORA visited him. He called on them for help with new county taxes assessed on inherited homestead properties. Nora, fresh from passing the Bar, realized that Sheldon was dangerously close to losing the house and property. He had failed for years to file many of the legal documents that he should have when his father died. Nora, no doubt assuming the property would eventually go to Lew and then to Amy, offered to spend extra time sorting out Sheldon's legal matters. This allowed Lew and Amy to return to St. Louis. Grateful for the help, Sheldon paid for her to stay on in the small motel at the edge of town where she'd be close to the county offices. Lew and Nora learned at that time that Sheldon was severely dyslexic and not the family idiot he was thought to be by his relatives.

Amy, then eight years old, likely doesn't remember much from that visit. If anything, she remembers Uncle Sheldon taking her down to the river where they caught small crawdads and big bullfrog tadpoles. He showed her how he puts crawdad tails on his fishing hook for fishing. He caught a flathead catfish, held it up and told Amy that the witch who lived across the river hated cats and turned them into fish. Amy loved cats and started to cry. She clutched her stuffed cat Purry to her chest and sobbed. Lew was on his way to Amy when Sheldon dropped the catfish in the water, fell to his knees and hugged the distraught child, saying he was sorry and just teasing.

"Please don't cry. I was teasing you. Catfish are fish, not cats. It's okay, it's okay," he pleaded. Sheldon was crying just as loud as Amy was. Lew started to intervene, but saw Amy returning Sheldon's hug. She was fine. That was the first time Lew saw a different side, a very sensitive side, of his Uncle Sheldon.

That trip was Amy's first outdoor fish-fry with what Lew and Sheldon caught. It was quite the adventure for her. For Lew and Nora it was a way to not deal with Sheldon's kitchen. He realizes that he made a lot of unfair assumptions about Uncle Sheldon and how he lived. Memories and revelations aside, living here is going to be a whole new set of realities and challenges for him and Amy.

Much of Lew's memory of that trip to Free Haven is how Nora stepped up to deal with Uncle Sheldon's problems, freeing him to focus on his exciting new job at the *Globe-Dispatch*. He had spent the previous six years working in communications in a corporate office, writing copy denying responsibility for the chemical disasters the corporation was in fact responsible for worldwide. Keeping the family afloat while Nora got through law school just barely offset Lew's self-loathing as he helped to deny and cover up the giant corporation's countless crimes. The new job as reporter at the *Globe* would not only help expunge his conscience but put him back on track with his original ambition to be an investigative journalist.

It felt like everything was finally coming together for him and Nora after a number of rough patches. She was clearly demonstrating her love and gratitude by helping with Sheldon's issues and allowing Lew to return home to the new job. Lew believed that this is the way marriages and families should work.

He didn't have much of a role model for marriage and family. His mom had never married. Christy doted on him and made the best home she could, but it always felt incomplete, especially when he visited friends' homes with two parents and siblings. He created an inflated sense of what he called *life-normal* in his mind. He was thinking of that when he met Nora in the diner where they both worked during college. She was a great waitress and especially good with families. He was taken with her simple beauty, freckled nose, long legs and lithe figure. He was drawn to her even more by the way she related to kids and they to her. He could see in her the very essence of *life-normal.*

Nora, on the other hand, didn't really notice Lew any more than the other guys in the diner. He was nice, a little taller than her by an inch or so. She was self-conscious about being taller than most guys she dated. The first time she really noticed Lew was the night the diner was robbed. They had closed for the night and the staff was cleaning up when a guy with a scarf covering his face walked in and produced a gun. He ordered the staff to get on the floor, then confronted Donna, the cashier. He told her to empty the cash register's contents into a bag. Lew was hauling trash out to the curb and saw what was happening inside. He quietly slipped back in and while the robber was stuffing cash into his bag, Lew grabbed the scarf from behind, jerking the man back while kicking the back of his knees. The crook fell hard on the floor. Lew stomped the hand holding the gun, knocking it away. He fell on the guy and put him in an armlock he had learned on the wrestling squad. By then, the cook jumped over the counter, picked the gun up off the floor, and helped Lew hold the robber until the cops arrived.

Lew was proclaimed a hero and made employee of the month. Nora suddenly noticed his soft good looks that recalled a young Harrison Ford. She made note of his shy smile, electric blue eyes, sandy blonde hair and long athletic body. She invited him to a campus party the next week and the two didn't look back. They moved in together a month after graduation. Soon after that, Nora was accepted into the Washington University Law School. They agreed that

Lew would work and support them while she focused on law school. Lew raised the matter of getting married, but Nora said it was unnecessary. "A marriage license doesn't mean we love each other any more than we do," she'd say whenever he brought it up.

Then Amy arrived. She wasn't part of the plan, but both were thrilled when she came into their lives. It meant a longer haul through law school for both Nora and Lew, but that's what families do.

A VICIOUS TERRITORIAL BATTLE BETWEEN A CROW and a blue jay erupts outside Lew's bedroom window, bringing him out of a deep sleep. In his sleep-state it sounds like another screaming match between the lesbians who lived in the apartment across the hall in St. Louis. He checks his phone. *Sheesh, 7:30? How the hell did that happen?* He's usually awake by 6:30, or sometimes earlier. It's hardly surprising. Yesterday was a long day. A good day, but physically and mentally exhausting. He sees that Amy is still sleeping soundly. He gets dressed and slips out the back door as quietly as possible. He's eager to go down to check out the river.

The river Saoirse is much as Lew remembers from their last visit. As a twelve-year old, the river seemed vast. Swimming across it was daunting until he got used to the constantly changing currents and eddies coming off the rocks upstream where Bymer Spring infuses the river with cool water. The local kids he played with then weren't intimidated at all by the river. Watching them boosted his confidence about diving in and taking his chances, even though he wasn't the swimmer the others were. But it didn't take him long.

Lew has always had a trim, athletic body. But he didn't swim or participate much in sports as a kid because he and his mom had to move around so much. While he had natural athletic ability, he lacked the finesse that comes from repeatedly playing sports with friends. Still, he was a quick study and always managed to catch up.

There's something about the cool spring water mixing with the tepid river water of spring and summer that keeps this part of the river crystal clear. From the bank, the river bottom appears magnified and the water only inches high when in fact it's five, six or more feet deep. Such deception can be dangerous unless you know how to read the water and river flow. Lew learned from his Uncle Dillard how to estimate the rate of drop-off by watching fish cruise along the sides searching for food. When bass, in particular, snag an unsuspecting crawdad or a tasty insect, they retreat into deeper water. You can discern water depths by how the fish appears to shrink as it dives down.

The big sycamore tree on the bank where the local kids suspended a rope and tire to swing out into the water is still there. Once settled in, he'll have to rig up a new rope and tire for Amy to swing on. And he may have to take a few swings into the water himself, just to make sure it works right.

Walking back up to the house, Lew is struck by something he didn't notice at all yesterday. Gran'mam's garden between the outhouse and tobacco shed that Sheldon kept up after she died is as lush and thriving as ever, and with all Gran'mam's favorites. The lettuces, cucumbers, radishes, green onions, zucchini, green beans and snap peas seem to be lined up in their proper rows, growing and beautiful. The row of corn on the back side is May-correct, about a foot high. Even the tomato plants have been staked and are set with small promising blossoms. The only thing missing are the rows of tobacco that supplied the men of the family with their smokeless chew.

Uncle Sheldon's been gone for more than a year, Lew's thinking. *Gardens don't voluntarily spring up like this. Someone has planted and tended this garden carefully and with knowledge of what goes where. Someone practically channeling Gran'mam herself.* He figures that sooner or later someone or something will account for how this garden is here. For now, it's a Godsend, considering their tight budget. *This being our property, if it's growing here, then it must belong to us, at least to share. For now, a nice green salad and some spring peas are going to look mighty nice on the table.*

STEPPING THROUGH THE BACK DOOR, LEW SEES AMY at the kitchen table, Purry on her lap. She has one of the old books open and slightly propped on the table. She doesn't look up.

"Good morning, sweetie. Good night's sleep?" Silence. "How about a little breakfast? I uncovered a toaster, so we can have your fave, toast with peanut butter and banana."

More silence. "Well then, how about banana, peanut butter and toast?" Silence still. Then he says in a high-pitched voice, "Why yes, thank you Daddy, and what will you have?"

Without looking up from the book, "Sorry, your sarcasm sucks."

"Well as they say in show-biz, a bad notice is better than no notice," he quips, plopping a couple slices of bread into the toaster.

"I hope you don't plan to audition," she says, without altering her gaze on the book. "Where've you been?"

He puts a pot of water on to boil for his instant coffee. "Down to the river. It's beautiful this time of morning. When I was your age, I'd go for a swim first thing in the morning. Before breakfast even. You're going to love the river Saoirse, Amy." He puts her breakfast drink, half root beer, half milk, in front of her. But she sits back in her chair, hugs Purry with both arms and stares out the window. He spreads two slices of toast with peanut butter, then chops up a banana between them. He places one in front of Amy next to her untouched drink and sits down with his toast and coffee. Sipping his coffee, he's bewildered. *How can she be here, so present one minute, and then gone the next? Gone somewhere.*

Amy has still said nothing about losing her mom or for that matter even spoken of her. But then they've been so consumed with adjusting and surviving her absence that they've talked very little about the loss. Lew was so shocked by Nora's death that he wasn't nearly as present or available to Amy as he should have been. He feels the weight of responsibility for the way she retreats into herself. Amy and Nora were close and shared things that moms and daughters keep to themselves. He's conscious about not pressing Amy to express her feelings until she's ready. He especially wants to make sure she's not made to feel she has to be there for him as he continues to grieve.

He knows that at some point, when she's hungry, she'll eat. In the meantime, he wants to flip through the phone book he found in the living room yesterday. It's several years old but there are still some names and numbers that might help finding work. He can't go long without some source of income and he's a stranger in town, at least for now. He'd prefer getting a job writing and editing. There's a weekly newspaper published here that he has to check out at some point. But the best first shot may be teaching English or writing in the schools on some level. Picking up substitute work would be a good start.

He comes across a listing for the Cloch County School District and the superintendent's office. *Might as well start at the top.* He dials the number and a woman answers. "Dr. O'Fallon's office, how may I help you?"

"Yes, hello. May I speak with Dr. O'Fallon, please? This is Lew Harra."

"Is Dr. O'Fallon expecting your call?"

"No, no he's not. My daughter and I just moved to the area and I wanted to talk to the superintendent about a possible teaching job."

There's a pause, and then: "I'm sorry, Mr. Lewarra, but there's only a week of school left this semester. The School District isn't hiring any new faculty now."

"I – I - I realize that," Lew stammers, "and that's Harra, Lew Harra. I was actually wondering about summer school, and the fall?"

"I'm sure we have our full complement of teachers for summer classes, Mr. Harris. You'll have to call back later about the fall. Thank you."

"I'd still to like to arrange an appointment with the superintendent to introduce myself."

"I'm sorry, Mr. Harris, the superintendent is very busy with graduation and end of year business. Call back later, in a couple weeks." She hangs up.

Wow, this is going to be a harder than I thought. He turns back to the phone book to see if there are any private schools in the area. The only one appears to be a Christian school affiliated with the Christian college in the next county. That can wait until he's a little more desperate.

He walks back through the middle room toward the kitchen. Out the window he sees Amy, Purry in the crook of her right arm, going down toward the river. It doesn't look like she touched much of her breakfast. But a walk to the river could help him clear his head.

Amy is at the edge of the river, looking down at the water. Lew walks up beside and bends over and picks up a couple of flat rocks.

"Do you remember me showing you how to skip stones when we were here before?" He sidearms the first stone upstream. It tilts left, hits the water, drops and sinks. "Okay, I'm a little out of practice." He flicks the second stone and gets a better result; the stone skims the surface three, four, five, six times. "Yup, still got it."

"I heard your call," she says. "What if you can't get a job? What if there is nothing you can do here?"

Lew's heart sinks. This is the last thing he wants. He spent most of his childhood worrying about his mom's work and fearing that they'd have to live in the car again. Or someplace worse. He knows now that living in fear is far worse than living in a car or a homeless shelter. You can eventually get out of those places. But fear and dread lives in you for a lifetime.

"I'm sorry you heard that. I should have known better than calling a school system this time of year. It'll be different later on. And there are lots of jobs I can get. I'm just getting started. I don't want you worrying about this. We're going to be fine." He reaches out to hug her.

Clutching Purry to her chest with both hands she pulls away. "I want to go home." She turns and starts heading up again toward the house.

Lew drops his arms to his sides watching her go, shaking his head. *Dear God, how close she can seem at times. And then so distant. What's it going to take to find that closeness we had before . . . before.*

BACK IN THE HOUSE, LEW IS DETERMINED TO DO SOME deep cleaning of the oven and refrigerator. Both appliances work, but he'll feel a lot better using them after confronting the crud. While he's working on the stove, he asks Amy to sort through some of the old linens in the utility closet for sheets and towels they can use. He's delighted that she's actually sorting some things as he asked. It's good to see her involved in something besides those old books or staring into space.

Lew is sitting backwards on the floor, reaching his gloved hand inside the oven, trying to avoid sticking his head in to confront who knows what when he sees Amy step up with a fishing rod in each hand.

"Look here, Daddy. There's all of this fishing stuff. What do we do with this?" Lew looks up and sees Amy holding the fishing rods. There is almost a slight smile on her face. Dear God, how he wants to see her smile. It hits him hard looking up, remembering that Amy has Nora's beautiful smile – when she smiles. There's no question that she's going to be tall and slender and, yes, beautiful like her mom.

Before he starts sobbing, Lew sets the sponge and steel wool aside and gets up. "I'll tell you what we do with fishing poles. We go fishing. And you know what, fresh fish for dinner would be a treat."

He's amazed that the River Saoirse hasn't changed over the years. Many of the local rivers and streams in Cloch County were diverted, reduced to trickles or simply subsumed into the lakes. Water rights have been a major source of conflict in the county since the Army Corps of Engineers began constructing the lakes. A number of farms were put out of business due to loss of water for farming and cattle. Others were taken over by eminent domain and are resting at the bottom of the lakes. Lew is well aware how lucky they are to have this river fairly untouched. And still clean enough for fishing and swimming.

The river is teeming with fish, mostly perch and blue gill, but also bass, crappie, carp, catfish and seasonal transient trout. Finding bait is no problem. Turning over a single shovel of black dirt on the bank yields a dozen or more nightcrawler worms. And rocks at the side of the river hide plenty of crawdads. Lew sets hooks and sinkers on each of their two poles. He overturns some rocks and traps a couple crawdads attempting backward escape. This is the technique he learned from Uncle Dillard years ago. Some things never change. He carefully baits the first pole and casts out about halfway across the river. He hands the pole to Amy,

"When you feel a tug on the fishing line, that's a fish. Just pull up on your pole and hook it and reel it in." Amy proves a worthy student and snags a sun perch on this first cast before Lew can even get a hook in the water. He's exuberant helping her bring it in. Removing the fishhook while Amy holds the fish, "Great job, sweetie! A few more of these and we've got a fine dinner."

Amy holds the small fish in both hands and looks up. Her eyes big as silver dollars. "No, NO! We can't eat her. She's too pretty." She flings the perch back into the water and runs up the bank toward the house. Lew starts to yell, but again catches himself. He remembers how sensitive she can be. *Damn, damn, DAMN!* he screams in his head. *Nora would have known better. And she'd know what to do now, dammit!* Looking up and throwing his arms out wide, "A little help from up there would be appreciated!"

He takes a deep breath, then another, calming himself. *Stupid, fucking stupid! Two steps forward and two steps back – again.* He turns back and looking down at the fishing poles, "Oh, and don't forget Lew-boy, you still have to figure out dinner – and no pretty fish."

Lew can't help feeling guilty for harvesting from a garden he had nothing to do with planting. But thank God for it. Until he comes up with a plan for how to put more food on the table without further alienating his daughter, they have to rely on fresh vegetables from the garden. Maybe if he can get to the river early enough in the morning and catch a dinner's worth of fish, he can clean them and have them stashed in the fridge ready for the evening's dinner before Amy is awake. That way she doesn't have to see the *pretty fish* any more than she did when they had fish for dinner in St Louis.

THREE

EW SETS HIS PHONE ALARM FOR RIGHT ABOUT
sunrise. He has his fishing gear set up by the back
door so he can quietly slip out while Amy sleeps.
The alarm goes off and he quickly taps it off, jumps
into his clothes, and in less than three minutes he's stepping
out into the cool morning air. He steps stealthily to the end
of the house and rounding the corner, "Aaarrghhh!" He's
face to face with someone. An attractive Black woman someone, as startled as he is. And a small black and white dog, who
starts barking at him. The woman steps back. "Hush, Bibi,"
she says. The dog looks up at her and then back at Lew but
stays on guard.

"Who are you?" Lew huffs.

Her hand on her chest, the woman exhales, "You scared
me, Mr. O'Hara. I didn't expect to see you up so early." She's
holding a garden hoe in her other hand.

Lew stammers, "Well, I, uh, I was going fishing and ...

hey, wait. How do you know me? But first, who are you and what are you doing here?"

She smiles, wipes her hand on her coveralls and extends it. "I'm Jewel Bennett, and this is my pup, Bibi. It's my day to tend the garden. Actually, I have three days, Mondays, Wednesdays and Saturdays," she says, matter-of-fact-like.

He grasps her hand and returning the smile, "I'm Lew, but it's Harra. Lew Harra. So, you're the secret gardener?"

She smiles. "Hell, there's no secret. It's just that Jeff and I both do the gardening early so we can go to work. You come out here any morning except Sunday around this time and you'll see us. Jeff is my nephew and your neighbor across the road down there. You'll have to meet him sometime."

"Yeah, I do," Lew says. "Say, can I go make some coffee and maybe we can talk?"

She steps to the side. "Sorry, but I really need to weed the green beans so I can get to work. But I'll try to drop by later, after work, if that's okay."

"Yeah, of course," Lew says. "That's great. Can I help you with the weeding?"

She laughs. "That's okay, it looks like you've got a date with a catfish. I'll see you later."

CONSIDERING THE AMOUNT OF TIME HE SPENDS OVER meals and meetings, usually one and the same, the presiding Commissioner of Cloch County, Davis Oakes, considers O'Byrne's Diner his unofficial office. Knowing this, the

O'Byrne family reserves Davis' favorite table in the corner window where he can sit and be seen without having to see anyone. He often dines with other county officials and sometimes business colleagues. Besides his commissioner position, he and his brother run a sod and topsoil business.

His most frequent luncheon date is June Eastman, an attractive widow who runs a chain of cabin rentals around the lake and a fast-growing real estate business. The two have been keeping company for several years, beginning shortly after her husband's fatal boating accident. There are still those in the area who mention Don Eastman's boating accident with air quotes, often followed by a snide comment about June. Don was a beloved local boy. June is neither beloved nor local. And the feelings are mutual. Davis and June usually dine alone, but today she's bringing someone to meet Davis. She mentions this in a text less than an hour before showing up.

June flings the diner door open, making her usual grand entrance, seeing and acknowledging no one except Davis at his usual spot. She waves at Davis as though he can't see or hear her black pumps quick-thumping the hard wood floor, announcing her approach. He could be blind and still know that June has arrived by the blast of White Shoulders perfume advancing her by three table lengths.

"Davis darlin', can we sit at that table back there, just this once?" she asks, but isn't really asking as she quickly pivots to the back of the diner. The tall, elegantly dressed man who followed her in continues following her to the back table. Davis stands and motions to the waitress that he and they are moving to the back.

June abruptly stops at the table and with a quick about-face presents her guest. "Davis Oakes, it gives me great pleasure to introduce Mr. Peter Umanoff, of Firebird Enterprises. Peter's company is going to change everything in this county and make us rich in the process."

Davis raises his eyebrows and extends his hand. "Well, nice ta meetcha, Peter. June has told me so little about you." Davis and June laugh nervously. Peter just scans the room. He stands about six-three, maybe six-four, and has a well-manicured two-day growth of beard, a short-sculpted haircut, penetrating dark blue eyes and flaring nostrils. He's wearing a black shirt with white vertical stripes under a black suit with black shoes so shiny they could pass for patent leather. It's obvious that Peter is not from these parts. And he is quite a contrast to Davis, who stands five-eight on a tall day and carries a slight paunch that hides the top half of the belt holding up his khaki slacks. Peter's long fingers practically wrap half again around Davis' pudgy hand.

"How do you do, Davis Oakes," Peter says, looking above Davis' head at one of the many old photos of O'Byrne's Diner that encircles the room. As the three sit the waitress approaches the table, water and menus in hand. They pause to view the menus. Eileen, the waitress, normally delivers the menus, then rushes away to help other customers. But today she stays put, staring at Peter, pad and pen in hand awaiting orders. June quickly orders her usual Cobb salad and Davis his usual burger, fries and Bud Lite. Peter glares at the menu, tilting it right and left like something logical will fall out of it.

Davis leans forward. "I highly recommend the burgers. Local beef, high quality."

Peter looks up and nods to the waitress. "I'll have the same as Davis Oakes, and a double shot of vodka with the beer." Davis and June look at each other. With wide eyes, Eileen retrieves the menus and hurries off.

June leans in, speaking in a loud whisper. "Davis, I want you to know that Peter and I have had a number of telephone conversations the last couple weeks. He is a partner in Firebird Enterprises, which is an international venture capital group. They develop luxury resorts and casinos around the world." She smiles, tilting her head toward Peter, trying to signal that he should make his pitch. Peter sits quietly with his hands resting on the table, still scanning the room warily. Davis now notices that he has clear polished fingernails.

"Peter," June presses, "tell Davis what you told me about your group. And your interest in Cloch County. It's very exciting."

Peter nods and looks at Davis. "Yes, yes, yes. We build hotels and casinos. For serious gamblers, you know." He continues describing several hotel sites in the U.S., Europe and Asia. Davis is trying to pick up his accent. It's kind of Eastern European, but not really.

Davis nods until Peter finishes. "Interesting, very interesting. So, Peter, where's your home office?"

"Brooklyn, New York. We have a European office in Budapest."

Davis nods. "And where are you from originally?"

Peter looks a little puzzled and responds, "Brooklyn. Brooklyn, New York City."

Davis has no way of knowing, but that accounts for the accent. Waves of Russian immigrants settled in Brooklyn as early as the late eighteenth century. With every political eruption in Russia comes a new wave of immigrants. The neighborhoods of Brighton Beach, also known as Little Odessa, and Sheepshead Bay are almost entirely made up of Russian descendants and expats. Even those four or five generations deep, like Peter, still speak in what they call a Runglish accent. And the Russian Mafia tucked within this small Brooklyn enclave became the most powerful and brutal in New York City the day John Gotti was arrested and the Italian Mafia splintered. A lot of Russian oligarchs commune openly and freely with the Brooklyn mafia. But Davis is less concerned with Peter's strange accent than why he and his group are interested in Cloch County.

"Your company and operation sounds impressive Peter," Davis says. "You're talking about some places I'd like to visit sometime. But none of that sounds a thing like our little village and county."

Peter sits up and leans forward, "It's a good location, Davis Oakes. Low costs. Cheap labor. It's like Croatia was after the war."

"Yeah, lot's changed over there after WWII," Davis says. Peter glances at June.

"Peter's talking about that other war, Davis. You know, the one in the nineties."

Davis purses his lips, "Oh, oh yeah, that one. Ahem, I guess the real question I have is whether there's enough here to attract serious gamblers from away, because they sure don't live anywhere close by."

The food arrives and June picks up the thread. "Peter's group deals in big projects, Davis. Projects that attract the attention of a lot people around the world. Firebird Enterprises knows all about bringing the big gamblers to their casinos. From what Peter tells me, they need about fifty acres of land, with access to the highway closest to the airport. They are also looking for a natural stream or river source for the water features that are trademarks of their resort designs."

June is working hard, but Peter is simply into his burger. "This local beef, ex'lent. Terrific burga'. I mean Shake Shack's got nothin' on this place." Peter takes a last bite. "You know, with this burga', this place would make a killin' in Brooklyn. I mean people would be lined up to Times Square."

June smiles stoically, frustrated that she's doing all the heavy lifting. She takes the opportunity of Peter downing the last of his beer to ask: "So, Davis, does that description sound like any place we know in the area?"

Davis gives June a skeptical look. "Yeah, maybe. But I think I need more information and time to think about this." He turns to Peter. "Has your group developed a prospectus or development schematic for this project?"

Peter is wiping grease from his fingers. "You want it, I'll get it for ya. Where's that waitress? I need another burga'."

Lew's been dreading having to deal with the legal transfer of the Free Haven property. But having settled into the house, knowing now who's tending the garden and actually putting the fish he catches on the table, he's feeling good about a lot. For the first time, it seems like he and Amy can actually live and function here. Still, this meeting with the county recorder to confirm ownership isn't his concern as much as finding out what the property tax situation is. When Sheldon asked Lew and Nora for help, Lew gladly turned the whole matter over to Nora the attorney and left her to deal with it. He's sorry now that he didn't pay more attention to how Nora was helping Sheldon.

Stepping into the County Recording Office, he's surprised to find that County Recorder Pat O'Neill is a woman. Over the phone, her three-pack-a-day smoking voice sounds distinctly male. Her weathered face has lost any trace of gender distinction. He doesn't let on.

"Hi, I'm Lew Harra. I'm here to record my name on the title to the family home, RFD 22, off Old County Highway."

Pat crushes a cigarette out in her twelve-inch diameter ashtray that carries about a half century and quarter inch of caked ash on the bottom. "Yeah, I know the place," she says, smoke streams punctuating each word out of her mouth. "Is that old house still standing, *kawhauff*?" she cough-asks, taking out another Benson & Hedges Menthol and lighting it as she looks down at her ancient Olympic typewriter.

"Yeah, the barn and tobacco shed too," Lew replies. "Worse for the years, maybe, but still standing."

Pat coughs again into her typewriter. "Well, good thing. Because in this county, original homesteads without permanent, operating structures and in arrears on taxes are foreclosed on and revert to county ownership. You might keep that in mind. Have a seat, Mr. O'Hara."

Lew pulls a chair up to the desk. "That's Harra, Ms. O'Neill, Lew Harra."

"Let me write that down," she says. "L-O-U-I-S .... "

Lew interrupts, "Uh, no ma'am. It's L-E-W, short for Lewellyn."

"*Kawhauffff.* What the hell, L-E-W, is fine." She thumbs through a few pages. "You're family, aren't you, Mr. Harra?"

"Yes, Sheldon was my uncle."

"*Kawhauff.* So, there's a name change through marriage?"

Lew is perplexed. "Well, no, not exactly. I mean, Harra is my family's name. As far as I know it always has been."

She flips through more papers. "Not according to the original documents filed by Hugh O'Hara in 1851."

She hands Lew the file. He flips through the yellowed pages in the file. "Yeah, it seems an 'O' was dropped and an 'R' picked up somewhere along the line. But where, and why?"

"*Kawhauff,* you'll have to figure that out elsewhere. The original filing is O'Hara and the property has been transferred through the family, all are named O'Hara." She hands him another file and coughs. "Allergies," She says. "Here's the property schematic from when Hugh O'Hara filed for homestead ownership."

Lew carefully reviews the pages in the file. It appears the house was built by Hugh O'Hara and his two sons. Hugh must have been his great-great-grandfather. Hugh and his wife Claire and their sons arrived in this area with a group of Irish immigrants in 1851 seeking land to homestead. More than likely, they were part of the wave of Irish escaping Ireland during the potato famine. This hilly, rock-strewn area of the Ozarks was one of the last remaining areas in Missouri where there was actual land to be legally claimed through homesteading. There was constant conflict with other long-time settlers in the area who didn't recognize the Homestead Act and saw it infringing on open lands. And since the Missouri Compromise in 1820, the region had been a roiling stew of personal interests and conflicting political alignments. A steady influx of abolitionists moved north into southern Missouri. They believed themselves more entitled to available land than immigrants of any kind. Consequently, the O'Hara house was situated defensively, just above flood level with the River Saoirse on one side and a rocky, vertical hill on the other side. The house faced out on the hollow, making it relatively easy to defend. The quarter-mile dirt driveway to the main house from the county road allowed a good opportunity to see who was approaching before they arrived in front of the house.

Lew looks up at Pat O'Neill. "So the property has passed all these years from one generation of O'Hara's to the next?" He wonders, *Why didn't Nora mention this difference in names which she had to know from helping Sheldon with the tax situation?*

She continues flipping through the files. "Seems so, there's nothing new or changed really, not until ..." She picks up another file. "...Three years ago, when the homestead tax law went into effect."

Lew nods. "Yeah, my wife helped Uncle Sheldon resolve that matter and get his name officially affixed as owner under the new law."

"Not quite," Pat says. "The tax matter was resolved, but Sheldon O'Hara's name was replaced on the title."

Lew sits up. "What? If not Sheldon, whose name is it?" Pat hands him another file opened to the title. It reads: "Nora Henderson"

L EW'S HEAD IS SPINNING ON HIS WAY BACK TO FREE Haven. *Why would Nora put the property in her name? More importantly, why didn't she mention such an critical detail about my own family's property?* More than anything, Lew is pissed at his own negligence, for not paying attention to what Nora was doing with the taxes and, clearly, what she was doing with the property. He completely, blindingly trusted Nora, believing he was in the loop about everything. That nothing was hidden. None of this makes sense.

He's deep in thought as he pulls up the drive behind a Dodge Caravan. He sees Amy sitting on the front steps, clutching Purry, as usual, and an attractive Black woman is weeding the small iris garden on the side of the house. As Lew starts walking toward the house, Bibi the dog comes running around the old brick and stone well toward him, barking like she did early this morning. Amy quickly stands, holding Purry like she's protecting a real cat, and runs into the house. The woman looks up at Lew and starts up the incline. "Bibi, stop! Come here, girl." And like this morning, Bibi stops and turns to look at Jewel.

Lew gets out of his head for the moment. "Jewel, hi! I forgot that you were going to come by." Concerned about Amy, "Can you give me minute? I need to check on something inside. I'll be right back." He finds Amy on her bed, clutching Purry to her chest. "Are you okay, sweetie?"

Amy stares straight up to the ceiling. "That dog scared Purry. She's upset and I have to calm her."

Obviously, it's Amy who's upset, about something. "Okay, just relax and stay put. I'm going to talk to Miss Jewel outside and I'll come back in when she leaves. I won't be long." It seems to Lew that every time Amy might be making progress, some stupid thing like the dog barking sets her back.

He hops into the kitchen and pours a couple glasses of iced tea and heads back outside. Jewel is sitting in one of the metal lawn chairs facing the river. Bibi is lying next to her. Before Bibi can bark, Jewel puts a hand on the pup's head. Lew hands Jewel an iced tea and sits. "I hope you like sun-brewed iced tea."

Jewel smiles. "Oh, I like all kinds of iced tea, thanks."

Lew smiles sheepishly. "Sorry I didn't recognize you at first. I mean you look really different than in the early morning light."

Jewel laughs. "Yeah, well, the overalls aren't quite appropriate for the history museum. I'm the director and curator there. Oh, and the only employee. But I guess in some ways the overalls might fit right in, given the farming history in these parts."

Lew is struck by how young and pretty Jewel is. And that's not just due to her changing out of overalls. She's a striking woman, mid-thirties like Lew, maybe younger. But she has a beautiful smile that cues big dimples and eyes that smile as well. Her perfect cornrow braids were tucked up under her straw hat before. The light green dress she's wearing reveals long, shapely legs. It's the first time he's felt a spark of attraction to a woman since . . . well, in a while.

Lew sits back, watching Jewel rub Bibi's black ear, then the black ear with a white patch. "Bibi's a pretty dog, is she a rescue?"

"Well, in a way. A couple years ago, during a time when I was feeling awfully down, I walked out onto our front porch one morning and here was this puppy. She was curled up asleep on my favorite chair. She looked up at me with those big blue eyes as if to say, 'I'm here, let's have fun.' So yeah, she rescued me." Bibi knows Jewel is talking about her. *Rrowr ruff.* "Yes, we're talking about you, but you don't get an opinion."

Lew smiles. "Do you know what breed she is? I'm no expert, but she looks kind of like a border collie."

Jewel nods. "She's a mix, but I'm sure there's some border collie. When a group of schoolkids come into the museum, she can't resist trying to herd them."

"Are you from this area, Jewel? I mean, did you grow up here?"

She sets her tea on the small metal table. "Born and raised on the small farm across the river there. In the winter, when there are no leaves, you can see our house. It's just me and my momma now. My older sister Mabel lives in that white house with blue shutters across the road. Her husband Lucas runs their farm and has a hay-baling operation in the summer. Their son Jeff, who I mentioned this morning, helps with the garden. He works at the Piggly Wiggly in the summertime when he's not going to school."

Lew sips his iced tea and notices Amy standing at the screen door. When she sees him look up, she disappears back inside. He turns back to Jewel. "I'll have to get up early tomorrow morning so I can meet Jeff. Pardon me for asking, but why do you and Jeff do this? Take care of the garden, I mean?"

"Well, it's family tradition, I guess. I know that my grandparents helped your grandmother with the garden and my mom and I helped your uncle. The garden gives us all plenty of great vegetables in the summer and extra to put up for the winter."

"Put up?" asks Lew. "Put up where?"

Jewel laughs. "'Put up' is country for canning. What we can't eat we put up, or can, for the wintertime. That's where all those canned goods in your cellar came from."

A tad embarrassed, Lew says, "Uh, yeah, all those cans, huh. So that's where all those cans came from."

Jewel laughs again. "Okay, I see you haven't been in your cellar yet. Follow me."

She stands and leads Lew up to the side of the house to the bulkhead doors that go to the cellar that Lew has conveniently avoided. She pulls the handle to open the first door, then unlatches and opens the second. She pulls the hem of her dress up, carefully stepping down into the cellar with Lew following. At the bottom of the steps, she flips on a light illuminating a large room spanning the space below the living room and middle room above. Wooden shelves line the front and side stone walls of the room, holding jars of canned tomatoes, green beans, beets, and pickles. Some old gardening tools and two broken wooden boxes are on the floor against the wall opposite the bulkhead entrance. Jewel walks over and takes a jar of green beans off a shelf.

"As you can see, we didn't quite go through everything this winter. This time of year, we usually take these remaining jars to the county food bank, and they give us last year's empty jars to use again. It's a good system. Oh, and that staircase leads upstairs. You don't want to have to go in and out of here from outside in deep wintertime."

Lew realizes that he's never been in this cellar, even as a boy that one summer. He didn't think there was anything here except the undercroft of the house. But it's a good-sized space. While shelves line three walls, on the fourth wall at the back is a wide door. "So, Jewel, what's behind that door?"

Jewel shrugs. "I don't know. It's never been open as long as I've been coming here. You should open it. There's probably another room. Could be a root cellar, you know where they once kept potatoes and root vegetables for the winter. Hey, maybe there's some hidden treasure," she laughs.

Lew smirks. "Or maybe some more tax bills." He walks over and lifts up on the old lever-style doorknob. The door won't budge. It's locked. "There must be a key for this somewhere," he says. "Probably in all the stuff of Sheldon's I haven't been through."

Jewel turns toward the doorway. "I need to get home, Lew. Momma will wonder where I am. I'm happy to help take these canned goods to the food bank when you're ready. I can introduce you to folks there."

Up at Jewel's van, Lew opens the door for her and Bibi is quick to jump in and sit in the passenger seat. "One more thing, Jewel. I was wondering if you know anyone at the local weekly newspaper. I worked for the paper in St. Louis and I really need to find a job. We're going through my stash pretty quickly. Talking to someone at the local paper is a logical first step before I start looking elsewhere."

"Yeah," Jewel says, sliding behind the wheel. "I know the owner and editor at the *Cloch County Times*, Evie Anderson. She was my board chair at the museum a couple terms and a good friend. Don't know if she's hiring, but I can put you in touch."

"That's terrific," Lew says. "Thanks for everything."

As Jewel drives away, Amy's at the screen door again, holding Purry under her arm. When Lew steps up to the door, "I don't like her. And Purry doesn't like her mean dog." She turns and walks toward her room. Lew opens the door and follows.

"C'mon, Amy, you just got off on the wrong foot. She's really very nice. I found out that she's the one responsible for the garden and supplying us with all the fresh veggies. She also showed me our cool cellar that you've got to see. It has a secret door. And that dog of hers is all bark and no bite. Nothing for you or Purry to worry about."

"I still don't like her," Amy huffs. "Momma wouldn't like the way she acts with you. Or the way you act with her."

Wow, that is the first mention of her mom that she has made. It just took a little jealousy to pull it out of her. He sees that as progress, but needs to be careful.

"Listen, Amy, your mom would like Jewel as I do. She's a friendly and helpful neighbor." With that, there's a knock at the door. Strange, two visitors in one afternoon.

Lew goes to the door and steps out on the porch. There's a middle-aged man in a white short-sleeved shirt, khaki chinos and a big smile extending his hand.

"Mr. O'Hara, Davis Oakes. I'm the presiding commissioner of the county."

Lew shakes Davis's hand. "Call me Lew," he says, not bothering to correct his last name.

Davis hands him several envelopes and a magazine. "I picked up your mail from the mailbox. Aubrey the mailman was just by. You know, his grandson was accepted into the Baptist College in Springfield for the fall. He's really proud."

Lew takes the mail. "Thanks, Davis. What can I do for you?"

Taking on a sincere look, Davis says, "First of all, Lew, allow me to offer my condolences. I knew your Uncle Sheldon a long time. He was a good man and he helped a lot folks around here. He's been missed."

"Well, uh, thanks . . . Davis," Lew says, not knowing what else to say about Sheldon passing over a year ago.

Davis continues, "You know Lew, I got to know Mrs. O'Hara, Sheldon's mom, a short time before she passed. Great lady, Mrs. O'Hara. But I never got to meet any of his other kin."

Lew's pretty sure this is Davis' circuitous way of asking about his relationship to Sheldon. "Yeah, I remember Gran'mam fondly from a summer I spent here as a kid. My mom was Uncle Sheldon's younger sister. But she moved to St. Louis years ago and that's where I grew up. My mom passed away a couple years ago."

"I see," says Davis. "So you're down here from the city. You know, Lew, I've never been a fan of big cities. Too much of a country boy I guess. Born over in Christian County. Been here for twenty-four years now. Had family here. It's all country though, Christian and Cloch Counties. But St. Louis is nice for a big city, with that big ol' arch and all. Always been a Cardinals fan. I reckon that most folks here are Cardinals fans. O'course, you got your Royals fans here and there. But those are mostly newcomers . . . I think," rubbing his chin.

Lew nods and smiles trying to figure out if there's a point to Davis' folksy stream of consciousness about whatever the hell he's talking about.

And then: "Well living as you are in St. Louis, I'm guessing that you might be looking to sell this place. I mean it's nice here by the river, as long as it don't flood. But it's hardly choice land. It's amazing that the O'Haras scratched out a living here as long as they did."

"Yeah, they barely scraped by those, what, almost two hundred years."

The sarcasm is lost on Davis. "Yup, I suppose this would be more than a hand full for an experienced country man to manage. Dang near impossible for city folks long-distance."

Lew's pretty sure he's just been insulted. "Well, my daughter and I understand it's going to be a challenge and . . . "

"I'm sure you do, Lew, but you don't have to worry about that. I want you to know that I am willing to give you top dollar and take this off your hands."

"You mean the county wants to buy this property?"

"No, not the county. Me. Me and my brother, that is."

Lew doesn't attempt to hide his skeptic surprise. "Really. You want to offer top dollar for poor land. That doesn't make much sense."

Davis shuffles his feet and changes his tone. "Listen, I didn't mean it's poor land. It's just that, well, it's hilly and rocky. It's really not good for farming or grazing. It's a lot of land with little you can do with it."

A bit defensively, Lew says, "Well then, why would you want it if it's so useless?" Before Davis can answer, Lew steps back. "But never mind, Davis. I have no intention of selling this land. It's been in my family for generations and now it's in my care. And we don't live in St. Louis, we live here now. I decided that this is exactly the place that I want for my daughter and me. So while I appreciate the offer, no thanks."

"Suit yourself, Lew. And forgive me if I offended you in any way. I just want to make sure that old homesteads like this stay in the right hands." He extends his hand.

Lew grasps Davis's hand. "Yeah, I appreciate that, Davis. I hope you'll come to see that this property continues to be in the right hands."

Lew watches Davis get back into his Jeep Cherokee and drive out to the main road. He sits on the stoop and flips through the mail Davis handed him. Half of it is mail forwarded from St. Louis. There are two official-looking envelopes. The first is from the county assessor's office. That will be a tax bill. Lew forgot to find out what kind of back taxes he owed when he was in the county offices earlier. Reluctantly, he opens the envelope and catches his breath. Free Haven is in arrears a year and eleven months.

Taxes and penalties come to just over $5,000. And when taxes go unpaid for two years, the property goes on the auction block for the taxes. Where the hell is he going to get that kind of money, and that fast?

He looks at the second envelope and his heart sinks. It's from the district court in St. Louis. He's been expecting this. Nora's family had threatened Lew that if he moved and took Amy, they'd sue for custody. He can't believe they have a case against him, but it's a problem that he's jobless and bereft of the resources that Nora's family can provide for Amy. And he and Nora weren't officially married. He leaves the envelope unopened.

"Somebody's coming up the road," Amy says, again standing at the screen door.

The memorable Dorothy Parker quote comes to Lew. *What fresh hell is this?* "Stay inside, Amy. I'll see who this is."

The Ford 150 pickup comes bounding up and skids to a stop in the circular drive. Two guys in dingy white T-shirts get out. The driver walks around the front of the pickup. Lew stands and walks down the steps. The driver extends his hand. "Howdy, I'm Jerry Lloyd." Lew shakes his hand. "And this is my brother Ernest."

Lew turns and shakes hands with Ernest. "Lew Harra. I'm Sheldon's nephew."

"Real sorry 'bout ol' Shel," Ernest says. "He was a good ol' boy and a good neighbor. We really miss him."

Jerry Lloyd picks up. "Yup, and he was quite the *ar-teeste*. I think of him every time I see one of those sculptures of his around town."

"Sculptures? Uncle Sheldon? I've not seen those, or maybe just didn't notice."

Ernest laughs. "Yeah, well except for those things at the courthouse and the firehouse, a lot of it's hard to see 'cause he made stuff out of what people gave him to work with. Maybe wood off an old shed, limbs from a tree, scrap metal. Hell, he could take anything and make an artwork out of it. But it does tend to blend with the surroundings."

As Lew thinks about it, he has seen a good number of sculptural pieces in yards in town that fit Ernest's description.

Jerry Lloyd points at the barn. "Yeah, I'm sure you've seen some of the stuff in the barn that he was working on when he died. He was doing something for our dad from parts off his old tractor. Guess that'll never get done, unless ..." he tilts his head at Lew.

"No-o-o-o, I'm no sculptor. Fact is I didn't know Uncle Sheldon was. I've not opened and looked in that barn. Guess I better get to it."

"Yeah," Ernest says. "It's like a goddam museum in there. But I'll tell you what, the thing we miss the most is the great 'shine your uncle brought to our group's meetings each month."

"Shine? What's that?"

The two laugh, "Moonshine, Lew. White lightening. Brain thinner," says Jerry Lloyd. "Sheldon made the best around. Authorities liked it so much they wouldn't think of shutting his still down. Uh, any chance ... "

"No, I'm sure I'd be worse at making moonshine than sculpting. But what are your group meetings?"

"The Province," says Ernest. "Didn't you and your uncle ever talk? Shel was our oldest member and served as Grand Giant for a while. We meet every ..." Jerry Lloyd hits Ernest in the stomach.

"Sorry, Lew, Ernest seems to have forgotten that meeting times and locations are for members only. Of course, if you're interested in joining up, we'd be happy to sponsor you for membership. Seein' as how so many of your family have been Province members over the years, I don't think there'd be anything standing in your way."

"Thanks guys. I'll keep that in mind. For now, I'm a little overwhelmed just trying to get settled in with my daughter. Speaking of that, I need to get busy with dinner. I appreciate you stopping by." They all shake hands and the brothers get back in their pickup and throw gravel behind them on the way back out the driveway.

Stepping back inside, Lew sees Amy sitting in a chair by the window where she's been watching and listening to everything.

"Those are bad men, Daddy. I've read about those men."

"They're country boys, sweetie. Down here they're called 'good ol' boys.' Obnoxious but ultimately harmless."

"You're wrong, Daddy. They're really bad men. I read about them in that book. It's on my bed, see for yourself." Lew shakes his head and walks into the middle room. There's a book on the bed opened to a chapter titled, "The Cloch County Province." He picks the book up and looks at the cover: *The Ku Klux Klan in Missouri* by George Anderson. He quickly scans the chapter and his eyes open, in more ways than one. Lew realizes that Jerry Lloyd and Ernest were talking about the Klan. And Uncle Sheldon was not only a Klansman, but he was head honcho, what they call the Grand Giant in the Cloch County Province. Unbelievable.

FOUR

J EWEL ARRIVES WITH A DOZEN FOLDED BOXES TO help Lew transport the seasonal surplus of canned goods from the basement to the county food bank. Lew slides the side door of the van open and wrestles an armload of the collapsed boxes out and down to the cellar. Bibi watches carefully from the passenger seat of the van, making sure that the boxes are all he's taking. She's still a little suspicious of Lew and protective of Jewel, but she's also warming up to him. By the time he gets to the last of the boxes, she's on the ground letting him pet her.

"You see, Bibi," he says bending over rubbing her ears, "steering wheel, spare tire – it's all there. You can trust me."

"Nice work, Lew," Jewel says laughing with her big smile. "But you actually won her over by not laying a hand on her food bag behind my seat." *Rrowrr-ruff,* "Oh, and Bibi thanks you for keeping that in mind."

Lew laughs. "Not to worry, Bibi, I'm not that hungry – just yet." He wrestles the last of the folded boxes down to the cellar and begins assembling them with masking tape while Jewel writes up an inventory and inspects the jars for spoilage. Lew is still frustrated that Amy refuses to be around Jewel. *I just wish there was some way Amy would let Jewel win her trust as I won Bibi over. If she could just give an inch.*

"I really appreciate your help with this, Jewel. And with everything you do."

"It's no problem. That's what neighbors do for each other hereabouts. Your uncle was the best of all. Momma and I could always count on him to help out with all kinds of things. He was a great handyman and could fix anything. We could call on him any time." Lew cringes inside a little, thinking about all that Jewel and her family don't know about Sheldon.

"Yeah, Uncle Sheldon was something all right. I, uh, I mean I just learned so much by going into the barn and his workshop. He was obviously skilled in a lot of things. There's power saws and welding equipment, a whole paint station with tons of paint and different colors. It's really less a barn and more of a big workshop and art storage area. There's a lot of his sculptures and works in progress. It's hard for me to tell the difference. Maybe it would help if I could. Who knows, I might be able to sell some of it to help pay the taxes."

"I remember you saying that your uncle wasn't exactly on top of the taxes. Mind if I ask what kind of tax situation you're dealing with?"

"It's a lot. I got a bill a couple days ago for over $5,000, taxes and penalties. And the clock is ticking to pay up or everything gets auctioned."

"Yeah, that's a lot. Sorry, Lew. Have you thought about selling some of the land, maybe just a few acres? You've got a lot of land here and that's especially prime land all along the river."

"Yeah, I've thought about that. I'd like to keep that option as a last resort, but I may end up not having a choice but to sell some." Lew is also aware and not mentioning that officially, he doesn't own the property. It's still in Nora's name and since they never married, he has no legal claim if he were to present Nora's death certificate to the county recorder. Her family has a greater claim than he does. He can claim common law rights. In Missouri that's cohabitation of seven years. But he still has to produce documentation, and the legal steps involved are costly and time-consuming. Maybe in time. But for the time being, selling the property is not an option.

Lew and Jewel haul seven boxes of canned goods up to Jewel's Dodge Caravan. The summer heat has brought a light sheen of sweat to the two of them. Lew can't keep his eyes off Jewel's shapely legs and backside in her tight-fitting cut-off jeans. Her short-sleeved blouse with the two top buttons undone reveals well-defined breasts and cleavage that channels the beads of sweat running off her face and neck. As they place the last box in her van, she pulls a blue bandana out of her back pocket and wipes the sweat from her neck and chest.

"Geez, Lew, how'd we manage to pick the hottest day so far to do a job like this?"

Lew wipes the sweat off his brow with his sleeve in a motion that he hopes will hide his staring at her breasts. "Yeah, timing has never been my strong suit. Will there be someone at the food bank to help unload this?"

"Oh yeah, no problem." And of course Jewel sees Lew staring at her as he has been all day. And every time she's been here.

"My sister and nephew Jeff are working the pantry today. You know she's still looking forward to seeing you again."

"Again? Have I met your sister?" he asks.

"Okay, Lew, I've been patient long enough thinking at some point you were going to remember me and my sister. But I guess it ain't gonna happen."

Lew cocks his head, seriously puzzled. "Remember . . . what?"

"When you were here for that summer years ago, we all played and swam together almost every day at the river. We caught frogs, lightning bugs and June bugs. Any of that coming back to you?"

"Oh my God, was that you? But your name . . ."

Jewel laughs. "Yeah, back then I went by Weegy – that's what my sister called me when we were kids."

"Yeah, yeah, and she was Missy! That was a great summer. But you look, um, so different now. I'm sorry, I just didn't recognize you. Although that great smile of yours has never changed. We had a good time that summer, didn't we?"

"Yeah, it was a fun time. I wonder if you remember that last night before your mom came to pick you up."

"Um, not really. I mean, I know I was excited about seeing my mom but not about leaving and going home. What do you remember?"

"Well, I remember that you were the first boy to kiss me. Big you did. On the mouth. And I kissed you back, big. Aaaannd, naughty city boy, you slipped your hand up inside my shirt. Another first. That's when my momma yelled for me to come in."

Lew smiles and genuinely blushes. "Yeah, oh boy, it's all coming back to me now. Somehow, I blocked that. Good God, how embarrassing."

"C'mon, Lew, we were kids. Hormonal kids. Back then kissing a boy and doing stuff was mysterious and exciting. And it was probably a good thing that you left the next day." They both laugh.

Jewel's van pulls away and Lew watches as she heads toward the road. And as she heads down the driveway, he sees Amy coming up from the river, Purry under her arm as usual. She approaches Lew.

"Your friend laughs like a witch. And she needs to wear more clothes. She looks like a tramp."

"Amy, please. It's hot, she's wearing shorts like you are. Give her a break. She's helping us with a lot of stuff. I wish you'd just give her a chance. I know you'd like her."

"Okay, it's hot. And she's helping. But I don't have to like her. I don't have to like any of these people."

He shakes his head. "Can you at least help me organize the cellar now?"

Lew folds up the boxes they didn't use and Amy helps him move the shelves back in place. Two jars of clear liquid are still on one shelf. Amy points at them. "What are those? Do they store water like that?"

Lew laughs. "I'm pretty sure that those are the last remaining jars of Uncle Sheldon's moonshine. I didn't think they'd want that at the food pantry. Wish now I'd given them to Tweedledum and Tweedle-dummer when they were here – they're big fans."

Amy goes over to the mystery door and flips the handle. "So what's behind this door? Did you look for a key to open it?"

"Yeah, I turned that bedroom upside down and there was nothing resembling a key in any of Sheldon's stuff. It's the kind of key that would really stand out too, given how old. My guess is that Sheldon's moonshine still is back there. He likely hid the key."

Amy says, "You know, one of the books upstairs had a little verse about a key that didn't make much sense. But it may be a clue to where a key is."

Back upstairs, Amy scans the bookshelf and points at what appears to be a farmer's log. Lew pulls it down and opens it. "This looks to me like Gran'mam's garden book," he says. "Every year she would enter her dates of planting, ripening, harvesting, that sort of thing. But the log dates are well before Gran'mam's time. This looks like the first entries may have been in the 1800s."

Amy reaches over and flips to the back inside cover, where a verse is written in script that isn't Gran'mam's handwriting.

WHERE ITS WIDE AND NOT DEEP,
FROM WHERE ITS DEEP AND NOT WIDE,
BRICK BY BRICK AND STONE BY STONE,
A KEY YE SEEK MAY REST BESIDE.

Lew reads the verse out loud and repeats the last words: "Hmm, a key ye seek may rest beside. A key ye seek . . . may rest . . . beside? Beside what? And what's 'wide not deep, deep not wide'? Is this a proverb, or maybe some kind of riddle?"

Opposite the verse is a roughed likeness of a well. Amy exclaims, "I've got it!" and heads toward the door. Lew follows outside to the old well. She stands back from the well, looking over it and toward the river. "Where it's wide and not deep. I think maybe that's the river. From where it's deep and not wide. That could be this well. Brick by brick and stone by stone – that third row there has two bricks and two stones. A key ye seek may rest beside."

Lew reaches down and jiggles the second stone. "This one's loose," he says. He pulls the stone out and in a space behind it is a key. An old key. Eyes wide, they look at each other. "Let's go try it," Lew says gleefully.

In the cellar, Lew slips the key into the keyhole and twists. It doesn't budge. "I'm sure it's not been opened for a long time. And it's rusted," he says. "Wait here, I'll get some oil from upstairs." After spraying some oil in the keyhole and around the door latch, he grips and twists the key again and shakes the latch. He can feel it giving this time, and then a click. He pulls the latch lever up and the door creaks out and open. As the door swings open they are welcomed with a mix of cool, musty air and smells. Lew feels inside for a light switch but there's only bare stone. "Hand me that flashlight on the shelf," he says. He clicks on the flashlight and shines it in the dark space.

"Wow!" they exclaim together.

Lew runs back upstairs and brings a lamp and extension cord down to illuminate the space. And what a space it is. It appears to be an additional apartment the size of the upstairs kitchen and master bedroom. There's no electrical wiring. There are two ancient oil lamps that must have been a source for light.

"It looks like this could have been a living space for someone," Amy says.

"I think you're right," Lew says. "That's kind of a kitchenette against the back wall. There are still some old cooking pans and utensils on that countertop."

Lew turns the flashlight toward the outside wall. Approximately below the upstairs breakfast nook in the kitchen is a small empty room lined with thick wood. Amy looks inside. "Daddy, is this some kind of closet?"

Lew peeks inside. "Yeah, in a way. It's an old ice closet. Before folks had refrigerators, they had to store blocks of ice in underground closets like this. They were kind of like walk-in coolers where they could store things that needed chilling." He points to the rusted box by the counter. "And that, my dear, is a true ice box. I've never seen a real one before. This is like a place frozen in time."

There's a small table and several wooden chairs in the middle of the space, plus an Adirondack-style chair and loveseat made from pine wood slats held together with tongue and groove fittings and not a single nail or screw. There's a wooden bed frame against the inside wall, but no mattress. Lew shines the flashlight in the back corner. There's a solid wooden chair with a hole in the center.

"Is that what I think it is?' she asks.

Lew laughs, "Well, if you're thinking toilet, then yep. That, sweetheart, is a gen-u-ine chamber pot chair. Your basic indoor mainstay of pre-plumbing toilets."

"Okay, that is really gross," she counters.

"Not if you really have to go and can't get to the out-house. And when there's no running water or flushing system indoors, you have what you need. That rusted out washtub next to it was probably for bathing. This space was completely left out of the house's electrical and plumbing updates for some reason."

Lew scans the back wall with the flashlight. Embedded on the right side of the brick and rock wall is another door like the one opening into this room. It has an old lever handle and lock much like the first one.

"Wow, there's no end to mysterious doors in this place," Lew says. "Let's see if the key works on that one." He sprays oil in the lock and on the latch assuming it's also rusted and requires lubrication. But unlike the first door, there's no give at all. He pulls the key out of the lock. "Looks like we'll have to find another key for this one. I'm guessing that's where we'll find Uncle Sheldon's still."

While Lew is fumbling with the door, Amy is inspecting the opposite end of the room. Standing against the inside wall is the single largest piece of furniture in the room, a pine-slat wardrobe. It's about six feet high, maybe four feet wide. "Hey, Daddy, look at this," she says.

"Is it locked? Can you open it?"

"No thanks," she says standing back. "I'd rather watch."

Lew scans the wardrobe with the flashlight, then grasps the knob and opens the door on the right. There are two rifles. He recognizes one as a .22 caliber. The second looks like a shotgun.

"Uncle Sheldon's rifles," he says. "I remembers him hunting rabbits with the .22 that summer when I was here."

Next to the rifles is a military uniform. "Was Uncle Sheldon in the army?" Amy asks.

"I guess, maybe. I don't recall anything about his military service. Of course, this could have been Uncle Dillard's uniform. I know even less about him." Lew pulls open the second wardrobe door and his heart sinks. There are half a dozen robes, all white except one that is blue, and a corresponding number of pointed hoods. Uncle Sheldon's Klan wardrobe safely hidden away. And maybe robes of other family members.

Amy clutches Purry and leans against Lew, "Is that ... I mean, do you think ... "

"Yeah, it's exactly what it looks like," Lew says. "Don't worry, I'll burn these at first opportunity. But I think I need to do a little more research."

"What research? Most of it is in those books upstairs," she says.

"Yeah, well, that's helpful information about the history of the Klan in this county. But I want to know more about the Klan here today. They are still active, according to Jerry Lloyd and Ernest. We need to know who else is involved? And what's the history of our family in it? I mean, was this room a secret meeting place, maybe a secret hiding place for some of their criminal element? Opening doors has only opened more questions. I need to know more than I did when I was talking to Oofus and Goofus."

Clutching Purry even tighter, Amy asks, "Are we in some kind of danger? I really think we should go home now. I want to go home."

Lew turns and pulls Amy to his chest. Purry is tucked between them. "Listen, sweetheart, this *is* home. For now. And we're not in any danger. I just want to keep it that way." Then he hears Jewel calling his name outside. "Sweetie, look around some more, but don't open anything until I get back." He heads up the stairs to the ground level.

Jewel is standing at the edge of the circle drive. "Oh, hey, Lew! I heard you talking. You and your daughter in the cellar? Is this a good time for me to meet her?" She starts walking toward the bulkhead door.

Lew quickly steps in front of her, holding his hands up. "Uh no, Jewel. This really isn't a good time," he says, fearing how Amy might respond. "Not yet, I mean. We're both really dirty, you know, working in the cellar and all. Not a good time. I'm sure you understand."

Jewel stops and tilts her head, "Uh, yeah, okay. I understand. I mean, you're the dad and dad knows best – I guess. Anyway, I just dropped by to tell you that I talked to Evie Anderson at the *Cloch County Times* earlier today and told her about you. And she would like to talk to you."

"That's fantastic, Jewel. Did she say when? Do I need to call her?"

"Here's her number. Just give her a call. Don't get your hopes up, though. She said they don't have any jobs available, but she's still interested in talking to you about freelancing if you're up for that."

Lew takes the slip of paper with Evie's number. "I'm very good with that. In fact, that's what I expected. Is there anything I need to know about Evie Anderson before talking to her? Any insights?"

Jewel rubs her chin, "I don't think so. She's smart and tough. Kind of what you'd expect of a woman running a newspaper. I think I told you the *Times* is a family operation. She told me once it's the only job she's ever had. Took over the operation right out of high school when her aunt, who was editor-in-chief, passed away."

"Wow, she's like the Katharine Graham of Cloch County," Lew says. "That's impressive."

"Evie Anderson is nobody's fool. She was a tenacious champion for the museum as our board chair. I was mighty glad to have her on my side and not against me."

Lew nods, looking down at the number. "Sounds like a straight-shooter. I like that. How can ever I thank you?"

Jewel turns toward her van with a suggestive look back at Lew. "Oh. I'm sure you'll think of something – or I will. Later, Lew."

BACK IN THE CELLAR, AMY WAVES LEW OVER. "DADDY, look at this." She pulls the Klan robes aside and at the bottom of the wardrobe is a built-in metal box. Lew tries to open it, but it's locked. "Great," he says. "Yet another lock and mystery."

Amy reaches above the robes and pulls open a small built-in cabinet door to reveal a row of eight binders much like Gran'mam's garden log. "Maybe there's something in one of these about the key to that box. And that other door too."

Lew opens one of the binders. It's full of old, yellowed paper with page after page of names, dates and indecipherable scrawls. "I have a feeling these could be the membership rolls of the Klan in Cloch County going back a lot of years. Maybe from the beginning. Why aren't these locked up, too?" He pulls out the rest of the binders, "Let's take these upstairs where we can get a good look at them."

THE NEXT MORNING, LEW CALLS EVIE ANDERSON at the *Cloch County Times* to set up a meeting. He's disappointed to learn that she's about to leave town for a publisher's convention and he won't be able to meet with her for a couple weeks. In the meantime, Jewel has put him in touch with her brother-in-law Lucas, who needs extra help with his hay operation. In these mid-June weeks, when hay grass grows fast, Lucas makes his best money if he can keep a crew on the ground and the weather cooperates.

Lucas works several hundred acres in the area, cutting, baling and stowing the old-fashioned way. He drives his old John Deere grass cutter and baler over fifteen to twenty acres at a time in the morning. His right-hand man Jesse follows, hauling a flatbed with two men, one bucking or throwing the bales onto the flatbed. The other stacks the hay on the flatbed. In the afternoons, Lucas delivers bales to the horse farms. Most all of his product goes to these farms nowadays. Lucas has one of the few remaining bale operations in the county. The horse farms favor the easily managed hay bales over the large hay wheels that most local farmers now prefer.

Lew helped Uncle Dillard in the hay field a couple times that summer years ago. He remembers bucking hay as hot, exhausting, and low-paying work. But money is money, and he needs it right now. A few weeks in the field will help a lot. Jesse's crew starts around seven a.m. and usually finishes in the field around noontime. This allows Lew to get in five hours of work and be back home not long after Amy is up and about.

Jesse's good about putting his young guy on the ground, allowing Lew to stay on the flatbed stacking bales. And when they're taking bales to barn stowage, he puts the young hand up in the barn loft where it's especially hot and dangerous. A single misstep between two loose bales can put a guy on the floor of a barn and out of the game real fast. Lew has no insurance to cover missteps of any kind.

Throwing the 60-to-80-pound bales around is a lot easier for Lew these days than when he was twelve. He didn't weigh much more than the bales at that age. And lifting and stacking the bales does have a way of building up muscle and stamina. After a couple weeks in the hay fields, Lew is looking and feeling more fit than he has since he was unloading delivery trucks at the diner back in college. And Lew's buff appearance hasn't gone unnoticed by Jewel on those mornings when she's finishing in the garden and Lew is on his way out to meet up with Jesse.

FIVE

EVIE ANDERSON'S OFFICE IS ON THE SECOND floor of the *Cloch County Times* building on Main Street in Cloch Village. The entrance to the second floor is up a stairway in the back of the building. Someone is coming out the door. Lew catches it and steps in. Inside the doorway he's met with the familiar smells of an old-fashioned newspaper operation.

He stops to take in the mix of acrid print ink, pungent newspaper pulp and pressed cardboard rolls. It's a smell long absent from most big city newspapers with high tech digital printing systems. He's transported back to his college days and the small, three-person newspaper operation. Lew was editor-in-chief his senior year and well remembers putting in long hours to meet print deadlines. He also remembers how Nora would come by and visit. Since it was the only place where they had real privacy, they made love there several times. That helped motivate Lew to keep a clean, uncluttered desk. Interesting how the aroma of the *Cloch County Times* not only brings back memories of being on print deadline but is slightly arousing as well.

Lew climbs the stairs and steps through the door on the second floor. An attractive woman sees him and motions for him to come to the front of the space to her glassed-in office. The second floor obviously serves as offices and records for the paper. Besides Evie Anderson's office, there are two other desk stations, both unoccupied.

"Hello, Mr. Harra, I'm Evie Anderson. Thanks for coming in." Evie looks to be forty-something, although she could be older. She's wearing stylish form-fitting jeans, a light-green blouse and blue and green silk scarf around her neck. Her hair is the kind of a blonde-gray that women of an age seem to prefer keeping their age nicely ambiguous. Her reading glasses hang on a blue beaded chain around her neck.

Lew accepts her firm handshake with a smile, "Thank you for your time, Ms. Anderson. And for getting my name right. I think you're the first."

She laughs, still grasping his hand. "Well, our friend Jewel made quite a point of your name to me. Come on in." She turns and walks briskly in her dark green pumps into her office. She exudes an air of cheerful confidence and authority, reflecting exactly the personality that Jewel described. She offers Lew a seat at a round oak table next to a large oak roll-top desk. The table is covered with papers that she appears to be editing.

"So, Mr. Harra, I understand you recently moved here from St. Louis. Are you experiencing a bit of culture shock?"

Lew smiles, "A little, I guess. And please, call me Lew. I had a pretty good idea what we were coming into, my daughter Amy and me. We're living in my late mom's family homestead. I was here one summer as a kid and again a few years ago. I forgot how beautiful the countryside is, especially this time of year."

"That's the old O'Hara homestead, isn't it?" Lew nods. "So, you're an O'Hara with a slightly different name. Jewel didn't mention that you had a daughter."

"Yeah, well, they didn't get off to a great start. But that's less about Jewel than my daughter. She's been struggling since her mom was killed in a car accident. So far, she won't talk to anyone but me. But I feel like we're making progress."

"I'm really sorry about your wife. Jewel did mention that. I'm sure your daughter will get more and more comfortable with Jewel. I mean, everybody loves Jewel." Lew smiles and nods.

"Let me get to the point, Lew. I don't have a job to offer right now. In fact, this paper hasn't had a full-time staff for a number of years. As I'm sure you know, print media has fallen on pretty hard times. But there's still a market here for this old weekly and I have a couple freelance writers who contribute articles and stories. I'm able to pay twenty-five cents a word, with a limit of a thousand words per article and two thousand words for feature stories I accept."

"Well, nobody gets into journalism expecting to get rich. That sounds fair. Do you want to see some of my clips?"

"Hey, if the *Globe-Dispatch* liked your work, I'm sure I'll have no problem. The challenge for you is that most county news revolves in and around the courthouse and my other two writers have that covered pretty well. You'll need to sniff out other news or find your own feature ideas."

"I understand. How do you feel about investigative reporting, Ms. Anderson? I've read a little about the history and activity of the Ku Klux Klan in these parts. I'm kind of interested in learning more about that."

"Please, call me Evie. As interesting as you may find the topic, those boys aren't very interested in being learned about. And they sure don't like investigators, of any kind. You can easily find yourself in a dangerous situation."

"I see. Has anyone done any recent investigative reporting on the Klan? There are a couple older books on the history of the Klan in my uncle's book collection."

"Yes, some historical writing. It's likely that one of those books you've seen is my father's. His name was George Anderson, and he founded this paper. He had no problem researching and writing that book. But it's more than likely that his continuing investigation cost him his life."

"Wow, I'm sorry, Evie. He sounds like an amazing man. Do you know if he was investigating something in particular?"

"No. He was conscientious about keeping the family out of that aspect of his work. Back then, though, the Klan was a lot less likely to go after family than a specific mark. That's changed over the years."

"Message received," Lew says, rubbing his chin.

"A good rule of thumb is to know just enough about the Klan to know when to stop poking around."

Lew nods. "The little I've read so far really surprised me. It seems that, for a lot of its history, the Klan was less racist than just purely reactionary. I mean the racism is always there, but there seemed to be more focus on resisting modern encroachments. You know, the gated communities popping up around the lake area, power boats outnumbering fishing boats, foreign investors of any kind. Oh, and the Arab horse farms. First I'd known about those."

"It's true, Lew. The Klan of fifty and more years ago that my dad wrote about is very different than the Klan of today. But there have been different dimensions to the Klan in this part of the country from the beginning. Differences that aren't subtle. The Klan changed as times changed. Of course, you can generally count on it reflecting the worst of that change, but you can't ignore the differences.

"Most people think of the Klan in its post-Civil War Reconstructionist phase, trying to hold on to Southern power. A big part of that was controlling the freed slaves and Northern attempts to remake the economy and culture of the pre-war South. A lot of that was gone before the turn of the century. A resurgence of the Klan occurred between the two wars, in the 1920s and '30s. My father's book is largely focused on that era.

"During that period, the Klan took on the role of self-appointed morality police, like ferreting out and helping capture bootleggers for local officials. They even monitored personal behaviors, like lovers parked on county roads. It's what they called *bushwhacking*. They would sneak up on a couple necking in their car and start banging on the hood and windows. If the occupants were doing, ahem, more than smooching, they might tip the car over on its side," She laughs. "But I guess that's not funny if you're in a car on its side with your pants down."

Lew laughs too, "That's pretty extreme. But what if they found one of their own Klan members in a car?"

"Oh, same treatment. When it comes to keeping their own in line, the Klan doesn't pull punches. Sometimes they punch harder. They take themselves and their work seriously and expect their own to lead by example. A Klan brother might get his car tipped, and then be pulled out of his car, stripped of his clothes and painted with molasses and covered with chicken feathers.'

"Wow! So they just inflict a sweet version of the old tar and feathers treatment?"

"Nothing sweet about it. Molasses is a lot cheaper and easier to keep at hand as needed than hot tar. If not, trust me, it would be hot tar and feathers. But then, Lew, *but then*, during the Depression, a horrible time in this county, the Klan helped organize food co-ops and distributions. They worked with local churches to keep folks from falling between the economic cracks and starving. In many ways, they looked little different than a local Kiwanis, Rotary Club, or church auxiliary."

"But that clearly didn't last, at least as a primary focus," Lew asserts. "Most people today equate the Klan with the Civil Rights movement. The Klan's images are all the hoods and robes, the cross burnings, the lynching's and assassinations. I read what your dad wrote about the Cloch County Province. And he didn't soft-pedal a thing."

"True, and that was likely his mistake. All that he wrote about the Province was true, but it sure set some pointy hoods askew. And it cost him dearly. My point being, Lew, the Klan is ever-changing in its response to the world, but what hasn't changed much at all are the central values. Those are indelible and you can see them from the beginning to today."

"I appreciate your sharing all this, Evie. A lot. But one last question. Do you know who's in the Klan locally and who's not? The two guys who visited us several weeks ago, Jerry Lloyd and Ernest, were pretty open, even proud to talk about their involvement. Of course, they were visiting to feel me out given Uncle Sheldon's long association."

"Yeah, the Ducker boys and their dad Owen wear their K's openly and proudly. My understanding is that Owen is currently Grand Poobah, or what they call the Grand Giant of the local Province. There's a long family tradition with the Duckers."

"I was disappointed to learn that Uncle Sheldon was a Klansman and Grand Giant at one time. Apparently, we too have a long family tradition."

"Trust me, Lew, there are varying degrees of commitment and involvement within the Klan ranks. Your uncle wasn't the Grand Giant that Owen is, not by a mile. But that can be as hard to know as who's in and who's not. I've always felt it safest to assume that if a man is white and has family roots in the area, he's likely a Klansman. But beyond that you can't make assumptions by what a person really believes or does.

"To share a bit of wisdom from my father, the thing that makes the Klan so dangerous is not the blatant racism alone. Underpinning the racism and the hate is the fear. St. Teresa of Avila said, 'I don't fear the devil, I fear the people who fear the devil.' Sad to say, Lew, fear is a big part of the Klan mind-set everywhere."

"Thanks, Evie. That's a lot to think about. I have one last question on another topic. I have an idea for a story about hay baling operations and the guys who do it. To make some extra cash, I just finished working several weeks on Lucas Thompson's crew over our way. It's hard but necessary work for farms hereabout. I thought folks might find it interesting."

"Interesting, yes. But this is a good example. Lucas Thompson is not a very popular guy these days because he basically turned his hay operation over to supplying the horse farms. A lot of folks associate the horse farms with the worst encroachments." She leans forward and says in a fake whisper, "Some of those farms are owned by A-rabs." She sits back, raising her eyebrows.

"I see," Lew grimaces. "Clearly not an advisable first effort."

Evie leans in again. "No. Lew. It is. But write it up from a first-person angle. Focus on the hard work aspect and the tradition. Folks eat that stuff up. If you can avoid mentioning Lucas' name, so much the better." Lew nods, taking that idea in.

"By the way," she continues, "the July Fourth parade and celebration is coming up. It's a very big deal in the county, something you and your daughter don't want to miss. And you might get some ideas for stories there – safer ones, anyway."

"Thanks, Evie. I hear you. I'll make sure we're there."

ALL SMALL TOWNS HAVE HOLIDAY TRADITIONS. IN these parts, the Fourth of July is second only to Christmas. For more than a week, Lew has been telling Amy about the parade and how excited he is for them to attend, "just like we're locals." Amy appears to listen but doesn't respond. Lew is thinking that this is a great opportunity for Amy to begin to experience a festive event in town. Maybe see and meet some kids her age. When it's close to time to leave, he finishes washing the breakfast dishes and steps to the middle room doorway, Amy's room. She's on her bed, still in pajamas, nose in a book.

Lew steps into the room. "Why aren't you ready to go? The parade starts in half an hour, and we need to find a place to watch."

"I'm not going to the stupid parade."

"What is this? We've talked about going to the parade for over a week."

"No, *you've* talked about going to the parade for over a week. I'm fine with you going to the parade. I'm sure you'll have a good time. If you won't let me go home, then I'm fine staying right here."

Lew works to keep a lid on his irritation. "But Amy, sweetheart, I'm not comfortable having you stay here alone. I would much prefer having you be with me."

She plops back against the headboard of the bed. "Holy crap, Daddy, I'm not a six-year-old. I'm old enough to stay by myself. I've got my cell phone and I'll call you if a squirrel tries to break in and steal some of your black walnuts."

Lew is really okay leaving her alone as he did when he was working on Lucas' hay crew. It's more about getting her out and seeing and meeting people. But he's trying hard to give Amy space and not hover. It's early in the day and he doesn't need to spend that much time at the parade. This is an opportunity to build some trust, or at least avoid a blow-up. He has to choose his battles.

FOLKS HAVE COME INTO CLOCH VILLAGE FOR THE parade and other Fourth of July activities from all over the county. Lew is surprised that he can't find a parking place on one of the side streets off Main. He decides to park behind the *Cloch County Times* building next to Evie Anderson's big white Cadillac Escalade. He figures he's kind of on assignment, given Evie's directive about attending the parade. He walks down Main Street and finds a good viewing spot in the partial shade of a large maple tree. The parade is just beginning. It's led by the Sons of the Confederacy drum and bugle corps. Lew wonders whether anybody besides himself, the local Black folks and Evie Anderson gets the ridiculous irony of such a thing. But traditions are traditions. Right behind the drum and bugle corps march the Veterans of Foreign Wars, then the American Legion, then the high school marching band playing patriotic tunes, which of course includes *Dixie*.

Trailing the band is a pickup truck driven by Jerry Lloyd Ducker hauling a flatbed wagon float with a hill of dirt and sod and three crosses. The faux-Calvary dirt mound is festooned with flags of various local community groups: the Boys and Girls Club, the Red Cross, the food bank and others. The name on the side of the float is Cloch Province Charities. Sitting on the front of the mound is Owen Ducker. On the sides, his son Ernest and several others are throwing candy to the crowd. Lew shakes his head. *Such good citizens. Who could ever think ill of these fine folks, at least as long as you can overlook the racism and violence?*

As Lew looks up and down the street at all the white families cheering and waving American flags and Confederate battle-flags, he recalls what Evie Anderson said. He has to assume that many, if not all, of these good family men are Klan. And regardless of degrees of allegiance, joining means suspending certain values of civility. Scanning the crowd, he's glad now that Amy chose to stay home. And for the first time, he wonders if this is really a place he can live and raise his daughter.

His thoughts suddenly shift to Amy's mental state. It seems like she's becoming more reclusive instead of coming out of her shell. If not for the fact that she seems so happy in her isolation, he'd be more concerned. He feels she needs more time, but it won't be long before they have to have a discussion about school and interacting with kids her age. That can have a good and bad side. But Lew also understands that his protecting Amy contributes to her isolation. Still, his instincts to protect his daughter outweighs everything.

As the final float passes by, Lew walks along with it, back toward the *Cloch County Times* building. He has an idea for a new story – maybe a series – and he wants to run it by Evie. She loved his thousand-worder on working the hay fields, and he sure appreciated getting a check unaccompanied by new blisters.

The building is at the end of the parade route and parade participants and families are milling around. The back door to the office is open so he goes in and heads up the stairs. He walks in and sees Evie and Jewel looking out the office window. Bibi is stretched out at Jewel's feet. "Hey there," Lew calls out. "Breaking news – the parade is over."

Evie turns and waves. "Hi, Lew, come on in. We're enjoying a beer and laughing at all the nonsense. Grab one out of the fridge and join us."

Lew helps himself to a Pabst Blue Ribbon, pops it open and raises it to Evie and Jewel. "Happy Fourth of July in bizarro country."

"Cheers," says Jewel.

"Slainte," says Evie. "This is a little tradition of ours: Watching the parade from here where we can see them, but they can't see us."

Lew steps forward. "How's that? Is this like those two-way mirrors that cops use?"

"More of a special tinted glass that allows me to see out but not be seen. I had it put in after my father was shot. He was sitting at his desk in the window. Officially, it's a way to block the direct heat of the sun. Unofficially, it's a way to watch the world and not be watched. Or be an easy target."

Jewel chimes in. "As you might have guessed, July Fourth festivities aren't exactly the best time for Black folks to be too public, what with certain drunken yahoos running around."

Lew nods. "Yeah, makes sense. I couldn't help but notice that most all the parade marchers and audience were distinct shades of pale."

"Right you are," Jewel says. "And welcome to my world. But I'm guessing the two of you have some business to discuss. I'm going to slip out the back before things start getting rowdy on the street. Oh, and Lew, I'm going to harvest a bushel or two of the green beans in the morning to take home so Momma and I can begin canning. It's that time."

"Great. I'll get up and give you a hand."

Jewel exits and Lew notices Evie looking intently at something below. "Now that's a sordid group I wouldn't want to encounter in a dark alley. But I'd sure like to be listening in to the conversation." Lew steps over and looks down. From this vantage point, they can see four people engaged in an intense conversation behind the Province float.

Evie points at the group. "You have here Owen Ducker in the blue polo shirt, he was atop the Province float. That's Davis Oakes in the white short-sleeve shirt, with June Eastman and a character I've seen on the street with June a couple times. He's not from around here."

"I know about Ducker and Davis Oakes," Lew says. "Who's June Eastman?"

"She's a local businesswoman who runs her late husband's lodging and real estate operations around the lake region. She and Davis are said to be an item. I'm pretty sure it's more of a business relationship. She's benefitted financially quite a lot from her close connection to the county government through Davis. And the tall guy in black looked questionable before; now he looks downright sinister in that group."

"Davis Oakes was out to see me not long after we arrived, wanting to buy Free Haven. He assumed I wanted to sell. As county commissioner, he knows all about our tax problems."

"Yep, that's how June scores a lot of her properties. You're sitting on a mighty attractive piece of real estate to someone like June."

"Well, I'm going to hold on as long as I can. But the man in black notwithstanding, would you say that thick-as-thieves klatch is discussing real estate or Klan biz? Or would those pretty much be one and the same?"

"You're catching on fast, Lew."

SIX

LEW HAS MOVED THE DINING TABLE FROM THE middle room, now Amy's bedroom, to the living room to use as a desk and to keep all his legal and tax documents organized. This kind of organization does not come easily to him. He's placed two of Gran'mam's garden baskets on the floor beside the table, one for bills and one for tax documents. There's a shoe box with a lid where he stashes the three unopened envelopes from St. Louis District Court and two unopened letters from Jane Henderson. He knows well what the court and the relentless Henderson family wants. *And the only way they'll get Amy is over my dead body.*

The most worrisome thing he's received to date is a thirty-day notice to pay all the property taxes and penalties or Free Haven goes on the auction block. It seems he has reached the point of last resort. Tomorrow he's going into town to talk to an agent at Mid-County Realty who Jewel turned him onto about leasing a portion of the property. He can't sell anything, since he doesn't officially own the property. But maybe he can get away with leasing some of it, enough to cover all their outstanding taxes and bills. After seeing the little confab Davis Oakes was having with Owen Ducker, Lew will do whatever he can to keep the Klan at bay.

For now, he has cleared the table so he and Amy can spread out the logs they took from the old wardrobe cabinet to try and decipher what is recorded in them. They realize right away that there are actually six logs filled with seemingly random names, one binder of old maps, and a Bible. Amy's interest in the logs and the books she's found in the library are heartening. It's the one thing that she wants to share with Lew. And it's about the only time when she sets Purry aside, although the stuffed cat is never more than an arm's length away.

The logs are old and the pages yellowed, brittle, and in fragile condition. It's like they were all written in approximately the same time period. Lew's theory that this might be Klan member rolls over the years doesn't jibe with the uniform age of the logs. And he has observed that some of the readable names appear to be those of women – but there are no women in the Klan. It appears that all entries include only a month and day and no year. Some list a first and last name, but most only a single name. There appear to be some financial records, too. Maybe the family was into loan sharking or money laundering for the Klan. That's been a part of the Klan's financial underpinning from the beginning. All that good Christian charitable work has to be paid for somehow.

The O'Haras may have been the bankers to the Province. Lew's concentration is broken as he looks up and sees a white Ford Bronco coming up the drive to the house.

"Keep studying, Amy. I'll go see what this is." As Lew descends the front steps, June Eastman gets out from behind the wheel of the car and the man in black emerges from the passenger side. The two of them approach Lew. June is still in her white cotton dress and the white sandal mules she was wearing on the street in town. She's an attractive woman, likely older than she looks. He's thinking that June and Davis aren't a very convincing couple. But business makes for strange bed partners.

June quickly steps up and extends her hand to Lew. "Hi, Mr. O'Hara, we haven't had the pleasure yet. I'm June Eastman."

Lew smiles and shakes her hand, "Please, just call me Lew."

"And this is Peter Umanoff. He's with Firebird Enterprises, a major international resort developer based in Brooklyn, New York." Lew shakes Peter's hand. Both nod and say nothing.

"So, what brings you to Free Haven this warm Fourth of July holiday?"

June rotates to Peter, hands up as though presenting him. "Peter's company is very interested in developing a luxury resort hotel complex here in Cloch County. Can we go inside and talk with you about their plans?"

"I'd love to invite you in, but my daughter is sleeping and, well, she's not feeling well. We can chat right here." Lew looks at Peter. "So, a luxury resort hotel here in Cloch County? That's a little surprising."

"Yes, yes, we see this is the next big place. Like a new Las Vegas, but classy, like Monaco."

"In time, of course," June quickly adds. "But for now, Lew, Peter's group is looking for about 50 acres of land to develop, ideally with a water source close by. With the Saoirse River right here, Free Haven fits that to a T. I think you'll find that they are willing to pay a very handsome price, *annnnd* throw in some nice incentives." She looks at Peter, nodding and cueing him to nod, which he does without expression.

Lew turns to Peter. "Umm, what kind of incentives are you talking about?"

June, feeling she has Lew's attention, steps in. "Peter, tell Lew about some of the good reasons why he wants to sell to Firebird Enterprises."

"Yes, yes, reasons." He looks at June. "Besides money, um, I don't remember, what did you say we'll do?"

With a distinct look of frustration on her face, June quickly turns to Lew, "Well, for one, I remember you saying that you would include an owner apartment in the complex for Lew and his family? So you see Lew, you could live there, rent it, or sell it if you like. Also, one of the permanent structures would be named for this property or the O'Hara family. There might be other ways to recognize your family. By the way, are any family members buried here?"

Lew remembers there's a family cemetery on the property somewhere, although he's not sure where. "Yes, there is a family cemetery. But let me stop you there, June. And

Peter. I appreciate your interest in this property. But no, I'm not interested in selling Free Haven, at least not in the foreseeable future."

Peter, sweat streaming from his sideburns, looks perturbed. "Don't be foolish, Lew. We'll give you a lot of money, a lot more than this land and that house is worth. You and your family can walk away and nobody gets hurt."

Lew, taken aback, looks at Peter, then June, and back, sharply at Peter. "That sounds like a threat to me. And threats have a way of really pissing me off."

June quickly interjects, "No, no Lew, that's not at all what Peter meant. It's a matter of translation, right, Peter? No regrets, no pain of regrets is what he means, right? And, oh my, look at the time, we really have to go," she says pulling Peter back toward her car. "It's just the translation, Lew. Please think about the offer so there's no regrets. Everybody can win, Lew."

It's a little after six a.m. and the sun is up. The heat can't be far behind. Lew steps out the back door and sees Jewel already squatting on her little garden stool plucking green beans, her beautiful long legs folded beneath her. He struggles to not be obvious looking at Jewel's body. It appears that she already has a half bushel picked. "Morning, Jewel. Did you sleep in the garden overnight?"

Jewel looks up from under her straw hat with a big smile, "Good morning, Mr. Harra. I had the misguided notion I might be able to pick two bushels before it gets too hot. Silly me." Bibi is busy snapping at grasshoppers in the pepper rows and abruptly stops and runs up to Lew. He's gotten into the habit of carrying dog treats for Bibi – at first to keep her from barking, but now they are just the best of friends. Lew drops a treat and Bibi snatches it when it's barely out of his hand.

"Easy, Bibi. Sit, girl. Do you want another?" Bibi obediently sits. *Rowrr ruff.* "Of course you do." Lew drops another treat and again she practically scarfs it up before it leaves his hand.

Jewel looks at them playing. "Here's an idea, Lew. Teach Bibi how to pick green beans, and this'll go a lot faster."

"Subtle, Jewel, real subtle." Lew kneels down in the furrow across from Jewel and starts plucking green beans. "I've a lot to fill you in on."

"Oh yeah?" she says, keeping her head down and not missing a beat with her plucking.

"Yeah. First off, we found a key to the mystery door in the cellar."

"You don't say. Where was it? What did you find?"

"I can't describe it. You really have to see this." The two stand and Jewel follows him to the bulkhead. They walk down to the cellar and through the mystery door.

"Come-to-Jesus, Lew! It's a whole apartment. Someone must have lived here."

"Quite a surprise, isn't it? There's an unpleasant surprise as well." He opens the wardrobe, revealing Sheldon's Klan robes.

Jewel grimaces. "Yeah, that's stinks. But you know, it's not terribly surprising, not in these parts."

"It's still disappointing. I didn't know Uncle Sheldon that well, but I felt he had a kind heart and was better than this."

"He did. He had a very kind heart, and he was better than this, Lew. My momma and I knew him well. He was kind and there wasn't a thing he wouldn't do for my momma and me. There's a lot of pressure on white men in these parts. They feel they have to go along to get along. Especially when there are certain family histories. Don't be too quick to judge."

"I guess. Evie Anderson said essentially the same thing, that there are varying degrees of commitment and involvement in the Klan."

"And a lot of different intentions. There are good reasons why the most devoted Klan racists are paranoid about infiltrators. It's pretty easy to get in but real hard to know everyone's intention."

"Yeah, that's a helpful perspective, Jewel. It always seemed to me that everyone in the Klan was coated with the same layers of hatred and evil. I guess I have to modulate a bit. And I have to share your thoughts with Amy. I'm afraid I've been laying my disgust with the Klan on her pretty thick."

"By the way, is that daughter of yours ever going to give me a chance to know and be friends with her? It's been a while now."

"Soon, Jewel. This move has been a difficult process for her. She still talks a lot about wanting to go home. But I feel her interest in Sheldon's books, the family logs and so on have opened her up more to being here. She was thrilled deciphering that riddle and finding the key to this room. And now we have to figure out how to find the key to the lockbox in the wardrobe, and the key to that other door."

"Oh my God, there's another door? I didn't notice it at first."

"Yeah. It seems like solving one mystery only presents us with several more. Hopefully we'll find more keys and that may be the key to bringing Amy out of herself. In the meantime, dear Jewel, we need to finish with the green beans. Then I've got to organize some things for my appointment with your realtor friend about leasing some of the property. Time is closing in."

"So sorry it's come to that, Lew. Hey, I'm good to finish with the green beans. Go do what you need to do." She reaches out and hugs Lew, he returns the hug, and what starts as a hug of comfort feels like something more. He feels Jewel's firm breasts pressing against his chest, her soft cheek brushing against his. He breathes in the perfume in her shampoo. It has been so long since he has held a woman in his arms. There's a warm rush of affection and arousal coursing through his body. It feels like he could melt into her. And then, he catches himself. What if Amy were to appear and see them like this? He abruptly pushes back and half smiles. Jewel smiles but with a perplexed look, trying hard to figure out what kind of relationship Lew wants with her. As far as she's concerned, he's the biggest mystery in this cellar.

THE REALTOR LEW TALKS TO IS ENCOURAGING, BUT realtors always are. It's frustrating because there's no easy way to divide the property and lease a portion that will have access to both the roadway and the river. And that combination will bring the best price. The only possibility is a kind of gerrymandered L-shaped strip that runs parallel to the house, then cuts across the back section to give limited access to the river. That would also include Luna's Leap, the high point that rises about two hundred feet above the river. It's the most dramatic and beautiful part of the entire fifty acres of land. Lew struggles with the notion of letting that go. But he may not have a choice. The realtor is eager to see the property. Lew agrees to have him come and survey the property tomorrow and then make a decision.

Leaving the realtors office, Lew is only a couple blocks from the *Times* building. He decides to go by and fill Evie in on his Fourth of July visitors, June Eastman and Peter Umanoff. Main Street is far quieter compared to the crowds and noise of the Independence Day parade. A lot of folks are back to work and the lake area is back in the hands of retirees and vacationers. With some time to spare, Lew walks a block away from the *Times* to the fire station to get a closer look at Uncle Sheldon's sculpture, the one that the Brain-Free Boys mentioned.

This sculpture is completely different than the one he viewed in front of the courthouse. It appears to be a five-foot wide section of stressed wood cut out of the side of a house or maybe a barn. The wood is thick, and it appears that Sheldon carved faces, possibly likenesses of some the firemen, into it from top to bottom. There are six faces altogether. They are so articulately carved that Lew can tell that two of them are older than others. And one fireman appears to be Black.

There's a small plaque at the bottom that Lew has to squat down to read: *In loving memory of our fallen brothers Alfred Lynch, Bobby Ball, Joshua Anders, Mick O'Brian, Tim Jones, Lee O'Byrne.* There's no indication on the plaque or sculpture that Sheldon created the work. Of the various pieces that Lew has seen so far of Sheldon's, nothing has been so figurative and finely finished. It's a beautiful and moving piece.

Lew walks back up Main in the direction of the *Times* building, crossing the street to have another look at the sculpture in front of the county courthouse. This is an abstract piece made of what appears to be a whole tree trunk of driftwood, about seven feet tall, with stones implanted randomly from top to bottom. It's a rough piece, except that Sheldon likely put four to six coats of lacquer finish on it. It's an amazing contrast in materials and textures that gives the piece a kind of depth, as though it's suspended in amber. In this instance there's no plaque, no indication of Sheldon's authorship, no name. Lew would love to have a conversation with Sheldon about these two works of art. Sorry he missed that opportunity.

He crosses back over Main Street and to the *Cloch County Times* building. The back door is locked, so he rings the buzzer. Evie comes to the second-floor window. "Hi, Lew." She looks around to make sure no one is in earshot. "Use the combination on the door. It's 2-4-6-7." Lew enters and climbs the stairs. Evie greets him at the top of the stairs. "I always keep the door locked when I'm here alone. Keep that combination in mind, but don't share it."

Lew nods. "Of course. Are there particular threats that you're concerned about?"

"Just threats in general. This may be a weekly paper, but it's still a newspaper, and we print news and stories that always set someone's undies in a knot." She sits down at her oak talk-table. "Do you have something for me, Lew?"

"No, not yet. But I thought you'd be interested in knowing that I received a visit yesterday afternoon from June Eastman and 'the man in black.' His name is Peter Umanoff and he's with an international resort hotel development group in Brooklyn, New York. They want to buy Free Haven to build a resort hotel." He hands Evie the business card Peter gave him.

"That's ambitious. And what's June's interest in this?"

"That isn't clear. Although she did most of the talking. When I said Free Haven's not for sale, this Peter Umanoff guy morphed from silent partner into thug. He actually threatened me. Obviously not part of the script because June quickly pulled him back to her car and left."

"Yeah, but a threat's a threat. I'll poke around and see what I can find out. I've got my sources."

"You should know that something complicating things is that I just came from the Mid-County Realty office. I'm talking to them about leasing a portion of the property so I can pay back taxes. Free Haven is two years in arrears and I got a final notice last week to pay or it gets auctioned."

"Is that your only option, Lew? Didn't Sheldon leave anything?"

"Nothing I know of. There's no record of a bank account or any liquid assets. Except for Free Haven, no assets at all, really. Which is strange given all the sculpture that my uncle produced. I was just up viewing the piece in front of the firehouse. Really beautiful and clearly a memorial to fallen firefighters."

"Right. Those men were all killed in the Adams' family barn blaze nine or ten years ago. All six were in the barn when the burning roof collapsed on them. Seemed like everybody in the county was related to at least one of them. You're right, it's a beautiful work."

"Exactly. But was Sheldon commissioned to do that? And what about the sculpture at the courthouse?"

"I have no idea, Lew. Someone in the courthouse like Davis Oakes might be able to tell you. But knowing this county, I'd say Sheldon didn't make a penny off the work. He either donated it, or maybe it's loaned."

"In any case, my bottom-line option at this point appears to be leasing a portion of the property if I can. It's a real challenge figuring out how to section off something that will lease quickly and generate enough to pay taxes and hopefully more. Are you familiar with the Free Haven property, Evie?"

"Oh yeah. I guess I didn't tell you that I knew your mom and your uncles. Your mom was my first babysitter, until I was, I don't know, maybe nine or ten. My dad dropped me at Free Haven to stay with your mom several times. It's a fun place for a kid."

Lew sits back, surprised by Evie's revelation. "Why didn't you tell me that before? You're the first person I've met here who actually knew my mom."

"Well, she left the area at a young age. So yes, I'm familiar with Free Haven and have fond memories, especially of the river. But speaking of your mom, I knew when she passed because Sheldon made a point of putting a small notice in the paper. I'm sorry for your loss. I never heard the cause of death or anything."

Lew looks down. "It was heart failure. She had a lot of health issues. Her life was hard as a single mom. She never had health care of any kind. Losing her was as bad as losing my wife. Nothing prepares you for those kinds of things."

"I'm really sorry, Lew. She was a good soul and such a happy and positive person."

"Thanks. I need to get home. But let me know if you come up with anything about June and her goon."

SEVEN

EARLY SUNDAY MORNING AND AMY IS STILL IN bed. No one works the garden on Sunday. Early morning sunlight is filtering through the trees and the cool of the morning is holding on a while longer. Lew doesn't need an alarm any longer. He's awake and up with the first light and the clashing sounds of birds, cicadas and frogs. He pulls on his cut-offs, pocket tee shirt and wading sneaks. It's kind of a routine now. Several times a week at this early morning hour, Lew quietly slips out the back door and heads down to the river. It doesn't take him long to catch enough fish for a couple of dinners and have them cleaned and in the fridge before Amy is up. As long as she doesn't witness the process of catching and cleaning the fish, she's fine eating them.

Lew knows how to vary the catch by the bait he uses. Crawdad tails are surefire for perch and bluegill; netting a few minnows is good for snagging the small bass. This time of the summer, a juicy grasshopper on his hook can attract the bigger bass. Catfish require digging for some plump worms to set on the river bottom, along with a bit of patience. Amy likes them all but favors fried catfish, just like Lew.

He takes to the well-worn path leading down to the river, fishing pole in one hand, tackle box in the other. It's the same path he walked that summer as a twelve-year-old. Mornings like this he feels more the twelve-year-old's anticipation of catching fish than a grown-up's chore of providing. He ambles down the hill, drinking in the sights and sounds of early morning, deep in his thoughts. *Oh Lordy, if only all day every day could be this peaceful. Just me and the river and the fish. I can't believe how I let so many years pass without fishing. This was the best part of when I was here as a kid. Getting up early and coming down to the river. This feeling, it never changes, never gets old.*

He stops for a moment, something on the ground catches his eye. There's a good size grasshopper, about two inches long, sitting on a long golden rod leaf. He slowly sets down the tackle box and in the same motion reaches forward and grabs it. He smiles at his closed hand. "Well little buddy, instead of chewing up the meadow grass, you'll be making a nice breakfast for a big ol' bass and that guy an even better dinner for us. Circle of life, pal." Holding the grasshopper gently in his fist he retrieves the tackle box with his rod hand and continues down the path.

Oh yeah, it's gonna be a good morning, I can tell. He stops in his tracks again. *Damn, this is a story. Why didn't I think of this before. I'll bet Evie would love a thousand words about this. Yeah, the early morning Everyman's River of Solitude, fishing pole in hand and his one and only concern – catching the big one. That Everyman, or woman – the barber, hair stylist, the banker, truck driver, store clerk, trash collector, delivery guy – arrives at the river's edge, the sun barely up, maybe not quite up. The noise, worry and chaos of life, a world away. He pauses for the moment, inhaling the moist, mossy, unmistakable smell of the river. He surveys the water. He's been here and seen this a thousand times, with his dad, grandpa, brother, uncle, best buddy. He knows this place like he knows his own backyard, but it's always different. The river, the water, always moving, always changing. What about today? What's hiding beneath that glistening, swirling surface? What's cruising the currents? Everyman-fisherman has rituals, most are part of readying the hook, line, sinker and bait for a showdown. But there are also rituals purely of superstition, guaranteed to help repeat his greatest fishing success – maybe. With the perfect bait or lure affixed, he makes that first cast. And then the watching, the waiting, the sensing, for the response. Some days no response. He doesn't want to think about that, not yet. But then, holy crawdad, a tug. A sudden rush of excitement runs up his spine to his brain. His pulse quickens, face flushes. "Come on big guy, take a big bite," he whispers like he's sending messages through the fishing line. Then, wham! The big bite, the snag, and the battle ensues as he reels and the fish fights. The screeching drag on his reel says it's a big one all right. "Just stay on the hook dammit. I've got plans for you." Oh yeah, that surge of adrenaline, the complete immersion in the moment, so visceral, so orgasmic. Yeah, almost sexual. Nope, better than sex. Hmm, I'll work on that last part. Mixing sexual metaphors, fishing and the river may be a bit of a stretch for the very proper Ms. Evie Anderson.*

The grasshopper suddenly jerks in his fist and he realizes he's been standing still in the path writing a story in his head. He holds his fist up, "Okay, Hoppity, we've got some fishing to get to, and then I've got a story to write.

About ten feet from the bank, he stops. On the opposite side of the river Bibi is engaged in her favorite activity, catching grasshoppers. *That's strange, I've never seen Bibi without Jewel somewhere close by.*

"Good morning, Lew," Jewel says, floating on her back in the river, au naturel. The water is crystal clear in this area, revealing Jewel's perfect round breasts, dark areolas and erect nipples as well as a small dark triangle of pubic hair between her legs. And he's feeling the effect of the sight between his own.

"How 'bout you put that fishing gear down and join me. The water's really nice. And that's not all."

Lew looks back up the hill, then up upstream and downstream. Satisfied there's no one around, he sets the pole and tackle box down and releases the grasshopper from his other hand. Removing his cap, "Okay, but you have to turn around."

Jewel laughs, "Oh brother," and whips around in the water. He kicks off his sneaks, drops his cut-offs and steps out of them, peels off his tee shirt and steps into the water. The river is cool and refreshing. Even in the worst heat of summer, this part of the river remains cool, fed by Bymer Spring. Lew walks into the water and then breast strokes to the middle where Jewel is still facing away.

She hears his splashing and turns, and without a word they come together, embrace and kiss, deeply, hungrily. Lew has been craving this closeness, this moment of intimacy with Jewel since the day he ran into her around the corner of the house. Jewel sensed that the time was right. She has been craving this just as much.

Lew plants his feet on the smooth river rock bottom, his shoulders out of the water. As they passionately kiss, tongue encircling tongue, Jewel wraps her legs around his waist and he grasps her round, firm bottom with his hands. While tongues dart and dance, Jewel reaches down between her thighs, grasps and strokes while positioning him just right to guide inside. He feels a taut resistance and whispers, "I don't think we can do this in the water."

"Shh, shh, shh – patience, Lew. Miss Puss has her way." With that he feels her open and welcome him in. With a deep kiss and deeper connection, they begin a passionate, rhythmic and intensifying water waltz.

On the riverbank, Bibi has stretched out and is watching the two lovers roil in the water. On the other bank, up at the confluence of Bymer Spring and Saoirse, Jerry Lloyd Ducker is also watching.

DRYING TOGETHER ON THE RIVERBANK, LEW IS stretched out on his back. Jewel rests on her side next to him. Her head is propped on her hand as her other hand traces figure eights across Lew's chest. Bibi is resting her head on Jewel's hip.

"Are you okay with this, Lew? I hope I didn't push you into something you weren't ready for."

Lew looks up and laughs. "Oh, I am so okay with this. Maybe a little more than ready." He pulls Jewel's head closer and kisses her.

"I'm glad. I wasn't really sure. So, I'm glad."

"Seems to me, Miss Weegy, that we've talked about my family and former life quite a lot. But I know so little of yours. Especially your social life and, mmm, romantic life? I mean, have you been married? Has there been a significant other, or two, or more in your life?"

Jewel looks up at the sky and laughs. "A significant other, two or more? That's funny, Lew. Sorry, but there's not much to tell . . . really. I mean, I hated high school. It was a god-awful bore. There were only six of us Black students. Two were guys. I think I had one date the whole time. I went to college up in Springfield. When I graduated, I started working at the city library there." She's silent for a moment, thinking and running her forefinger up and down Lew's bicep. "I guess there was one guy, for a while, at the university. He was a graduate student in business. His name was Kwaku. He was from Ghana and in the U.S. just for school. He was a drummer and son of a tribal chief. I attended some of his drumming circles. And we dated some."

Lew looks up at Jewel. "He sounds like an interesting guy. Son of a chief *and* a drummer. Impressive. What happened?"

"Well, we were getting pretty close, I guess. But when he graduated, he had to go home to Ghana. That was a big factor. And then my momma completely lost her eyesight and I had to come home to take care of her because my sister had her own family to care for. Kwaku and I talked about staying in touch, but you know how it is. The distance was just too much. No big whoop."

"Well," Lew says, "in my experience there's whoop and then there's big whoop. Whoop always seemed good enough for me."

"Okay, let's just say it wasn't enough whoop for me. Can we drop this, please?"

"Yeah, okay, consider it dropped. But I can say with some authority now, that Kwaku clearly didn't appreciate the incredible whoop he missed out on." Jewel laughs and punches him on the arm.

"Ouch! Okay, okay. I'm really sorry, but I need to get dressed and up to the house. Amy will be up soon and looking for breakfast."

Jewel smiles. "Yeah, and I have to get ready for church. I'm sure Momma's wondering where I am."

Lew stands up to cross the river for his clothes on the other side. Jewel continues relaxing on her side for the moment, then she jumps up and they embrace and kiss. And kiss. And kiss, pressing their bodies firmly together. Jewel starts feeling his body responding anew. She pulls back and places her forefinger on his lips.

"Sorry to shatter the moment, but I want you to know that I told my momma about the room you and Amy discovered and some of the things in it. You know, of your Uncle Sheldon's. She said there are some things that she feels important to tell you. I really think you need to come over and hear what Momma has to say."

Lew is intrigued. "Of course. I'm grateful for any information that's helpful. There's obviously a lot that I don't know. When can I come over?"

"Let me talk to Momma and I'll let you know. Just a reminder, she's blind and has some problems moving about. But her mind is as sharp as ever. She's also not given to sharing information lightly or generously. In fact, I've never known her to offer information – she usually holds on to it as tight as a blue tattoo on a brown butt. You should feel honored."

"That's a little intimidating. I really want to hear what your momma has to say. But right now, I'm more curious for you to turn around so I can see that tattoo." He tries turning her around and she pushes back laughing.

"It's just a saying, I have no tattoos. Now get across that river before I tattoo your butt." "Okay, okay," he says, backing away with hands raised in surrender, "Just let me know when I can come a visiting. I can't wait to meet your momma."

LEW RETURNS FROM THE RIVER WITH A BOUNCE IN HIS step but no fish to show for the outing. He slips in the back door as quietly as possible, expecting Amy to still be sleeping. But he sees from the kitchen that she's up and sitting at the table poring over the logs again.

"Good morning sweetie, you're up working on those logs awfully early."

Without looking up, she says, "And you and your girlfriend were up pretty early too." Lew stops breathing for the moment. Amy continues, "I found something here on the back of this map binder. It's another reference to a key." Lew starts breathing again, hoping she was just making a snide remark and didn't see what he and Jewel were doing at the river.

"It's another verse kind of like the one about the well. See here," she says, motioning to the binder for Lew to see.

THE BOOK IS GOD'S LAW AND SO DEMANDS,
THE PATH TO DELIVERANCE IS FINDING,
WHETHER READ FROM BEGINNING, MIDDLE OR END,
HOLD STRAIGHT YE FIND THE KEY MOST BINDING.

Lew reads the verse out loud, and then again. "Okay, it sounds almost like a religious dictum of some sort. Again, it's more like a riddle. What do you make of it?"

"A riddle . . . could be. But it's not that hard," she says. "Hold the Bible upright on the table and pull the covers out straight without tearing it."

Lew sets the Bible upright on the table. It's fragile and its pages are yellowed from age. The spine bows out in back.

"Okay," she says. "Now, can you hold it like that and pick it up?"

He lifts the book off the table and a key falls out of the bowed binding and bounces on the table. "Ha! Amy, you're a genius. How did you figure that out?"

"Kind of a no-brainer. If you just read the verse like directions and not like it's mystical or anything. You know, like the last one."

Lew kisses the top of her head. "Sarcasm aside, I still say you're a genius. Let's go see if this opens anything."

Lew goes right to the locked door, hoping that the verse and key they found will mirror what happened the last time. He inserts the key but it doesn't connect and the lock doesn't budge at all. He doesn't want to twist in a way that risks breaking the key or lock or both.

"It doesn't work. It doesn't really fit." he says.

"Okay, try it on the lockbox," Amy says.

They cross the space to the wardrobe and Lew squats down and inserts the key in the lockbox. There's an immediate *click*. He lifts the heavy leaded lid.

"Wow!" they exclaim together.

It appears that the lockbox hasn't been opened in quite a while. Maybe for a very long while. There are yellowed blank forms that look like legal stationery of some sort, and a half dozen or more metal stamp plates, like what old time notaries would use to officiate documents.

"It looks like there may have been a lawyer in the family at some point," Lew says. "Or someone who clerked in a law office or perhaps for the county." Under the first blank forms there are also what could be blank birth certificates for Cloch County.

Lew nods, "Yep, at some point the family had someone working in the local government. And maybe someone forging legal documents for the Klan."

Shoved down beside the forms and stamps is a canvas bag with a pull string tied in a knot. Lew picks it up. "Wow, it's heavy." He plops it back down and it makes a sound like it contains a chain. He tries to untie the knot in the pull cord, but it's like it's been permanently sealed by time and age. He pulls out his Swiss Army knife. The cord is so old he has to strain to cut through it. Finally, he pulls the bag open.

"My God! I don't believe it."

"Daddy, what is it?" Amy asks with a bit of alarm in her voice.

Lew reaches in and pulls out a large coin. "It's a silver dollar. A really old silver dollar." He rubs the coin with the hem of his shirt, trying to read the inscriptions and date. 'This is a Civil War era dollar that appears to have been minted in 1852 or 1853. I can't really make it out."

Lew hands the coin to Amy and she looks at one side, then the other. "Do you think it's still worth anything?"

Lew nods vigorously. "Oh yeah, it's still worth something, and likely a great deal more than a dollar. And look at how many are in the bag. We have to go count them."

UPSTAIRS, WITH BETTER LIGHT, LEW CAN SEE THAT these are in fact silver dollar coins minted in Philadelphia in 1852. He pushes back the logs and Bible and empties the bag out on the table.

"Eighteen silver dollars and two gold pieces. I'll bet those are worth even more."

Amy inspects several of the coins. "Do you think Uncle Sheldon knew they were in there? That box has been locked for a long time."

"I don't know. Hard to believe he didn't know. But why wouldn't he have used them? Or maybe he did, and these are all that remain."

"How do you find out what coins like this are worth?"

"I'm not sure," Lew says. "I know there are coin experts and collectors who would know about these. We need to find someone who can discreetly examine them and let us know what we have here. This could be the solution to some of our tax problems. Seems to me the logical thing to do is take a couple of these coins to the bank and see if someone there is knowledgeable enough to help." He sits back, tapping a coin on the table and thinking, "But you know, after some of the things Evie Anderson has said, I'm not really comfortable with who may see this and especially who may be talking to whom." He pulls his phone out and calls Evie Anderson.

"Hi Evie, Lew Harra. We just found some old coins here in the house. Do you happen to know anyone who is an expert in coins, especially old ones? Someone who can be trusted. I'm a little leery about going to the bank."

"That's smart, Lew. If you don't want your business shared with a lot of the wrong people, stay away from the bank. I have a friend who works in the library who is a certified numismatist."

"A new what? I'm not sure what you just said."

"A numismatist. She's a coin expert. She's collaborated on several books. Let me call her and see if she can come by after work today and you and your daughter can come in and see her very discreetly."

"Fantastic, Evie. I knew I could count on you." He hangs up and turns to Amy. "Evie's got a friend who's a coin expert.

She going to arrange for us to go see her later. This is exciting!" But in an instant, Amy pulls Purry into a tight clutch, steps back from Lew and runs into her room. His heart sinks. He follows her and she's on her back in bed in her usual uncommunicative position. Lew sits on the side of the bed.

"Sweetheart, I'm sorry if I upset you. I am only suggesting that you go with me to town and meet someone nice. Someone who can help us. You know, it's been a while now since your mom passed. We both miss her so much. But we have to go on. You know that she would want you to go on with your life, meet new people, make new friends. There's nothing for you to be afraid of. Nothing will harm you. I promise. I love you more than life itself. I really want you to go with me. I want my new friends to know how special you are. They are eager to meet you."

He waits for an answer, for some indication that she's hearing him and understands how much he loves her and will protect her. But she lies still, clutching Purry, staring at the ceiling. Lew's phone rings and he returns to the living room and answers.

"Yes, Evie, oh, that's great. Thanks, thanks so much. I'll see you soon."

EIGHT

L EW USES THE COMBINATION EVIE SHARED WITH him to enter the *Times* building's back door and climb the stairs to Evie's office. There's a woman sitting with Evie at her big round table. The two appear to be enjoying cocktail time. Evie waves him in.

"Lew Harra, this is Doreen Leach, my old high school friend and the only numismatist I know."

Lew smiles and extends his hand to Doreen. "So nice to meet you and thank you for making time to help us."

Doreen grasps his hand and smiles. "Not at all. I'm happy to help anytime a meeting is important enough for Evie to break out the good Scotch. I understand you've come across some interesting coins."

Lew reaches in his pocket and starts to place several coins on the table. Doreen quickly holds up her hand. "Wait a second Lew. Let's do this the right way." She opens her briefcase and brings out a small leather pouch. From that she pulls a green felt square and unfolds it on the table. "Okay, let's see what you've got there." Lew gently sets two silver dollars and a gold piece on the green felt. Doreen pulls a small magnifying glass out of the leather pouch and begins examining each coin on both sides.

"Well, Lew, you've happened onto some really nice specimens here. The two silver dollars are nearly mint condition and part of the highly collectible Liberty Seated series. I believe that series was struck from about 1840 to 1870. These two coins are the 1852 Philadelphia Liberty Seated edition. Depending on various characteristics they can range from pretty valuable to extremely valuable."

'Which means . . .?" Lew leans in.

"Which means, somewhere between five or six hundred dollars a coin to several thousand dollars. There's a big range. I have one in my personal collection that I bought ten years ago for six hundred. It's not in nearly such good condition as these. The gold coin is Confederate issue and harder to value because gold Confederate coins sometimes contain only small amounts of gold. It's also in poorer condition. It could still fetch a good price from a serious collector. In both cases, Lew, it would take a more informed eye than mine to authenticate and estimate the value."

"That's incredible, Doreen. Right now I have a need for some quick cash. How do I go about exchanging these for money?"

"It's a process. Not difficult, but not one you can count on for quick cash. To get top value, you need to have a coin grading service review and certify authenticity. At best, that can take a few weeks. But it could take longer. When it comes to selling the coins, I'm happy to broker a sale for you for a small fee. I've done that before. Once authenticated, I might like to take one off your hands as well."

Evie leans over and eyeing the coins, "Are these all you found, Lew, or are there more? You don't have to say how many, but I know you need the money for the property taxes. Do you think you might have enough for that?"

Lew smiles. "Oh yeah, enough for the taxes and then some. But the problem is time. I have two weeks to pay the taxes and fines or everything goes on the auction block."

Evie turns to Doreen. "And how long before these coins can be certified?"

Doreen sits back. "To be safe, I'd say give it a month, maybe more. The closest quality grading service I know of is in Little Rock. I can put you in touch with someone there and you can take your specimens directly to expedite matters. It's less than a two-hour drive. But for now, I need to be going. Oh, and Lew, I suggest that you wrap these coins in some soft material and keep them separate. You don't want to lower the value by having them clanking around in your pocket." She smiles and pushes up out of her chair. "Thanks for the Scotch, Evie, and thanks for sharing this great find, Lew."

Evie walks Doreen to the door and then returns. "You have a few more minutes, Lew?" Both sit back down. "What do you need to resolve the tax matter? I'm guessing you must be at least two years down."

"Actually, a little more than two years of taxes and fines. I need just over five thousand bucks."

"Tell you what. If you're willing, I'll make you a personal loan – very quietly and off the record. Then when you get the money you need out of these coins you can pay me back. No interest."

"That's incredibly generous of you, Evie. I don't know what to say. But I think I should pay interest or do something."

"How about letting me meet that daughter of yours. I'd say it's about time."

"Yeah. About that. I feel like I need to find a counselor to work with Amy. I thought she was making progress for a while, but now, I don't know. She may be getting worse. I mean she'll barely leave the house, and any mention of leaving or seeing anyone sends her to her room angry and silent. I'm at a loss for what to do."

"That sounds serious. Lucky for you I know everyone there is to know here. I have another friend who is a counselor who specializes in grief. Come by tomorrow morning and I'll give you his information. And I'll have a check ready for you."

THE NEXT MORNING, EVIE HAS A PERSONAL LOAN agreement for Lew to sign and a bank check drawn from one of her business accounts for the exact amount needed for the property taxes and penalties. Lew signs the agreement and takes the check across the street to the bank and deposits it. From there he goes directly to the county courthouse and county clerk's office and writes a check for the taxes and penalties. He hands over the check and instantly feels a weight lift from his shoulders. He tucks the tax receipt into his briefcase and returns to his old Toyota, where Amy and Purry are waiting. He starts up the engine and points the car south down good ol' Highway 65, toward Little Rock.

Doreen Leach called him last night with the name and address of the coin grading firm she spoke of when they met. She also set up an appointment for Lew with the firm's partner, a Mr. Durand, who specializes in Civil War-era Federal and Confederate coins.

It occurs to Lew that for every despicable character he's encountered since being here, he's met at least two truly wonderful people. He had no idea or expectation that he would encounter someone as amazing as Jewel. And what a blessing Evie Anderson has been. She alone may be the difference between Amy and him making a life for themselves here. Somebody upstairs must be watching out for them.

Aside from his excitement and nervousness about getting the coins authenticated, Lew's thrilled to share the experience of the Ozark countryside south of the Missouri border with Amy. This will be his first time in Arkansas. The highway to Little Rock is not as winding and challenging as it appears on the map. He stops off at one of the roadside scenic outcrops so they can get out of the car and take in the vista. He's so pleased Amy can be here to see this.

"You know, sweetie, the Boston Mountain range of the Ozark Plateau is said to be the oldest mountain range in North America. And many of the big rivers are among the oldest in the country, etched out long ago by receding glaciers."

"Yeah, it's beautiful. But your Dad-splaining doesn't make me like it more. It's still not home. I miss my friends. I miss Momma. It's fine that you get so excited about new stuff. But I miss home. I just want to go home."

Lew puts his arm around her and hugs her to his side. She pulls away, staring straight ahead and clutching Purry tightly. He turns to her. "Okay, I get it! You miss home. I miss home. I miss a lot of things. It doesn't change a da . . ." He catches himself. He takes a breath and turns back toward the view. "I mean to say, it's natural to miss things. There are loved ones like your mom and Grandma Christy who we will never, ever forget. We just have to be open to new things, new places and people. You're young and there's so much of the world I want you to see. Places, people and things I didn't get to see. I want your life to be full and wonderful. So please forgive me the transgression of the occasional Dad-splain."

He smiles, feeling her step back and lean against him, Purry tucked in her arm between them. "Okay, as long as it's only an occasional Dad-splain."

Back on the road, Lew's pleased that Amy spoke of her mom. And he's all the more saddened that he didn't get the opportunity to bring Nora down to this stunning country-side. It simply didn't occur to them to sightsee on their trip four years ago. It was all business. Get in, fix things and get on with work and life back in St. Louis. He never thought of them being on a treadmill and oblivious to all this beauty around them. But that's one of the things that a jarring loss brings into full relief. Too often a little late. But not for him and for Amy. He can do better. With the tax nightmare resolved for now, he can put his focus and energies in better directions. Like getting Amy the help that she needs. And getting to know Jewel better, and more intimately.

THE COIN GRADING FIRM IS IN A SMALL STRIP MALL ON the northern outskirts of Little Rock, making it easy to reach from the highway without having to deal with Little Rock traffic. Lew encourages Amy to stroll the strip mall and check out some of the shops while he meets with Mr. Durand. But as he expected, she and Purry remain in the car.

Mr. Durand is a short, fastidious-looking middle-aged man with a gray goatee and wire-rimmed glasses who calls to mind the Gringotts bankers in the Harry Potter movies. He ushers Lew into his office and seats him at a small round felt top table. There are framed photos of various coins hanging on the walls. Lew opens his briefcase and pulls out a small bag with the coins he brought. He places them on the table, explaining just enough to let Mr. Durand know to take this grading process seriously. He is back in the car with Amy and heading home in less than twenty minutes. It's a little after lunchtime, so Lew pulls off the highway and finds a picnic area alongside the Buffalo River.

The length of the Buffalo River in Arkansas is a designated national park and it's a lush and beautiful area. Lew's research before their trip indicated that this was the first river in the U.S. to receive National Park designation – a factoid he'd love to share with Amy, except for her admonishment earlier. He instinctively knows that Dad-splaining has to be far worse than any other kind of 'splaining. He keeps the fascinating little nugget of history to himself as he pulls out the lunch of bologna sandwiches he made for the trip.

Amy loved bologna sandwiches when he made them for her in grade school. He's pretty confident that her advancing age and independence won't alter her taste. He also breaks out some potato salad he made last night for dinner. They both love potato salad.

While Lew doesn't enjoy getting called out by his tween-aged daughter, at the same time he basks in her intelligence and self-possession. She's demonstrating self-confidence in a way that suggests she's definitely making some progress. In these positive moments he sees more and more of Nora in her, both in manner and appearance. Her lengthening arms and legs and compact, athletic torso are just like her mother's. Lew knows that Amy's at the brink of independence, and he has to accept what this age brings. He recalls all too well what he and his mom went through. But he also knows it's a temporary stage. If he keeps his balance and perspective, she'll find her way back to him. At least that's what's supposed to happen.

There's no rush to get through lunch, but Lew wants to get back into town before the post office closes. Aubrey the mailman left a note in the last delivery that he has a package to pick up. Depending on who and where it's from, it may or may not get opened. Like always the return trip seems shorter. He pulls the old Toyota off Highway 65 and into town and merges onto Main street of Cloch Village. The post office is in the center of town on Main Street. Lew turns into one of the slanted parking spaces in front of the late 19th century structure, one of the first buildings in town that was built to serve the purpose it continues to serve. How he'd love to share that little tidbit with Amy. But he's stoic. He unfastens his seat belt.

"Wait here, sweetie, I have to run in and pick up a package. Won't be a minute."

There's no line at the post office window. Some of the realities of small-town life still fascinate Lew. He pushes the package notice through the window slot to Marvin, the eighty-something clerk who has probably worked in this job since he was eighteen. Marvin shuffles back behind the original wooden racks and works his way down, trying to match the notice with the package. He pulls something out and triple checks the notice and package address, then shuffles back to the window. He pushes the notice back to Lew. "Sign right there." Lew picks up the chain-anchored pen and signs the notice and Marvin pulls it back. Lew looks at the address.

"Hey wait, Marvin, this isn't addressed to me. I mean it's my address, but this is to a 'Ward Sheldon.'"

Marvin shuffles back to the window, turns the package around and studies it. "Hmmm, no see, it says here below, *In lieu of addressee*–your name's Lew, isn't it?" Marvin looks up with a sly smile. Before Lew can say anything, he hears someone calling his name. Standing at the door is June Eastman, waving furiously at him.

"Hey Lew, have you got a minute?" At that instant, Marvin shuts the window and closes up shop.

Lew turns, tucks the package under his arm and walks to the door. "Hi, June, how are you?"

June has no time for social salutary conventions. "I've been meaning to come see you again, Lew. I'm sorry about that little misunderstanding with Mr. Umanoff. You know he's one of those foreign fellas who doesn't know how to speak good English."

"But I thought the guy was from Brooklyn."

"Exactly. But Lew, you need to know that your property is just perfect for this resort hotel project and believe me, they are willing to pay you twice or more what that property is worth."

"Now, June . . ." She holds her hand up.

"Wait, Lew. Just think about it. Besides getting a primo apartment in the new resort, you can buy another place twice the size of Free Haven, build a beautiful new home, or you and your family can take a trip around the world. Or all of those things. Just think about that, Lew."

"I appreciate your efforts, June, and those are all really interesting things to think about. But I'm simply not interested in selling. This family homestead dates back almost two hundred years and has been entrusted to me. I don't believe entrusted means making the biggest profit I can. It's still no! No thank you."

June's realtor smile disappears and she instantly turns sullen. "You are making a big mistake, Lew. I don't think you understand how important this project is to the economy of this area. This could mean a lot of jobs for people who need work. It's going to bring a lot of money into the area. And if you stand in the way of this happening, well, a lot of people are going to be really angry. It's not good to have so many people that angry with you in this county."

Lew purses his lips. He looks away and then back at June, not wanting to respond too angrily. "If I misinterpreted Umanoff's comment as a threat, there's no question about yours. I'm not sure I can say this emphatically enough, but if you and people here are unhappy with me for not selling my family's home, I really don't give a blue opossum's ass. And I'm positive that needs no translation. Excuse me, my daughter's waiting in the car."

DETERMINED NOT TO LET THIS DUST-UP WITH JUNE dampen his mood, Lew gets back on track with his plan for dinner. With the promise of financial relief coming from the sale of silver coins, Lew decides to go a little deeper into their dwindling savings and splurge on dinner. He stops off at the Piggly Wiggly. While Lew's shopping The Pig, as locals refer to the store, Amy and Purry stay in the car – as usual.

Inside, Lew wheels his cart directly to the meat counter. It's been a long time since he and Amy have enjoyed a thick ribeye steak smothered with mushrooms, and a baked potato oozing butter and sour cream. A rich, sweet cherry pie for dessert is but a faint memory.

Jewel's nephew, Jeff, is at the check-out. "Hi, Mr. Harra, looks like a special night at your place."

With pride of possibilities, Lew stacks his items on the belt. "Yep, Jeff. Having a special night with my girl."

Jeff smiles big. "Oooh, Auntie Jewel is coming over?"

Lew is taken aback. "Uh, no, Jeff. I mean my daughter Amy and me."

Jeff, embarrassed, laughs, "Yeah, yeah, I was teasing. You know, I mean I know, I mean everybody knows, how much, uh, uh, Auntie Jewel and well your, uh, you know . . ."

Lew packs up his groceries and smiles. "Thanks, Jeff, we're good. See you later."

"Yeah, Mr. Harra, thanks for shopping the Pig."

It's been a while since Lew has grilled a steak, but some things never change. And the smell of a good steak over a hot wood fire provokes appetite and memories of every succulent steak ever grilled. Amy gazes at the twilight sky as Lew grills, both enjoying the warm summer evening. Lew waxes on about how much he enjoyed the Little Rock excursion. Amy clutches Purry and continues staring at the sky. He jokes about the nerdy little man, Mr. Durand, who almost got emotional seeing the mint-condition silver dollars placed before him.

"I have a feeling we'll get a grading pretty fast out of this guy. Like Doreen, I half expect an offer from him to buy the coins he's assessing. That's fine by me." Lew feels that they had such a good day together, Dad-splaining notwithstanding, it seems a good time to broach the matter of the counselor.

"You know, when I was meeting with Evie Anderson a couple days ago, she asked how you are doing. She expressed concern about you because she had her own experience losing a parent when she was not much older than you. She said it was hard for her and, well, she really benefitted by talking to this counselor here in town. He knows a lot about how young people deal with loss. I was thinking maybe you might like to talk to him. No pressure, of course, but we can afford something like that now . . . I mean, if you'd like to talk to someone besides me."

Amy sits silently, continuing to stare out at something, at nothing. Without altering her posture or stare, "I think you need to talk to him, Daddy. I think you should. I'm fine and I wish you'd stop worrying about me. I don't want to talk to anyone. Not because I can't, but I don't want to. I don't like your girlfriend. I don't like the people who come here. I don't like anyone here. I want to go home, that's all."

Lew turns the steak one last time. "Sweetheart, we are home. And I know you miss your friends in St. Louis, and maybe we can make a trip there to see them sometime. But this is home for now and will be for a while. As soon as school starts, you're going to make new friends." With that, she gets up and goes into the house without another word, leaving Lew to finish the steak. Discussion over.

NINE

IN MID-JULY, THE COOL OF THE MORNING DOESN'T last long. Once the sun is up, so is the temperature. Lew is sitting at the kitchen table gazing out the window onto the garden. He's watching Jewel plucking suckers off the tomato plants. She's picked about a bushel of the Kirby cucumbers that are just right for canning pickles. She's wearing her short cutoff jeans that show off her legs especially well. Her faded yellow tee shirt is wet with sweat and clinging fast around her round breasts. He's feeling a spark of arousal watching her and looking forward to their early morning swimming date tomorrow. It looks like she's about finished, so he pours a couple glasses of iced coffee to take outside.

Seeing Lew approach, Jewel smiles her beautiful whole face smile. "Good morning, handsome. You guessed right again about what I need . . . for now." She takes a glass and drinks deep, then holds the chilled glass to her forehead. "Was your trip to Little Rock successful?"

Lew nods. "Oh yeah, the guy Doreen set me up with was immediately impressed. I think we'll hear something soon."

Jewel dabs her face and neck with her neckerchief. "That's great. Momma and I are going to do some serious pickle canning a little later. If you're free, why don't you come over and pitch in? It'll give you a chance to meet Momma and talk."

"That sounds perfect. I've got to do a little repair work on a couple of the shelves in the cellar before you start loading them up with more canned goods. I'll call and come over as soon as I finish."

JEWEL AND HER MOM LIVE JUST ACROSS THE RIVER from Free Haven. Lew could probably hit their house with a rock thrown from the front circle driveway. But to get there, he has to drive out to County Road, cross the bridge over the Saoirse River, drive about a hundred yards, turn left and drive up about a half mile to their house. As hilly and rocky as Free Haven is, this area is flat and serves Jewel and her mom as a source of market hay. Her brother-in-law Lucas handles cutting, baling the hay and selling it for both their properties during the entire summer growing season. Given the controversy around Lucas selling hay to the thoroughbred horse farms on the western side of the lake, Jewel and her mom prefer to stay at arm's-length from the transactions.

The house looks about as old as the Free Haven house, probably built about the same time. But this is a much smaller house with a good-sized covered porch, a chain-suspended bench swing, and two rocking chairs. Lew parks in front next to Jewel's van. As soon as he steps up on the porch, he hears Bibi barking. Jewel comes to the door, now dressed in a yellow cotton sun dress. She's also wearing a blue denim bib apron suitable for canning. She looks much cooler and just as sexy to Lew. She smiles big and opens the screen door, leans forward and kisses Lew, something they wouldn't think of doing where Amy might see them.

"Come in and meet Momma." Jewel's mom is sitting in a kitchen chair by the table where they have a couple dozen jars ready to receive the season's pickles. She looks to be in her sixties, maybe younger, maybe older. Her striking silver hair is pulled back tight in a bun. Jewel bears a strong resemblance to her mom, although her mother's skin is darker than Jewel's. They have the same pronounced cheekbones and smiles that charm and disarm.

"Momma, this is Lew Harra from across the river. Lew, my momma Berta." Her eyes stay closed.

She extends her hand. "So nice to meet you, Lew. Jewel has told me so much about you. But I guess not everything." She turns toward Jewel. "I heard that little kiss, you know."

Jewel laughs. "Momma, I don't tell you everything because you always know everything."

Lew shakes Berta's hand. "So nice to meet you and I've heard wonderful things about you from Jewel. I really appreciate getting to talk to you and learn more about my own family, especially about my Uncle Sheldon."

Berta motions to a chair. "Sit, Lew, I got things to tell you. And you got things to tell me." Jewel continues working on the pickles, and the pungent aroma of fresh dill hangs in the kitchen air. Berta starts telling Lew of her family's history and experience with the O'Hara's. Lew has brought along a pad and pen to take notes, not wanting to rely on memory for such important information.

"Well now Lew, don't you know that our family history runs like a deep stream with the O'Hara's. I mean to tell you that our grandparent ancestors came to this area with the O'Hara family and helped homestead Free Haven."

Lew looks up at Jewel, suspecting and dreading what he hears next from Berta:

"Yes. Our family was your family's slaves." She senses Lew's discomfort and places a hand on his forearm on the table. "It was our lives and reality at the time, Lew. Now, if this makes you uncomfortable, that's good. It means you're hearing me. Besides, if you didn't know this before, then it's high time you learn about it. But there's more for you to know." She goes on to describe the early years of settling the area, building the house and the original barn.

"The first barn they built burned. Don't you know it was struck by lightning and was full of fresh hay putting off swamp gas. Apparently that ol' barn took off like a rocket ship." She laughs and slaps Lew's leg. They all laugh.

Lew holds up his hands. "But wait, wait a minute, what's swamp gas? Remember, you're talking to a city guy."

Berta leans in. "Gas, Lew, gas. It builds up and then it's kinda like the barn farts, big time!" She laughs and slaps his leg again.

"Momma, please. In spite of how many times I've explained it," Jewel says, "Momma still enjoys repeating that old farmer's tale about wet hay producing methane gas and causing fires. The truth of the matter, bacteria in hay bales that are put up too wet will grow. When that growth accelerates, at a certain point it generates high enough heat for spontaneous combustion to occur. Often in an explosion that makes you think it's gas or dynamite."

"I didn't think spontaneous combustion was a real thing," Lew says. "Does that really happen? I mean hay just bursts into flames on its own?"

"Oh, it's real," Berta says. "Next time you see Lucas have him tell you about his experience with barn fires."

"Yeah, it's a serious problem," Jewel says. "I'm surprised Lucas didn't tell you about measures he and Jesse take to make sure the hay isn't too wet when baled and stowed. The worst barn fire we've had in this area was not that many years ago. The old Adams barn went up in flames. Our fire department lost several men in that disaster. Terrible tragedy."

Lew nods. "It had to be. I saw that memorial sculpture to those men that Uncle Sheldon made outside the fire station. So that was caused by wet hay. That's amazing."

Berta continues, "Okay, Lew, pay attention. I've got more to tell you. As you must know, Missouri was a slave state, but horribly conflicted. In this area, most slaves, like my ancestors, were domestics and worked the farm like field hands. After completing the Free Haven house, ol' Hugh O'Hara and his sons helped my grandfather-ancestor build this house for his family. That was soon after the war broke out – you know, the big one, between North and South."

Lew smiles. "Yeah, I've heard of that one."

Berta laughs and slaps his thigh again and keeps her hand there. Lew looks up at Jewel and she turns her head and winces with an embarrassed smile, saying without saying, *Yup, Momma kinda randy.*

Berta sits up. "Anyway, Lew, after the war started your grandfather-ancestor Hugh gave my grandfather-ancestor his manumission."

Lew tilts his head. "His manu-what?"

"Manumission. It's the document given to slaves by slaveholders granting them their freedom. He gave one to my grandmother-ancestor too."

Jewel pours three glasses of lemonade and plops ice cubes in each. She sets a glass down for her mom and one for Lew. "Take a deep breath, Lew, there's more to come. Go on, Momma."

Berta sips her lemonade. "As I hope you can see, Lew, our families worked together and relied on each other for generations. And they shared a very big and important secret all those generations." Lew sits upright again. "Jewel told me about the hidden room you found in your cellar and some of the items in that lockbox. Tell me, Lew, who knows about that room?"

Lew thinks for a moment. "Well, my daughter Amy knows, of course. She found the key to the room and the lockbox."

Berta smiles. "Clever girl."

Lew smiles and nods. "Yes, she is. Who else? Well, Jewel, and Evie Anderson at the *Cloch County Times*. That's really it. Oh wait, Doreen Leach knows we found the silver coins. But I didn't tell her about the room."

Berta nods. "You have to make sure the information goes no farther. Because, you see, Free Haven was a way station on the Underground Railroad from when your ancestors arrived until the end of the war. Your family came here and much like the Irish newcomers of that time, many of them were abolitionist. But you don't announce those things, especially in a slave state and most especially when the new migrants aren't welcome to begin with."

Lew shakes his head. "Wow. I mean, wow! That's amazing. Do you know how they became part of that underground network?"

Jewel interjects, putting on her historian hat. "It's a common belief, Lew, or more like a myth, that the Underground Railroad was a coordinated and organized effort among White abolitionists. It definitely wasn't that. The fact is the Underground Railroad was organized and largely run by free Blacks in various partnerships with White abolitionists, including the Quakers. The O'Haras were partners and provided a safe space and some resources. But they also kept themselves a safe distance from direct association in case the way station was found out. Not that there is a *safe distance.* Fact is, anyone assisting slaves to escape in any way, Black or White, ended up dead."

Lew nods. "Yeah, I can well imagine. I think I have a lot to learn about the whole movement. But I have to say, it helps me feel better knowing I come from a family that actually freed slaves and worked in partnership to try to free others. It all makes sense now. The names on the logs we found with the lockbox were escaped slaves making the transition to freedom."

Berta smiles. "Through *Free* Haven," she says, emphasizing the word *Free.*

Lew almost jumps out of his seat. "So that's where the name came from." Lew is trying to digest all this new information. "I get the part about how that room could be a safe place to stay and hide for a while. But where did they go from there?"

Berta shakes her head. "That part is hard to know. Once they left, there's no record of them after that. No way of knowing."

Stuffing a dill frond into a jar of cucumbers, Jewel adds, "We know that they had fewer options after the Fugitive Slave Act was passed in 1850. Before that, all a runaway had to do was get to a free state. But after 1850, they could be captured and returned to the slaveholder from any free state. There was no safe haven. So the runaways passing through Free Haven pretty much had to find the best route they could to Canada, where they couldn't be captured and returned to the slavers. From here that was most likely into Illinois, a free state where they could find more way stations, then up through the Detroit area. That was a mighty long and dangerous trek. I feel sure that's why our ancestors started giving runaways forged manumissions to carry."

Lew interrupts. "Yeah, we found blank official-looking stationery and metal stamps they must have used to forge the manumissions. I'm guessing then that each runaway would get a manumission, a map, and probably a silver dollar, which back then was worth a lot more than a dollar today. All that gave them a reasonable chance to gain their freedom."

Berta smiles. "Probably less than a reasonable chance, Lew. The odds were still stacked against them. One of the hardest things to do was get the runaways safely out of the area while staying off the roads. On the roads, not just bounty hunters but local police could capture and return them. That's where the river became vital."

Jewel chimes in. "I was fascinated to learn from local history books that those early Irish who settled in this area named the river Saoirse, which is the Irish Gaelic word for *Freedom*."

"It was the river, Lew, where my people played a really key role," Berta says. "It was my ancestor's risky job to get runaways safely up the river to points where there were fewer police and bounty hunters. The runaways had to get up to Luna's Leap and from there take the path down to the dock on the river."

"You know, I wondered about that name, Luna's Leap. I first thought maybe someone didn't know how to spell 'Lovers.'"

Berta laughs and slaps Lew's thigh again. "You're hilarious, Lew." She turns to Jewel. "You got yourself a funny one here." Jewel rolls her eyes. Berta continues, "Well, Lew, I don't know what stories white folks tell, but amongst Black folks, Luna is a folk hero. She was a runaway who had a knack for escaping her slave owners. But the third time she escaped with her infant girl, when the bounty hunter's dogs were closing in on her, rather than being captured and returned again to the punishment and having her daughter torn away from her, she chose the freedom of leaping and dying from what we now know as Luna's Leap."

"That's amazing, Miss Berta. And incredibly sad. I'm sorry I was so flip. I'll tell Amy that story so Luna will be our hero as well."

"Well, for those runaways who did find their way down the path from Luna's Leap, ol' Hugh O'Hara had a keel boat moored at his dock that was used to ship goods up to Springfield and the Atlantic Street Market by the train station. That ol' boat had a false bottom to hide the runaways."

"Fascinating! But what kind of goods did the family have to ship?"

"Oh, a variety of things. Fruits, vegetables, tobacco. But the important product was corn whiskey, always on board in good supply to reliably distract any official getting too curious."

"Yeah, apparently Uncle Sheldon continued the proud tradition of producing corn whiskey and moonshine."

"He sure did. I still have some if you'd like to try a little."

"Thanks, but no. It's a little early. And I think I have a couple jars of White Lightning left in the basement. Everything you're saying makes sense, Miss Berta, and clarifies a lot for me. But I still don't understand how they managed to keep such an operation a secret back then and for so long after."

"It was a simple strategy of hiding in plain sight. From all outward appearances, the O'Hara family was solid South. They owned slaves. Hugh's two sons were said to have joined the Confederate Army in North Carolina, when they actually joined the Baldknobbers over in Taney County. The Baldknobbers were a vigilante group that scouted and provided underground support for the Union Army in Southern Missouri and Northern Arkansas. They gave protection to runaways when they could and sometimes took out bounty hunters poking around the area. And from that time up to

Sheldon, the men of the O'Hara family have been members in good standing in the Klan. But like Sheldon, not committed Klan. There's a big difference, Lew."

"I'm understanding a lot more now. My head is swimming with all this information and connecting so many of the dots. But right now, I really need to get home. I told Amy I'd be back before now. She and I were going to do some more work on finding the key to that last door. I left her poring over more of the logs that we found. She's become a little obsessed about ferreting out clues to hidden keys. But I have so many questions and, well, I'd like to hear more. Can I come see you again?"

"Of course. Any time. I'm sure Jewel appreciates your help with the canning."

Jewel looks up while twisting on a jar lid. "Oh yeah, thanks for all the help, Lew."

TEN

FINDING THE SILVER DOLLARS WAS LUCKY BE-yond belief, but Lew still has to make money. He would prefer cashing in no more of the silver than he has to for the time being. He hoped to have more stories to take to Evie since the hay-baling piece. But his enthusiasm for the Everyman fishing story waned in light of his and Jewel's river activities and then finding the lock box key and coins.

When he swings by the library mid-week to report to Doreen Leach about his trip to Little Rock, it occurs to him that a feature story about Doreen and Civil War era coins might be of interest to Evie. It would also cover his tracks explaining to any who might be curious about his sudden interest in silver coins. Doreen is pleased and not surprised with the response he got from the expert at the Little Rock grading firm. And she's flattered by Lew's wanting to write about her. Librarians and numismatists pretty much move through life invisible to the public.

Lew spends enough time with Doreen to get what he feels he needs for about a thousand words. He spends another hour at the library writing the story up. Even as rusty as his writing chops are these days, this piece practically writes itself. Doreen loans him several great photos of coins, Civil War era Federal and Confederate, and a fairly old photo of herself when she started working at the library.

Before leaving the library, Lew checks out a couple books on the Underground Railroad. Now that he's the keeper of a way station, he needs to know a lot more about the history and nature of the system. There's a lot that he still has to understand about the secret room, not to mention what may be on the other side of that still-locked door.

From the library he goes directly to the *Cloch County Times* to see Evie and offer her the article on Doreen. Evie is meeting with a woman who appears to be about her age. She sees Lew walk in and waves him up to her office.

"Come on in, Lew. I want you to meet Erin Oakes, one of your fellow writers and a dear friend of mine."

Erin stands and extends her hand and Lew grasps it. "Nice to meet you, Erin. Any relation to Presiding Commissioner Oakes?"

"Yes indeed. Davis would be my dear cousin."

"That must make getting scoops at the courthouse a little easier."

"I wish. Most of the time I feel like I'd be better off being a reporter that he couldn't ignore as easily as his cousin."

"I doubt that, Erin," Evie quickly interjects. "Davis Oakes dislikes and ignores reporters of all kinds – kith, kin and faceless stranger. You do a great job in spite of the relationship."

"Well, it's great meeting you, Lew. Sorry I have to run now, but I hope we'll get a chance to get acquainted. I'd love to hear about your experience at the *Globe-Dispatch*."

"You bet. I look forward to finding some time."

Evie waits until Erin leaves, then turns to Lew. "Before I tell you what I've got, tell me what you have."

"That sounds ominous. But I have a couple things. For one, I thought an article about Doreen Leach would be interesting to folks, especially given her knowledge of Civil War era coins. I interviewed her, got some great photos and I have about eight hundred words."

"That's terrific, Lew. People like Doreen never get a light shined on them. It's just the kind of writing I was hoping you'd bring me."

"I have also learned more about that cellar room we uncovered from Jewel's mom. But that's a longer story. Maybe you should tell me what you've got first."

"Yeah, because this is something you need to know about. Word got to the county commissioners about you paying your taxes and penalties and getting in the clear."

"I'm surprised any of them would be paying attention, except for Davis Oakes, and for his own reasons."

"Oh, they are all very interested, Lew. Because there's a lot of interest in the Firebird Resort Hotel project happening. And all of them have been focused on Free Haven as not just the best site for the development, but the only possibility."

"Sorry to disappoint so many important people. But I'm not selling and at this juncture there's not much they can do about it."

"Actually, Lew, there is something they can do. In fact, my sources tell me that they have already started the process of acquiring Free Haven through a writ of eminent domain."

"Eminent domain? Really!" Lew's eyes bulge and his face reddens. "How the hell can they make a case for eminent domain? The Firebird project is purely a private money-making venture by a bunch of shady New Yorkers and God only knows who else."

"Easy, Lew. You've got to get smart, not angry. Keep in mind that eminent domain has been central to economic development in this county for a lot of years. Thousands of acres on the bottoms of those lakes were acquired that way. And while the Army Corps of Engineers designed and undertook the lakes projects to serve as a fresh water supply, the driving force of county officials from beginning to end was economic. You need to find an attorney if you plan to fight this. And that will be a challenge because lawyers around here are gun-shy about going up against county economic interests."

"Yeah, I get that. I have to go think this through." Without telling Evie about what he learned from Berta, Lew heads home. He's angry, scared, frustrated. But mostly he's angry. He's also wondering if he should tell Amy about the county commission's actions at all. On the one hand, it would be giving her another reason to say they have to leave. And she gets so emotional and fragile when she feels they are being threatened. Her well-being is still the most important thing. Besides, how the hell does he go about explaining something like eminent domain to a twelve-year-old? Truth is, he doesn't fully understand it himself.

He drives past the history museum and turns onto County Road. Then it hits him: *What if a property is an officially designated historic landmark, like a hub on the Underground Railroad? Can eminent domain be enacted on such a property? As director of the history museum, Jewel knows more about historic landmarks than anyone.*

He pulls the car over and stops. Jewel's van is still in the museum parking lot. He makes a quick U-turn, shoots into the museum parking lot and parks next to the van. It's a little after four p.m., so Jewel has probably closed the museum for the day. Lew goes to the service entrance and dials Jewel at precisely the instant she opens the door to leave. "*AAEY-HHH!*" It's like the first day they ran into each other. Bibi even starts barking. "Shhh, Bibi. Lew, what are you doing? You scared the bejesus out of me."

"Sorry," he says, smiling and holding up his phone. "I was trying to call you to let you know that I was here, and then you opened the door."

"Well, what is it? Is something wrong?"

"Can we go back inside? I need to fill you in on what Evie Anderson just told me and I feel a little exposed out here." Inside, he relates what Evie told him then describes his idea about securing historic landmark status for Free Haven as a way station on the Underground Railroad.

"The key question is, can Free Haven qualify for historic landmark status in the first place? And then, can that status block an eminent domain claim? And then, if the answer is yes to the first two questions, what's involved in securing landmark status?"

"First of all, Lew, take a deep breath and calm down. Those are several complicated questions. I'm no authority on landmark status, but I know quite a bit. The answer to your first question is absolutely yes. Any documented Underground Railroad station qualifies on the National Registry. The second question is a legal matter. An attorney familiar with eminent domain would have to answer that one. About the third question, I believe I have the forms on file that you need to apply for historic landmark status. I went through all that getting this building landmarked several years ago. Follow me."

She walks back into the museum space and toward her corner office as Lew follows. He hasn't seen Jewel in her stylish work attire in a while. She looks positively cool and elegant, not to mention sexy, in her light beige, form-fitting slacks, with a yellow, lavender and white patterned silk blouse and beige sandal heels. She's striking and very much the woman in charge.

She leads Lew to a standing file cabinet next to her desk. She turns to him, "Before going further, has it occurred to you that applying for historic landmark status completely exposes generations of your family for who and what they really were?"

"Yes, of course that occurred to me. And it opens me up to Klan retribution here and now. It's risky. But considering the risks all those generations of family before us accepted, I feel like this is the only thing I can do. And, by the way, on some level don't those generations deserve credit for what they did?"

"Okay, Lew. I just want to make sure you're considering all the dimensions of what you're about to do." With that, Jewel opens a file drawer and thumbs through several files, eventually pulling a folder out. "Yep, it's right here. This form describes the four steps in the process. This one's the application form. Here's the documentation form, which is crucial of course. And this one is for your personal and legal connection to the site, and a supplemental page to list credentials and references. And this form here is the menu for the Piggly Wiggly deli. Damn, I've been looking for that for weeks. Oh, and I think I just found Obama's birth certificate."

Lew laughs, sets the forms on her desk, and then takes Jewel in his arms. They press their bodies together and enjoy a deep, warm kiss. Except for their Sunday morning river liaisons, there have been no private opportunities for them to enjoy a moment of intimacy. It reminds him of similar moments with Nora in college when he worked late at the newspaper office. There is something particularly innervating about intimate experiences in public places suddenly made private. It's deliciously naughty, and nice.

Jewel is caught off guard by Lew's sudden shift of mood from high anxiety to high passion, but she's good to go with it. It feels a little strange doing something like this in the museum, but the doors are locked. She is so fixated on the intense kissing, tongues turning and teasing, retreating and seeking, that she doesn't notice Lew unfastening her slacks, but can feel his hand sliding down, inside her panty waistband and, oh yeah, there. It's the first time Lew has felt

Jewel's natural wet response since they have only been in the river before this.

Every nerve in his body is lighting up. He eases down to his knees, gently pulling panties and slacks down to the floor with him. She steps out of them, separating her thighs so slight. Lew leans in, tasting as well as feeling her passion. He feels and hears her shudder responding to his oral entreaties. Standing, he lifts her up on the edge of the desk, and pressing forward between her legs, he proceeds with something now deeply familiar and craved by both of them.

On their way out of the building, Jewel stops and locks the service door. Lew slides his arm around her waist, as they walk to their cars. "I have to say, Madam Director, this has been the most enjoyable and rewarding visit I've made to a museum in many years."

"I'm pleased I could make your visit so enjoyable, Mr. Harra. I look forward to having you come again." They share a knowing laugh as Lew opens her van door and Bibi jumps to the passenger seat.

"I hope we left everything around your desk in good order. That area is pretty open."

"It's fine. I just have to remember to check the security video first thing tomorrow morning and do a little editing and erasing – unless of course it's really interesting, and then I'll be sure to make a copy." They smile, nod and enjoy a last kiss before Jewel slides into her van and Lew closes the door.

IT'S BEEN THREE WEEKS SINCE LEW'S TRIP TO THE COIN grading service in Little Rock. He's feeling anxious and can't help getting paranoid that maybe the coins don't have the value they hoped. And it's been ten days since he and Jewel completed and mailed the historic landmark application materials to the National Historic Landmark Registry office in Washington, D.C. Jewel assured him that the office is usually prompt in confirming receipt and acceptance of applications. A notice of receipt but rejection of the application could either mean Free Haven doesn't qualify, or for some other reason the application is unacceptable.

Lew has grown accustomed to, although not entirely accepting of, the erratic mail delivery system whereby he only gets mail delivery twice a week. Due to the lack of postal carriers in the county, Aubrey the mailman can't cover every route every day. And going to the post office to get mail doesn't help, because the lack of staff there means most days no one is at the window to help. It's just one of a few instances in which Lew's big city sensibilities and expectations clash with rural realities. He feels that he's adjusted pretty well. But the mail situation, especially when he's awaiting something crucial, can make him want to take his frustration out on an unsuspecting opossum. But those docile creatures don't deserve such treatment any more than Lew deserves being tortured over his mail delivery.

Jewel is in the garden early this morning, picking the bumper crop of ripe tomatoes that have set on the vines. The tomatoes are delicious and the local raccoons, in particular, have developed a voracious appetite for them. Some mornings Lew has come out to find a dozen or more half eaten tomatoes that the raccoons have helped themselves to overnight. Once again Jewel explains to Lew that one of the reasons for canning the tomatoes is to not forfeit good fruit to entitled raccoons.

Lew's not a big fan of weeding and tending the garden in the way that Jewel and Jeff do so well, but he does enjoy helping harvest for canning. So far, they've canned several dozen jars of green beans and a couple dozen jars each of dill pickles and bread and butter pickle slices. In another few weeks, things will get frenetic as corn ripens, cabbage is ready for sauerkraut, banana peppers reach peak color and flavor, and beets grow to just the right size. Then, it will be all hands on deck at Jewel's house. But for now, the only urgency is beating the raccoons to the tomatoes.

As they are carrying two full bushel baskets of tomatoes to Jewel's van, she casually jabs Lew with her elbow. "Hey Lew, Momma wanted me to remind you that there was more that she wanted to share with you about your Uncle Sheldon. And you did promise to come back and see her."

"I know. I've been thinking that I want to get back over and hear more from your momma. Thanks to her knowledge of Free Haven and all that family history I feel there's a chance of holding on here. There's just been so much else going on. And I've been trying hard to spend as much time as I can with Amy."

"Yeah, I know all about that. What happened to the grief counselor that you were going to have her see?"

They set the bushels down and Lew opens the back hatch. As usual Bibi jumps in first and goes to sit in her spot in the passenger seat.

"No luck on that end. Every time I bring it up, she either gets irritated and tells me I should go see the counselor myself, or she just clings to her stuffed cat and walks away without saying anything."

"And you don't think it would help if I could talk to her? Or if she spent time with anyone besides you?"

"Sorry, Jewel. At this juncture, she is so jealous and suspicious of you, that would be a nightmare. From the time she saw us together, she picked up on our attraction to each other. She's a twelve-year old kid, but pretty damned astute. Anyway, I'm curious about how you and your mom can tomatoes. Do you think I could come by later and help with the canning and talk some more with your mom?"

Jewel shuts the hatchback. "You know where to find us. And trust me, you will actually help with the canning this time. Just don't wear anything you don't want tomato stains on."

ELEVEN

BIBI IS STANDING INSIDE THE DOOR PRACTI-cally vibrating as Lew approaches and *tap-taps* on the door. "Back here, Lew," Jewel calls out. Bibi circles in place in anticipation as Lew opens the screen door and steps inside. Carrying puppy treats has pretty much guaranteed Bibi's devotion and eliminated her barking each time he's around. Except, of course, when he's a little too slow producing the treat. So, he quickly pulls a treat out of his pocket and drops it just above Bibi's head. She jumps, snatching it out of the air an inch from Lew's fingers.

"Your timing is good Lew. The tomatoes are ready for peeling."

"Your sous chef is coming to the rescue," he says. "Just one more kibble for sweet Bibi."

"Hey, Chef Harra, you're on the clock. And I'll thank you to stop spoiling my dog."

In the kitchen, sterilized jars are again lined up in rows on the table. Next to them, Jewel is carefully dumping hot tomatoes into a pot with water and ice to cool them. For this canning job Jewel is wearing black bib overalls and a red halter top underneath. Lew smiles at Jewel, thinking, *This woman would look sexy wearing an army puptent.*

Berta is sitting in her usual chair, supervising. "Hello, Lew. Nice seeing you again. Wash your hands and Jewel will show you how to peel the tomatoes so she can pack them into jars." Lew washes his hands at the sink, dries them and turns toward Jewel with his hands up like a surgeon ready to go to work.

"Okay, watch this," Jewel says, holding one of the tomatoes and a paring knife. "The tomatoes have boiled briefly. The ice water stops the cooking and now the skins are loose. I need for you to strip the skins off the tomato like this." She peels the skin of the tomato down like a banana, pinches it off at the core nub, then gently drops the peeled tomato into a glass bowl. "Once I place the tomatoes into a jar, all they need is a little lemon juice and kosher salt. We have to work quickly so that once the skins are off the tomatoes don't oxidize."

"Okay, I think I can handle that. But this seems like an awfully simple process. Can you be sure these are really safe to eat in four months?"

Berta interjects, "It is simple, Lew. But you have to keep in mind how many years and how many generations learned about these things. In some cases, the hard way. And they've passed all this knowledge on to us. The ancestors knew a lot about how to sterilize by boiling and how to cook using acid and preserving with salt. They didn't need fancy chemicals because they didn't have any. When we don't practice what we've learned from the ancestors we lose that knowledge and the connection. We lose respect for the ancestors, and then ourselves and each other."

After a few fumbles, Lew is getting the hang of holding and peeling the warm, slippery tomatoes. "I hear you, Miss Berta, which I guess brings us to the subject of Uncle Sheldon."

"Yes, it does, Lew. And don't you know, your uncle Sheldon was an amazing man. I've been eager to tell you more about him. I don't know if you realized, but he grew up with a learning problem. He was called names and treated horribly."

"I know a little about that. When my wife Nora and I were here several years ago helping him with his taxes, we figured out that he was severely dyslexic."

"Yes, but he wasn't stupid. No sir. He was smart and caring and talented. And yes, he joined the Klan like a lot of young White men around this area. But keep in mind, a big part of the family's history from the beginning has been to blend, to appear to be among the slave holders and the Klan. But to use that cover to work *against* the evil. And that's exactly what your uncle did. He spent his time in the Klan using information to mess up a lot of what they were doing. Every day, his life was at risk if he'd been found out. He couldn't stop everything the Province did, but he managed to do a lot and most likely spared lives in the process."

"But it does beg the question. How did he remain undercover so long if he was working so actively to undermine Klan actions?"

"He worked his way into trusted leadership positions." Berta stresses the words *trusted leadership*. "When he became Grand Giant, he got the Province involved in very public charity work."

"Yeah, I saw all those charity flags on the Province float in the July Fourth parade. But my impression was that it's all public relations and a way of making an evil outfit appear to be angelic. To justify their existence. It struck me as a complete contradiction between what we know of the Klan and what they actually do."

"You're not wrong, Lew. But keep in mind, when you look at all those charities, who in the community benefits. It's White and Black folks alike. But more to the point, the community at large benefits. The Province put a lot of money and good work into the community thanks to Sheldon. Don't we all wish that that's all they did."

"Okay, I get that. It's not a purely black or white situation, so to speak."

"Your uncle was also a talented artist. Why, his work is strewn all around town and the county."

"Yeah, that was a shocker. I had no idea about that. And the more I see, the more impressed I am. A lot of the sculptures, especially in front of the buildings in town are really beautiful works."

"What you may not know is that any money he made on the sculpture he sold, he used to help poor folks who needed a hand. If he heard of someone with a health issue, someone needing help paying bills, especially anyone needing food on the table, those folks would mysteriously get the help they needed. He always did it quietly, and nobody knew that he was the one helping them."

"That's amazing. But I can't believe he made that much money off selling art. And how is it you knew of Sheldon's good acts if he was so discreet?"

"There are some things you don't need to know. But what you *do* need to know is that your uncle was one of the most remarkable men I, or anyone in the county, has ever known."

Lew nods and stops peeling. Jewel taps his shoulder. "Okay, Lew, you need to listen, think, and peel tomatoes at the same time. We've only one more jar to fill."

"Can I talk to you a little about your momma, Lew?" Berta asks.

Lew gives Jewel a perplexed look, then turns to Berta. "You knew my mom?"

"Ha! Christy and I were best friends growing up. It was one of the saddest days of my life when she left the county."

"I'm sorry, Miss Berta, but she never mentioned you, to my recollection. But she talked very little of home and growing up. I tried to get her to tell me about my father, but nothing. When I asked, she'd get really quiet and almost act hurt. It was easier to avoid the topic."

"Yeah, well, unfortunately, when your momma got pregnant and wasn't married, the family took it as a disgrace. Your grandfather and Uncle Dillard mostly, not Sheldon. They all but disowned her. She came here to live. My momma took her in. As luck would have it, my momma was a midwife and delivered most of the Black babies in the county. She delivered her share of poor white babies also. Did your momma ever tell you where you were born?"

Lew peels the last tomato and hands it over to Jewel. "Mom told me I was born here in the county, but that's all." He washes and dries his hands then walks around the table and sits in front of Berta.

"You were born right here in this house Lew, in Jewel's room. That's the bedroom on the left down this hall." Lew's and Jewel's mouths fall open.

"Did you know this, Jewel?" Lew asks.

Jewel shakes her head. "No, I didn't! Momma! You've never mentioned this before."

Berta turns in Jewel's direction. "Well, you didn't need to know.'

Lew sits silently, thinking about finding himself in the place of his birth, literally.

"So, this right here was my first home," he says, leaning back and holding his arms out. "Miss Berta, you've just told me more about my momma and her life before than I've ever heard. What else can you tell me? I mean, what was my mom like when she was young? What kinds of things did she like to do? When did the two of you first meet?"

Berta smiles and puts her hand on Lew's thigh. "As soon as you stop asking questions, I'll tell you more. I can't tell you exactly when Christy and I first met, because I knew her earlier than I can remember. My first memory of the two of us together was playing in the dirt over at Free Haven while my momma and your Gran'mam worked in the garden. I remember us playing with pill bugs, or what we called roly-polies, seeing how many we could touch and keep rolled in balls at one time. No batteries needed for that kind of fun. And

I guess those bugs were harmless because I'm sure we ate a few." She slaps Lew's thigh and laughs.

"Your momma and I grew up more like sisters than friends. We were in and out of each other's houses constantly. In summer, we'd swim across the river to see each other. Other times we'd walk across on the fallen trees above Bymer Spring. And it didn't occur to us that we were at all different until we started first grade together. The White kids teased Christy for holding hands with me and being friends. Back then, schools hadn't been integrated all that long. We Black kids were always put in the back rows. I remember our first day of first grade when the teacher put your mom in the second row in front and me on the back row. When Teacher left the room, your mom pulled her desk chair back beside me. With all those kids in the room, Christy thought Teacher would never notice that she'd moved!" Berta laughs and slaps Lew's thigh again.

Lew smiles. "Yeah, I guess my six-year-old momma didn't see black and white so the teacher must not either. I can just imagine."

"Exactly. Well, Teacher did notice and made Christy move her chair back up front. After about the third time Christy moved back by me, teacher made her sit on a stool in the front corner of the room and put on a dunce cap. Do you know what that is?"

Lew sits back thoughtfully and looks up at Jewel. She raises her eyebrows and shrugs. "No, I never heard of a dunce cap," Lew admits.

Berta laughs again. "C'mon, Lew, don't be a dunce about

being a dunce!" She delivers another blow to Lew's thigh. "I'm funnin' you."

"Momma, if you don't stop funnin' and slapping Lew on the leg he'll end up with a bruise and never come back to see us again."

"Oh, hush. Lew's a big strong man and can take a little fun slappin', can't you, Lew? Yeah, I knew you could." Lew looks at Jewel and they exchange smiles.

"Anyway, a dunce is a stupid person, someone who does shameful, stupid things. And in the first grade when you did a shameful, stupid thing you sat on the dunce stool, in the dunce corner and had to wear a tall pointy dunce cap until Teacher decided you could rejoin the class. It's funny 'cause that ol' dunce cap looked a lot like one of those pointy Klan bonnets. So I guess they got the dunce cap part right!" and Berta laughs slapping her own knees. "When Teacher couldn't get Christy to stop moving her desk chair next to mine, she took Christy home. She told your Gran'mam what a terrible, unruly child Christy was and how she kept moving her desk chair back with the colored seating. Apparently, your Gran'mam gave Miss Teacher an earful about who's a dunce and who ain't, because after that she left your momma alone and we sat together from first grade to eighth."

Lew smiles up at Jewel, then back at Berta. "That's a great story, Miss Berta. It sounds just like Momma. But it says just as much about Gran'mam. She stood up in a courageous way for her little girl. But I'm guessing that didn't last."

"Well, yes and no. Don't get ahead of me, Lew. If you want the story, you're going to hear it the way I tell it." Jewel muffles a laugh. "And you keep quiet, Miss Eyerolls. Keep that up and your eyeballs will get stuck and your brain won't know where to find them.

"Where was I? Oh yeah, things started changing in high school. Your momma was a pretty girl and was real popular with the boys, especially the athletic boys. They were also the bullies. It was boys like that Owen Ducker so's you know what I mean. There was a lot of social pressure, and back then there sure was no socializing or dating between Whites and Blacks. It was especially dangerous for a Black boy or girl to be seen too much with a White one.

"I also had my own group of Black friends who didn't look kindly on mixing things up. During those years me and Christy kept our friendship close to home and out of sight, mainly to protect me, but really both of us. Don't you know that the Black boys were allowed to play sports, but Black girls couldn't be cheerleaders or be on the pep squad? Even after Jim Crow was outlawed, things didn't change very much around here."

Lew leans back in his chair and looks up at Jewel. "I guess things changed quite a bit by the time you started school. I mean, my high school in St. Louis was completely integrated. The Black students did everything the White students did."

"Well, that could be the difference a couple hundred miles makes," Jewel says. "But I suspect if you talked honestly with some of your Black classmates, you'd hear a very different story. And yes, a lot of the pressures our mommas experienced may have officially lifted. But don't kid yourself, the pressures are still there. There are still divisions, separations, distinctions. And there can still be serious consequences for Blacks and Whites mingling."

"Yeah, I'm sure you're right," he says. "Granted, not many folks around here have seen us together. But we've been together in town. I mean, it's not like we've been hiding our friendship."

"Right. And have you been approached again about joining the Province?"

"That's true. I've had no more visits from the Wit brothers – Half and Dim. Miss Berta, I'm still curious about why my mom felt she had to leave the county. I mean it sounds like you and she developed pretty thick skins. And Gran'mam stuck by Mom, at least early on. Something must have changed. There must have been something more that forced her to leave."

"Yes, there was something – *you*! But there's more to every story. Your momma was a talented artist. Did you know that?"

Lew nods. "Oh yeah, she loved to sketch and paint. She was especially good with portraiture. She sketched me on my birthday every year from the time I was one until I was in high school. That collection of sketches is just one of many of Mom's artworks we lost in an eviction. We watched as they pulled up a dumpster and hauled off most of our stuff, including dozens of Mom's sketches and paintings. It was heartbreaking."

"I'm so sorry, Lew," Jewel says. "How old were you then?"

"High school sophomore, I believe. Maybe fifteen. I was big enough that the apartment landlord assumed me to be a threat, so he took out a restraining order on us. Then he hired a security team to forcibly remove us from the apartment. It was the second time we moved into Mom's old Oldsmobile. So yes, Miss Berta, I knew Mom to be a talented artist. Sadly, I didn't inherit any of her artistic talent."

"Your momma's talent and good grades got her a scholarship to go to the state college in Springfield. She was the first in your family to graduate from high school. Her older brothers never got beyond the sixth grade. She was your grandparents' pride and joy."

"And then . . . "

"Yeah, and then she got in trouble. When she knew she was pregnant she told me and my momma. Like I told you, my momma was a midwife and like a second momma to Christy."

"And she didn't tell you or your mom who the guy was?"

"Uh, no, Lew. She was close-lipped about that. I had my suspicions. I guess everybody who knew about her had suspicions. But she said nothing. My momma finally convinced her to tell her mom and dad she was pregnant. That turned out to be a mistake. Your grandad was furious with Christy. He insisted that she not destroy her future and get an abortion. Your uncle Dillard insisted she tell him who the father was so he could beat him up and make him do the right thing and marry her. Gran'mam wanted Christy to have the baby and let her adopt and raise you. Christy felt like everything and everybody was stacking up against her. That's when my momma offered her to stay with us. Your uncle Sheldon was the only family member who knew where she was. I'm still amazed we kept her hidden from the family and others so long."

Lew looks down and shakes his head. "It's amazing how fast people, especially family, can turn on you. I mean, for a young, unmarried pregnant woman, nothing could be more important than family. To have to hide from your own family at such a time is worse than rejection – it's a denial of everything you ever believed you knew about the most important people in your life."

"You're right, Lew," Jewel says.

"It's a kind of abandonment you can't imagine happening, until it does. And then what?" Berta says. "Well, my momma told Christy that she could live with us as long as she wanted. She's our family and nothing would change that. But Christy couldn't see any way forward. College was impossible with a baby and no job, even with a scholarship. And just trying to live and work in the county would be inviting shame and more rejection for herself and for you. She felt her only option was to leave. To keep you, to protect you, to live her life without shame or family interference, she had to leave the county."

Jewel puts her hand on Lew's shoulder. "Sounds a lot like someone else we know, doesn't it, Lew?"

He puts his hand on hers and looks up. "Yeah, it sure does. It makes a lot of sense now." He reaches over and grasps Berta's hand. "Thank you, Miss Berta. You've given me a big part of my momma's life that I could never have known about otherwise. Do you remember how long after I was born that Mom took me and left?"

Berta leans back rubbing her chin, "Seems to me that it was only months after you were born. Out of the blue, at least to me and Momma, a generous person gave Christy the money to move to St. Louis. We all assumed it was your natural dad who did that. But Christy never let on. Once she left,

I didn't hear or see her again until that summer she brought you to stay with your grandparents. She came by here for a short visit before she picked you up. And that was the last time I saw or heard from her."

"It didn't occur to me before, but my staying with Gran'mam and Grandad that summer must have meant there was some kind of reconciliation. Don't you agree?"

Berta nods. "Oh yeah. But it was your grandparents who tried to get Christy to come home many times, especially after your Uncle Dillard was killed in that accident. She always refused and only made the exception that one time when she needed a safe place for you to stay while she was recovering. And I can't say what kind of reconciliation there was, if any at all. Your momma was deeply hurt. Someone like your mom doesn't get over that kind of hurt quickly or easily."

Lew sits silent again for a moment. "I don't know what to say, Miss Berta. This is all so new, so unexpected. Do you have any idea when Mom changed her name, our name, to Harra?"

"Yes, I do. Do you remember me telling you about the manumission that granted my ancestor his freedom? I have it, and it's framed and hanging on the wall in the living room. I want you to go look at it."

The document is very yellowed, and the script is hard to read, but Lew can make out the word *Manumission*. And Hugh O'Hara's name stands out, as does the raised stamp next to Hugh's name. But the name that really gets his attention is Lewellyn Harra.

"Lewellyn Harra? Is that your grandfather ancestor, Miss Berta?"

"Yes, Lew. Slaves often took the name of their owners, or variations on it, especially if they were freed as our ancestor was. The name went by the way in our family through a couple generations of marriage. But when your momma was faced with moving and starting a new life, she decided to take a new name. And she was so grateful to my momma and me for taking her in and caring for her, she named you after our great-ancestor."

"I am honored to know that, Miss Berta. It's always been annoying that nobody can spell my name correctly. They assume it's short for Louis. I'll never be annoyed by that again. Thank you, Miss Berta, for all of this."

BIBI STANDS AT THE DOOR AND WATCHES LEW DRIVE away. She whines and circles in place, whines and circles again. "Bibi!" Jewel shouts from the kitchen. "Stop that whining, it ain't gonna bring Lew back to give you more treats." She shakes her head and stacks the still-warm jars of canned tomatoes in a box. "That dog has gone stupid-gaga over Lew and his treats."

Berta laughs. "Well, I'd say she's not the only one."

"Excuse me. What do you mean by that?"

Berta shakes her head, "Oh please. I may be blind, but I can see that you are school-girl crazy about Lew. The treats are just different."

"I'll have you know that Lew and I enjoy each other's company. And I guess we're reliving a simple summer flirtation. Kinda like when we were kids."

"If you say so, baby girl. But that lilting hum I hear as you are getting ready for church after your Sunday stroll to the river sounds like a lot more than a simple flirtation. And I feel pretty sure it's a lot more than that to Lew too."

"Well, it's not, Momma. Lew is completely absorbed with his daughter. And trying to make ends meet. I don't think there's enough room in his head for more than that."

"For goodness sake, Jewel, it's not what's in a man's head, it's what's in his heart. And where he thinks about such things, in his loins." Berta laughs. "C'mon, girl, you weren't born yesterday, so don't talk to me like I was."

Jewel laughs and sits down. Bibi runs in from the living room and jumps onto Jewel's lap, her favorite place. Jewel rubs Bibi's ears and strokes her head. "To be honest, Momma, I don't know what to think about Lew. Every time I feel there's something happening with us and we're making a connection he seems to veer off on something to do about his daughter. Or about Free Haven. Or sometimes he just stares off into nothingness. It's like he's somewhere deep in his head where only he can go. We can enjoy wonderful, intimate moments, but we can't seem to talk about them and what they mean. Sometimes I feel like I'm in love with two different men. And I never know for sure which one will show up."

"So, you admit you're in love with Lew."

"What? No Momma, I didn't . . . I mean, I'm not saying that at all."

"Except you just said it. You just said you are in love with Lew. Which is exactly what I thought. And Jewel, baby, it seems to me that he's in love with you. But there is a lot going on in that man's life. You are probably the only one he can talk to about anything. And you know, there are bound to be things he's not yet ready to even talk to you about."

Bibi jumps down from Jewel's lap and walks over to her empty food dish. She looks back at Jewel. *Rrowr rurff.*

"Okay, Bibi. I swear, that dog can tell time better than I can." She gets up and walks to the pantry for a can of dog food.

"I guess you're right, Momma. I've been holding on to a thing for Lew for years now. He didn't experience the same feelings I did back then. He didn't even remember." Jewel opens the can and fills Bibi's food dish. *Rur ruff.* "You're welcome," Jewel says as Bibi dives into her dinner.

Berta gets up and takes her empty glass to the sink. "Of course he didn't experience what you did. Back then, Lew was just a boy and you were a young woman. There are big differences at that age. Young women feel things with their hearts; boys feel things with their hands," and they both laugh. Berta leans back against the counter and crosses her arms. "Have you told Lew about the African prince?"

"Yes, I have. Lew asked me if there had been another man in my life and I told him about Kwaku."

"Good for you. And you told him everything?"

"You said it yourself, Momma. Not everyone needs to know everything. I simply told Lew about a man from Africa I kept company with for a while. And that things didn't work out because I had to come home and take care of you."

"Hold on right there! A man you kept company with!? Seems to me that being just days from marrying that man is a little more than keeping company. And where do you get off playing Madame Martyr over me? You know damned well that you came back here because you had to. If anything, I was the one taking care of you."

"Yes, Momma. You did and you *are* taking care of me and I love you for it. But as I keep reminding you, 'close to married' isn't married. I just see no reason to discuss the episode with Lew. He doesn't know the difference, it's irrelevant. Can we please just drop it?"

TWELVE

Jewel and Bibi retreat to the front porch, to Jewel's favorite chair, Bibi's favorite lap. The sounds of a mid-summer night can be deafening. The tree frogs and bullfrogs find kinship riffing baselines as the cicadas and crickets weave dissonant waves of melodies. It's truly beautiful – until it becomes annoying. But tonight, sitting and dwelling on the conversation with her mom, Jewel is oblivious to the nighttime serenade. She's deep in her thoughts and memories. Momma won't let her forget something she has tried hard to forget. Something she so wishes she could just erase from her life altogether. Intellectually, she knows that she was young and fell victim to a dizzying mix of romantic infatuation, flattery and dreamy aspirations of an exotic life of love and privilege. But emotionally, she still carries resentment, guilt and disbelief that she could have been so willfully gullible. That time seems to live on a loop in her brain like no other time of her life. Of course, no other time so affected her life that followed.

JEWEL WAS COMPLETING HER THIRD YEAR AT THE university in Springfield. Final exams were a week away. After one more summer of classes, if all fit into place, she'd be able to graduate at the end of the fall semester. She had been assured that a job awaited her at the city library, where she'd been working part-time for the last year. This would allow her to continue at the university with graduate studies in library science and education.

She's been studying so intensely that it's a relief when her roommate Sharon, a Black dance student from Memphis, invites her to a drumming and dance circle in a nearby park. Sharon tells her that the drummer, a musician named Kwaku who plays for her Afro-Haitian dance class, is from Ghana. And he has invited some of his African drummer friends to make a traditional drumming circle. All who want can join the circle, either drumming or dancing. Or just listening. Sharon excitedly explains that Kwaku is a real African prince.

"He's the son of a chieftain in one of Ghana's richest regions. Oh, and he's gorgeous." Jewel is less interested in the gorgeous drummer than participating in a genuine African drumming circle. She loves being at the university with such a great community of both African-American and African students. She has a far larger circle of friends here than she grew up with in Cloch County. And she has been drawn into the group's deeper sense of connection to African cultures.

Jewel and Sharon can hear the drumming several blocks from the park as they approach. The circle won't be hard to find. She's a little surprised that the drumming circle is in fact a real circle. The ten to twelve drummers, playing on everything from bongo drums to congas, are in a semi-circle. Mirroring that is a semi-circle of mostly students, but also a number of folks from the community, sitting and standing, clapping and moving to the rhythms of the drums. Jewel recognizes three of Sharon's fellow dance students in the center improvising African dance movements. There is a bonfire in a large barrel directly behind the lead drummer, who Jewel immediately recognizes as Kwaku. Sharon still points him out. "There, there he is, Jewel, that's Kwaku."

"Yeah, Sharon, I kind of figured that out." Jewel can tell that Kwaku has noticed Sharon pointing. He looks up and smiles, not at Sharon but at her. She can feel herself blush. Sharon was right, he is gorgeous. He's wearing a traditional Ghanaian striped dashiki and black slacks. Jewel tries not to notice that he keeps his gaze on her as she and Sharon approach the circle and find a place to stand on the perimeter. Sharon hands Jewel her shoulder bag, throws her hands above her head, and dances into the circle to join her dance friends.

Jewel claps to the drums' rhythms and keeps time in place, watching the dancers and trying not to notice that Kwaku is still staring at her. After a minute or two, Kwaku drums the call to end the piece, and the drums are instantly silent. Almost deafeningly so. Everyone cheers and claps. Kwaku stands and stretches his hands and arms out to his sides, as though embracing the gathering.

"Greetings to all, old friends, new friends." He speaks with a distinct African accent and a deep, resonant voice. "You are not only welcome to our circle, you are the circle. We began with a traditional welcome, the rhythms you would hear if you were approaching my home in Ghana as a guest. Notice, please, that the rhythms sing the rhythm of your heart as it quickens when you see a friend approaching." Jewel is mesmerized and finds herself in thrall to this tall, and yes, gorgeous man.

"We will now bless the circle with drums of greeting," Kwaku continues. "And I will demonstrate our traditional dance, which is our way of opening our community and our hearts to new friends." He turns and claps a three-phrase rhythm sequence. The slender drummer that was sitting next to Kwaku picks up the rhythm, and then all join in.

With that, Kwaku turns to face Jewel. "Please, help me demonstrate this greeting, beautiful Miss?" A chorus of *oohs*, *eees* and *ahhs* envelop Jewel. It is special to be singled out by this charismatic African Adonis to demonstrate one of his traditional dances. Jewel can see Sharon's eyes bulge and her mouth fall open from shock, and jealousy. But Jewel is coping with her own shock and not feeling up to demonstrating a dance of any kind. She looks up at Kwaku with her whole-faced smile and shakes her head.

"I-I'm not a dancer." She points at Sharon. "Ask her. She's really good."

"She is, Miss. But I know her. You are a new friend, and this is a dance for new friends." He steps back into the center of the circle, the fingers of both hands beckoning her to join him in the circle and follow his movements.

Without another word, Jewel steps into the circle, responding to Kwaku's entreaties and mimicking the rhythmic sway of his hips. He points to her left foot, indicating for her to follow his right foot as he steps back. Then he steps in place, then forward, back in place, and to the side. Jewel follows likes her limbs are attached to his with strings, stepping in synch, mirroring his movements and gazing into his eyes. She mimics his movements of greeting, receiving and returning without touching. She can hear the drums but nothing else. Her eyes are affixed to his and everybody else disappears. Then the drums stop, the silence envelopes her and she catches her breath. Then the circle erupts with whooping and cheering and she exhales. Kwaku bows to Jewel, his right hand over his heart.

"I am Kwaku, son of Olija, and your servant," he bows. Jewel again mimics Kwaku, placing her hand on her heart and bowing.

"I am Jewel, daughter of Roberta, and I thank you." Kwaku smiles and walks back to his place at the head of the drumming circle.

The drumming circle continues well into the night. As much as she'd like to stay and perhaps have a more private conversation with Kwaku, Jewel has a test to study for and an early breakfast call to work in the dining hall. She gets Kwaku's attention and waves a shy goodbye, wishing there was way of waving goodbye and see you real soon, question mark. Kwaku smiles and nods to her, then continues leading the drumming circle.

Jewel hopes she might see Kwaku on campus or that he might come around. It would be unseemly for her to call on him. But the last two weeks of the spring semester are frantic with final exams and everyone planning their summer or the next fall. Caught up in her own finals, she has all but forgotten her magical night at the drumming circle.

Then, the afternoon before her last final exam, she gets a call from the front desk of the dorm. "You have a guest, please come to the lobby." She hastens down the two flights of stairs, wondering who it could be. All her friends would have just come to her room.

As she bounces down the last few steps, she sees Kwaku. He's wearing black slacks and a short-sleeved, Western-style shirt, but with a narrow, brightly colored Kente cloth around his neck. She's suddenly embarrassed, realizing she's wearing a Steak & Shake tee shirt and she can't remember what shape her hair is in. Kwaku sees her and smiles as big as that night in the drumming circle. Jewel walks up to him.

"Hi, Kwaku, what are you doing here? Uh, I mean, it's nice to see you."

She looks at the student at the desk, who is carefully studying them, then turns back to Kwaku. "Did you call for me?"

"Yes, I did. Your friend told me where to find you. I wanted to see you again. I hope you don't mind."

"No, no, I don't mind. I was studying, and . . ."

He interrupts. "Can we walk?"

Jewel turns to the girl at the desk. "We're, uh, we're going to walk, and uh, I'll be out, uh there."

The girl tilts her head. "Yes ma'am. I'll hold your calls." Two girls standing close by start laughing hysterically.

They step out the front door of the dorm and Kwaku points in the direction of the park. Jewel notices that a woman in traditional African attire is following about eight feet behind them. "Excuse me, Kwaku, is that woman with you?" Jewel asks.

"Oh, yes, that is Nijila. She has to walk with us because I can't be alone with a single woman."

"So," Jewel says, raising her eyebrows, "she's kind of a chaperone? Should I not feel safe with you by myself?"

He laughs. "No, no, you are perfectly safe with me. She is watching to make sure I'm safe with you."

That stops Jewel in her tracks.

"Let me explain," he says, "but as we walk, if you please." Kwaku explains that he is the eldest son of a tribal chief in Ghana. While in college in the U.S., he is accompanied by several members of his father's household whose job it is to help and protect the tribe's future chief. He explains in rich and colorful detail what a beautiful home he and his family have in a sub-region just west of the Oti capital of Dambai. His family has ruled the sub-region for many generations. It is a pivotal economic center of the larger Oti region and consequently the tribe wields far more influence than its size might suggest.

Jewel is mesmerized by this son of an important African chieftain. She had fantasies as a young girl about a great African king who would reveal himself to be her father and take her and her mom and sister away to his kingdom in Africa. Kwaku's story comes awfully close to Jewel's childhood fantasies.

In the park, they stop and sit on the playground swings, gently swinging so they can talk. Nijila sits on the fulcrum of the teeter-totters twenty feet away. She's pretending not to watch them, but she's watching them. There's something about seeing this African prince in a child's swing that allows Jewel to ask, "So what is an African tribal chief-in-waiting doing attending a southern Missouri university? I mean, why aren't you at Yale or Harvard?"

Kwaku laughs. "A good question, beautiful miss – and one I would expect an American to ask." Jewel furrows her eyebrows at what may have been an insult, but she's not sure.

"In my country and province," he says, "a degree means little, a big-name university even less. Knowledge is everything. It's all that matters. This university has a good business school. I need to learn all I can about running my family's business. Because my family business is the provincial business and our authority rests on how well we conduct business. If we don't conduct business well, then we don't just have unhappy stockholders, we have rebellion. People die. Far, far worse, you see."

Jewel looks down. "Wow, okay. Yeah, that's pretty real."

"I didn't come to see you to discuss tribal business, beautiful miss . . . "

Jewel interrupts. "While I appreciate the compliment, do you think you can call me by my name? Jewel."

"Yes, yes, beautiful Jewel. I can do that for you because you are truly a beautiful jewel."

Jewel can't help blushing at that comment but tries again. "Just *Jewel* is fine, please."

"As you wish, Jewel. I was about to say, I wanted to see you again. I was sorry we didn't meet before the drumming circle. I didn't come to see you after that because it's the end of semester. But your friend tells me that you will attend summer school."

Jewel sways in her swing. "Yes. I'm hoping to compile enough credit to graduate in December."

Kwaku smiles. "Wonderful. Please tell me I may call on you."

"Uh, yes, that would be fine, I guess, that you and Nijila can call."

"Oh no, just me. I believe she can see that you are no assassin."

"Egads, Kwaku, is assassination a worry?" Kwaku just laughs.

AFTER A WEEK'S BREAK TO VISIT HER MOM, JEWEL IS back for summer classes. And right away, she and Kwaku begin a whirlwind summer romance. She is soon invited to his residence, an eight-room suite at a nearby hotel where he lives with his six-person entourage. Nijila and another woman apparently keep things in order. Two of the men are armed security, and two other men are more like friends and fellow drummers in the drumming circle, which now takes place every Friday night. As the summer goes on, community locals begin to outnumber the students at the circle, some bringing drums to play.

During the break between summer and fall semesters, Jewel invites Kwaku to Cloch County to meet her mom and her sister and family. They arrive at Berta's house in two vehicles, one a limousine carrying Kwaku and Jewel that is followed by an SUV with the security detail and Nijila. Berta's eyesight is failing, but she can see that Kwaku is a big, attractive gentleman. According to custom, he brings gifts to the family and he is at his charming best. All are impressed with Kwaku and the entourage . . . except for Berta. While Mabel's husband Lucas is showing Kwaku and the security team his hay-baling operation, Berta tells Jewel that Kwaku is not sincere.

"He's charming, and he's very handsome. But something's not right, Jewel. I can feel it. He doesn't care for you in the way you think he does."

"How can you say that Momma? You just met him, and you haven't known him long enough to make such a judgement. Kwaku is very formal and he stands on long traditions."

"I don't care if he stands on water like Jesus himself. I can sense things about men that you're too young to understand. Besides, Jewel, where is this leading? Do you honestly think you're going to go with him and become the Queen of Sheba or something? He's just dallying with you."

"So what if he is? Maybe I'm dallying with him. You always think the worst, Momma. I don't know why you can't be happy for me."

When Kwaku returns from his tour with Lucas, Jewel cuts their visit short and insists that they head back to Springfield.

Jewel graduates as planned in early December. Berta and Mabel attend her graduation. Kwaku has returned to Ghana for a visit. After the holidays, Jewel starts working at the library, but decides to hold off grad school until the next fall. She needs a break from school and wants to settle into the job and enjoy more time with Kwaku, who is back and beginning the last semester of his MBA program. They pick up with their romance as before. Jewel rents a studio apartment close to the library and university, and she and Kwaku spend as much of their time together at her place. Jewel feels that it may be because of a new cast of characters at the residence.

Except for Nijila, a whole new entourage accompanied Kwaku on his return from Ghana. The other woman managing the residence, Amma, is older than Nijila and seems to be in charge. Jewel and Nijila have become friends and Jewel can tell that Nijila is not fond of Amma, or of having to take orders from her. Things feel and seem different, but Jewel can't tell exactly why.

During spring break, Jewel and Kwaku spend a long weekend in Memphis at a jazz festival. It's as much time as Jewel can get away from the library. During their last night at dinner, Kwaku informs Jewel that after his impending graduation, he will return home to Ghana to assume his official role in the tribe. Jewel gets a sinking feeling hearing this. She senses that this is where the handsome prince turns her back into a frog and sends her hopping away.

Instead, Kwaku smiles and locks his eyes on hers, "My beautiful Jewel. I want you to accompany me home to Ghana. And you can only do that," and he moves from his chair to kneel in front of her, "if you are my wife. Will you be my wife, Jewel?"

Jewel is stunned. She didn't see this coming at all. She's relieved, but in the moment far more stunned. She's also confused and conflicted. What does being his wife mean? Going home to Ghana is going to his home. What about her home? Her mother and sister? She hasn't allowed herself to think about marrying Kwaku and all the implications. There are so many questions. She sits expressionless, staring at Kwaku. He tilts his head and raises his eyebrows as he sees other diners noticing how long he's been on his knee awaiting an answer. Still looking at Jewel, but with smile faded, "Am I doing this right? Did you hear me, Jewel?"

She starts to speak, and nothing comes out. She clears her throat. "Yes, yes, I will be your wife." She lurches forward, hugging and kissing him, and cheers go up around the room.

On their return to Springfield, in the privacy of the limousine, Jewel begins talking about wedding preparations, setting a date, booking a site, organizing a wedding party. There's so much to do.

Kwaku interrupts her laughing, "My beautiful Jewel, my darling, there's no time for an elaborate American wedding here. We will have a traditional week-long wedding celebration in my village when we return there. But for you to accompany me there, we must first be married here. I believe we can do that at the city hall very quietly."

"But what about my momma? My family and friends?"

"We will bring your family to Ghana for the wedding celebration. Your friends will be welcome to join us. It's a beautiful place to visit for a wedding. But for now, we need to be married and you will receive some necessary instruction from Amma when we are back. She will speak to you of wifely responsibilities and protocols."

IT FEELS TO JEWEL LIKE THEY ARE ELOPING UNDER THE cover of silence so a celebration for others can take place in Kwaku's village. Receiving instruction from severe, prim Amma sounds daunting, and disquieting. But Jewel does her best to shove negative thoughts aside, partly by thinking about life with her husband Kwaku, a chieftain, and she, whatever a chieftain's wife is called. There's enough of her childhood fantasy in this to keep her excited about getting married and not dwelling on the rest.

Returning to Springfield, she is excited to tell Nijila about Kwaku's proposal. It will take her a day or two to pump up the courage to call her momma with the news. When she does, she receives the upbraiding she expected.

"This is too fast! You're too young! Africa's too far away! What do you really know about this man! Why can't you wait a while? I'll never see you again!" But then, accepting the inevitable, Berta calms herself and simply says, "Oh Jewel, baby girl, I wish you wouldn't go so far away. But if he makes you happy, that's all I care about." Jewel hangs up the phone feeling relieved.

With only a month until Kwaku's graduation and their departure for Ghana shortly after, Jewel has many details to take care of. She resigns from her job, breaks her lease midyear, and makes arrangement to travel to Africa. She's never before been out of the country. Kwaku gets the Ghanaian consulate in New York to help facilitate a visa while Jewel quickly applies for a U.S. passport.

Jewel's instruction with Amma is also about to begin. While Nijila is helping Jewel pack up her apartment, she asks her new friend for insight about what she is to learn from Amma.

"Let's sit. I will tell you," Nijila says. "Most of what Amma must teach is about ceremonial protocols. For example, how you greet his father and other elders. That is a very important thing in our country."

Jewel nods. "Kind of what I thought. You know, I just started thinking about when Kwaku and I have children. It hadn't occurred to me if both a boy or a girl will be in direct line to succeed him one day as tribal chief. How does that work?"

"I know it is very important to Kwaku that you have a son who is an American citizen. That means high status in our tribe. But it is Kwaku's son Addae who is first in line for chieftain after himself."

"Son? Kwaku has a son? He's said nothing about having a son."

"I'm sorry, Jewel. I thought that you knew."

Jewel is stunned. "Tell me, Nijila, who's the mother and when was the child born? And what happened to her? Did they divorce or what?"

"Oh no. Addae's mother is Adonde, wife number one. Their marriage is the union of the two major provinces in Oti region."

"Wait. You're telling me that Kwaku already has a wife? I'm about to marry a man who is already married?"

"I'm sorry, Jewel. I've upset you. And I've told you things that I shouldn't have. I'm sorry."

Jewel stands up. "No, Nijila, these are things I need to know. Things I must know. Things Kwaku should have told me. I mean, does he want to marry me just so I can give him American children, with full citizenship? And he already has a wife? I mean, these are pretty important details."

"Well now, and only because you'll find out sometime, he actually has two wives. I am wife number two."

JEWEL IS BADLY SHAKEN BY NIJILA'S REVELATIONS. She calls her sister Mabel to come get her to take her to see her mother so she can process all that Nijila has revealed. She spends a week, mostly in silence, reliving in her mind the drumming circles, the walks and the conversations with Kwaku, alternating emotions wildly swinging from deep hurt to intense anger, and back. There's no question now about marrying Kwaku, but how she will tell him and how can she retrieve the life she erased in order to marry Kwaku and move to Ghana.

Returning to Springfield, Kwaku tries to explain to Jewel that his two existing marriages are little more than business arrangements between tribes. And tribal succession demands that a son of pure blood is in place and prepared to lead. The reference to *pure blood* doesn't sit well with Jewel at all. She is direct and clear with Kwaku. Marrying him is impossible under these circumstances, and most especially his lack of honesty.

Following graduation, Kwaku and his entourage return to Ghana. Jewel returns to the library hoping to get her old job back. But the director has already moved to replace her, and there's no budget for new hires. Nor can she get her apartment back. It feels like doors are slamming in her face at every turn, except she was the one who slammed them shut in the first place. The only option remaining is to return to Cloch County and live with her mom. At least until she can regain some sense of balance in her life and make a new plan.

BIBI PRICKS UP HER EARS THEN RAISES HER HEAD at a sound in the darkness. Likely a skunk or opossum stalking grubs. She lowers her head again on Jewel's lap. All is calm. As it was, it is. Jewel lightly strokes Bibi's head, thinking, *Yeah, as it was it is.* Just like returning to Cloch County. Until Lew.

THIRTEEN

L EW HAS BEEN CATCHING AND PREPARING FRESH fish for dinners three and four times a week. He's starting to run out of ways to prepare his catch so that Amy will eat it without questions. The most reliable presentations are the fried catfish and sun perch, or as she calls them, the *pretty fish*. Fortunately, she doesn't have to see how pretty they are once fried and served with pan fried potatoes like his momma used to make. And, of course, with fresh tomatoes from the garden. As luck would have it this morning, the sun perch are running. When they're biting, it takes only minutes to catch what's needed. He's conscientious about catching no more than they need. With a sufficient stringer resting in the chill river water, he lingers for a while just enjoying the beautiful summer morning.

Arriving as they did in May has meant getting to spend the best time of the year in the county, and by the river. Lew has never been here in the fall, but he knows it will be beautiful when the maple, ash and elm trees erupt with an incredible array of colors on the hills. He's hopeful about the prospect of sharing the change of seasons with Amy. She's bound to fall in love with autumn in the Ozarks.

Reflecting on all that Berta told him about Sheldon and the good work he did in the community, Lew regrets even more not getting to know Sheldon better rather than writing him off as so many in the family did. It's a reminder that a disability doesn't prevent an ordinary person from leading an extraordinary life. But he's also troubled by the contradictions. While he can understand how Sheldon could be in the Klan and still do good community work, there's also the generosity. Making art for folks who give him personal items to work with is one thing. But paying people's bills, giving money away when he wasn't paying his own property taxes is another. And he left nothing for his own family, or anyone, to pay those taxes and hold on to Free Haven. This is a clear case in which charity should begin at home to some degree.

Then Lew remembers the package he got addressed to Ward Sheldon when they returned from Little Rock. Suspicious of such packages, Lew set it aside unopened. Maybe it deserves a look. Maybe there's something that can shine some light on the contradictions.

Returning to the house, Lew stashes the cleaned sun perch in the fridge. He puts a pot of coffee on. It looks to him like Amy hasn't budged a bit as he quietly tiptoes into the living room. The package is behind the shoebox of unopened mail. The return address on the package has been torn off. He quietly cuts the package open and pulls out a beautifully produced exhibition catalogue from a museum. The catalogue is for an exhibition, *Rural Visions.* Enclosed is a letter from the exhibition curator on the letterhead from The New Visionary Art Museum in Durham, North Carolina.

Dear Mr. Sheldon,

It is with great pride that we provide you with this souvenir catalogue from NVAM's *Rural Visions* exhibition as a reminder of what critical acclaim this exhibit received two years ago. Your two works, *River Life* and *Cloch Children,* loaned to the exhibition by Lowell and Janet Field, were vital to the exhibit's success. I am writing now to invite you to participate in a new project my team and I are mounting. Our working title for this exhibit is *Visionary Masters: In Their Own Works.* We hope to include artwork from master artists' personal collections. Since we are well-acquainted with your work, we are happy to include whatever work you would like to share for this exhibit. The museum will cover all costs of packing, shipping and insurance and will strictly adhere to any special handling that you require. I would very much appreciate the opportunity to speak with you or your representative about this exciting project. I sincerely hope you will want to be a part of another wonderful New Visionary Art Museum exhibition. I look forward to receiving your call very soon.

Yours Most Sincerely,
Nancy Wallace
Senior Exhibition Curator

Lew tears into the cellophane wrapping and opens the catalogue, searching for the works of Ward Sheldon. *River Life* is a large sculpture that looks to be made of a center section of three long pieces of driftwood, one painted black, one white and one natural. Interweaving the driftwood appears to be three strips off an old tire holding a variety of colored plastic bottles and cans against the wood. Ward Sheldon's work is certainly similar to what Lew has seen of Uncle Sheldon's.

Cloch Children is a playground setting with six-inch driftwood figures that look like they have arms and legs with small river stones with natural human facial features attached for heads. A little creepy but also interesting. There must be forty or fifty figures playing on stick and stone playground equipment, including a teeter-totter, slide and a merry-go-round. This piece doesn't look like anything of Sheldon's that Lew has seen.

Lew quickly turns to the *About the Artists* section and the page about Ward Sheldon. It's a photo of Uncle Sheldon in his overalls standing at the door of the barn workshop. Lew shakes his head – Ward Sheldon, the artist, is Uncle Sheldon. Why didn't he know this? Why didn't somebody know this? And why the different name? He remembers that Sheldon's first name is Edward. For his artistic pseudonym he must have adopted the *Ward* from his given name and made *Sheldon* his surname. But why?

When Lew sees that Amy is awake, he fills her in on this latest surprise about Uncle Sheldon and shows her the catalogue. She seems more fascinated with the other work in the catalogue than Sheldon's. Lew figures a call to this Nancy

Wallace is in order. While he waits on hold, instead of the usual annoying background music, there's an informational recording about the museum:

Welcome to the New Visionary Art Museum in historic Durham, North Carolina. Ours is a museum, education center and repository dedicated to intuitive, self-taught artistry. The New Visionary Art Museum considers visionary art that which is produced by self-taught individuals, without formal training, whose work arises from an innate personal vision that revels in the creative act itself. Visionary art listens to and speaks from the inner voices of the soul and is often not thought of as art by . . .

"Hello, this is Nancy Wallace. With whom am I speaking, please?"

"Oh hi, Ms. Wallace. This is Lew Harra. I'm calling you from Cloch County, Missouri. I am the nephew of Sheldon O'Hara, who I believe you know as Ward Sheldon."

"Yes, of course, Ward Sheldon! A talented artist whose work I admire very much. I've yet to meet Mr. Sheldon. I didn't realize that he goes by an artistic pseudonym."

"Frankly, I didn't either . . ."

"But that's not unusual, Mr. O'Hara. As you may know we are hoping that Mr. Sheldon will agree to contribute some of his work to a new exhibit that my team is developing. Sorry to say we are now on a very tight timeline. May I assume you are representing Mr. Sheldon?"

"Yes. I mean, no. I mean, uh, my Uncle Sheldon passed away over a year ago."

"Oh dear. I'm so sorry, very sorry for your loss. And it's a loss to our field. Mr. Sheldon's work is so insightful, so raw and honest. His craft is impeccable. I'm so sorry, and so sad to hear this. I'm surprised that we weren't notified about his passing."

"To be honest, Ms. Wallace, I nor anybody close to my uncle knew about his life as Ward Sheldon, at least as far as I know. Receiving the catalogue you sent of the last exhibition was the first I've learned of this. I mean I knew my uncle made art projects. He made sculptures for people all over the county. Some of his work is on display in town. The barn is full of his stuff. I thought it was more like a pastime or hobby of his rather than serious art. That recording I listened to while waiting for you told me more about artists like Uncle Sheldon than I ever knew."

"I know, Mr. O'Hara. That's the tragedy of how art is understood and treated in this country. The fact is we don't treat acknowledged, trained artists well. The self-trained, intuitive artists like your uncle are completely ignored and lost in the shadows. That's what this museum is all about."

"Sorry Ms. Wallace, but my name is Harra, not O'Hara, and, well, that's a completely different story. Please, just call me Lew. But I assure you, I've developed a whole new appreciation for my uncle's work, not just getting to see more of it but in making this phone call. I'm sorry I didn't know before."

"Please don't think me insensitive, Lew, but who is in charge of overseeing Mr. Sheldon's personal collection and his estate? Because if that's you, I want you to know that we are still interested in including your uncle's work in our show. And perhaps we can discuss acquiring his work for our permanent collection."

"I'll have to get back to you on that because I need more information myself. That couple mentioned in your letter who loaned my uncle's work to the museum before – the Fields? Can you give me their contact information so I can find out more about how they acquired that work?"

"I'm sorry, but I can't give out that information. However, I can contact them and have them contact you if they are willing. They are lovely folks and avid collectors of visionary art. I'm sure they would want to be helpful."

"Thank you, Ms. Wallace. I appreciate all your help."

He hangs up and sits back. *Well, that solves some of the mystery behind Sheldon's generosity and ability to help so many people in the county. He was selling his artwork. And he may have been making a lot of money as Ward Sheldon, visionary artist. But now, how do I find out about Ward Sheldon's assets? And what of Sheldon's personal collection in the barn is complete and can be sold?*

DON'T THE CRAWDADS KNOW THAT EVERYBODY knows they swim backwards to get away?"

Lew is listening to Amy and watching her taunt crawdads with a stick as she squats at the river edge. She's holding Purry in the crook of her left arm.

She continues, "I can't think of a better case against the theory of evolution than a creature like the crawdad arriving at this point in history, having to scurry for its life backwards in clear water, unable to see where it's going, while anyone watching knows exactly where it's going and how to capture it. I have a feeling that the crawdad is the reason why it's still called the *theory of evolution* and not *the law of evolution.* There are too many exceptions. Too many crawdads out there. Too many people like crawdads, running backwards to get away and no idea where they're going."

Lew squats down beside her. "That's a very interesting, but awfully cynical observation of the world for a young woman your age. I might disagree, except it sounds exactly like something I would say."

Amy tosses the stick and stands up, "Well, Daddy, I guess that's what they mean when they say the apple doesn't fall far from the tree."

"Ha! Yeah. Where'd you hear that old saying?"

"Grandma Christy used to say that about you and her. Since you don't seem to think I'm old enough to take care of myself, or make good decisions for myself, it's a good way to explain the unexplainable. So – I'm like you. Just trying to help you out."

She turns away as Lew stands, thinking, *Wow, okay. That is a well-conceived broadside on parental intelligence, feelings, and authority. And a solid shot it is – quick, cutting and complete, especially the unassailable part about grandmotherly wisdom. Yep, smart and well-played. And I'm not about to take the bait.*

"Well then, Professor Amy, have you fully considered the crawdad's speed in the water? And the defensive aspect of its pincers, with their capacity to inflict agonizing 'ouchies' on anyone foolishly grasping them the wrong way?"

"True. But his pattern never changes, and his defenses don't improve. He sure doesn't get any smarter. I still think it's a wonder that crawdads have managed to exist all this time."

Lew's cellphone begins vibrating in his pocket. He's relieved to answer the phone rather than Amy.

"Hello? Lew Harra here."

"Mr. Harra, this is Lowell Field. I received a call from Nancy Wallace at the New Visionary Museum about the Ward Sheldon art collection."

"Yes, thank you for calling. Can you hold a minute while I go to my office?" He turns to Amy. "Sweetie, I have to take this call in the house. Try to focus more attention on the frogs, okay?" That earns a highly evolved eyeroll from his daughter that makes him smile.

Inside, Lew pulls out the New Visionary Museum catalogue. "Thanks again for calling, Dr. Field. Did Ms. Wallace mention to you that I am Ward Sheldon's nephew and his only remaining family member?"

"She mentioned that you are his nephew, but that's really all. Let me say how sorry my wife and I are for your loss. We really enjoyed getting to know your uncle and we greatly admire his work."

"Obviously, considering that you own two of my uncle's works."

"My wife and I actually own four of his works. The two we loaned the museum for their exhibit were the first two we purchased. Ms. Wallace has asked us to consider donating them to the permanent collection. We are in fact considering that possibility."

"That would be very generous of you. I'm going to be honest with you. I didn't know my uncle was such an accomplished artist and only recently, very recently, learned that he is Ward Sheldon. His real name is Sheldon O'Hara."

"Not unusual, Mr. Harra. A lot of visionary artists' families don't realize or understand the vision and value of their work. They are sometimes, in fact often, considered childlike or unstable family members. And we knew your uncle worked under another name. We first met him as Sheldon O'Hara."

"Interesting, Dr. Field. Can you tell me more about how you came to know my uncle's work and purchased the work that you have?"

"Sure, happy to. My wife and I were on a fishing weekend with friends who have a place in West Branson. Our friends wanted to show us more of the region, so we spent one day driving through the area around the lake. As we were winding our way through Cloch Village, we were immediately impressed by a number of sculptures we saw in people's yards and especially the piece in front of the county courthouse. I believe that one is called *Rocks of Ages*, the old tree with stones embedded randomly from top to bottom, and heavily lacquered. We were hoping we'd find a piece in your uncle's collection like that one. But when we met him, he was clear about the fact that he never repeats himself. We certainly understand and respect that point of view."

"From all the work I've seen, he didn't sign anything," Lew says. "By the way, this is the first time I've heard the name of that sculpture. So, how did you meet my uncle?"

"Serendipity, pure serendipity. My wife and I, and the couple we were with, were admiring the sculpture at the courthouse. My friend and I were looking up and down for a signature. A man came out of the courthouse and stood watching us inspecting the piece. He asked me what we were looking for and I explained that we were interested in knowing who made the work. With that he yelled across the street to Sheldon and waved him over. Your uncle just happened to be standing on the other side of the street talking to his sales representative."

"Uncle Sheldon had a sales representative?!" Lew exclaims.

"I'm not sure how official a sales rep she was. The two of them came over and we told him how much we admired his work and would like to see more. He asked us to follow him and his rep out to his farm and the workshop in his barn. That's when we saw the first two pieces we ended up buying. I asked him point blank about his price points. He didn't understand what I meant about price points. His rep explained that we were asking the price of his work.

"Now this part is kind of funny, Mr. Harra. Sheldon started to say that he didn't sell his work, but if we liked it, he'd give it to us. But then the woman interrupted and pulled him aside. You know, it's not unusual for visionary artists to give their work away. And trust me, we would never have allowed your uncle to just give us his work. As lovers of visionary art, my wife and I want to see these artists recognized and paid for the work they do. As collectors we also want the work to have and retain value. That can't happen if the work is given away free. After they talked things over, they came back to us. The rep quoted us a price range on several of the pieces. We agreed on what we all felt was a fair price for each work and we made arrangements to have the two pieces shipped to our art warehouse in Boonville."

"Dr. Field, this is absolutely amazing to learn. But I have so many questions. I'm curious about this sales rep. Do you remember her name?"

"You know, I'm going through the file even as we speak because I don't remember ... oh wait, here it is. Her name is Nora Henderson. We had a sales agreement and receipt from her waiting for us when we got home to Columbia. My wife and I are both faculty at the university. Anyway, Ms. Henderson was right on top of things. That was when we first realized that we owned work by Ward Sheldon and not Sheldon O'Hara."

Lew looks up, shaking his head, recalling that time. *This transaction obviously took place while Nora stayed to help Sheldon with the tax situation and when she took ownership of Free Haven. And in the same way she said nothing to me about what she'd done.*

"Dr. Field, may I ask how much you paid for Uncle Sheldon's sculptures?"

"You may ask, but I'm afraid part of our sales agreement with the Ward Sheldon Trust is a clause of financial non-disclosure."

She thought of everything, Lew's thinking. *She's managed to cover her tracks on every account.* "Dr. Field, you said you own two other works of Sheldon's. Can you share with me what those are?"

"Sure. We have the exclusive right to show and share the work at our own discretion. We just can't disclose what we paid for it or, if we sell, what it sells for. We have our entire collection of art on display in our own warehouse in Boonville. That's just a few miles west of Columbia. All of your uncle's work is on display there. We're happy to have you pay a visit anytime you'd like to see his work."

"Thank you, Dr. Field. That's very kind. I'd really like to bring my daughter for a visit and see the work sometime."

"Great. I'll send you information about the warehouse and some photos and information about all the work. My wife and I are co-curators of our entire art collection. It's a labor of love for the two of us."

"One last thing, sir. You mentioned the Ward Sheldon Trust?"

"Yes, the transactions were all through the Trust."

"Do you have information on the Trust, you know if I wanted to make contact with them?"

"Sure thing. In fact, I got something from the Trust not so long ago. The new director is a Jane Henderson, Esquire. The address is in St. Louis. I'll include one of her cards with the other information I'm sending."

"Thanks, Dr. Field. You've been very helpful and gracious. I'm pleased to know my uncle's work is in such caring hands as yours and your wife's."

Lew hangs up, throws his phone on the table and collapses back in his chair. *Every turn, every fucking turn, Nora's ghost and her family are closing in. It's like they won't rest until they have everything of mine, or ever could be mine. What did*

I do to deserve this? What did I ever do to Nora besides love and adore her? But now, how the hell can I hold on to the one thing those infernal Henderson's want most, but can't have – Amy?

FOURTEEN

Mid-morning, Lew sees Aubrey the postman stopping at their mailbox – finally. He runs out to the mailbox as Aubrey is pulling away. The box is packed with about four days of mail jammed together. A lot of it is junk mail but mixed in are some official-looking documents. He pulls out the large envelope from the coin-grading firm in Little Rock and rips it open. There are two certificates, one authenticating the silver dollars, the second authenticating the Confederate gold coin. "YES!" he shouts.

There's a cover letter from Mr. Durand, the expert who reviewed and certified the coins, giving his opinion of value. The two silver coins Lew provided for inspection were in good but not mint condition. Durand's estimated value for each is between $700 and $800. The gold Confederate coin he estimates to have a value of $80 to $100, although he points out that the value of Confederate coins can vary greatly depending on collectors. He reiterates his interest in acquiring the coins if Lew is interested. He offers $700 each for the silver dollars, $80 for the gold coin, and will waive his fee for the grading service. Now it's just a matter of how many coins need to be sold and contacting Doreen Leach to begin that process.

But there's more. Lew holds his breath as he opens the envelope from the National Park Service, Office of Historic Landmarks. Yes, it's good news; they've accepted his application. The letter instructs him to provide detailed descriptions of the site, documentable evidence of authenticity of the site and contents, photographs, and any additional supporting materials. And until the office can conduct a site visit, no construction or alteration of the site should be undertaken. He can't wait to tell Jewel and Evie. Now they can proceed with filing an injunction to prevent the county commissioners from imposing eminent domain on Free Haven.

But Lew's joy is quickly tempered. There's another letter from the St. Louis District Court and one from Jane Henderson. Those will go unopened in the shoe box with the others.

Lew is so preoccupied with the mail that he fails to notice a car has pulled up behind him at the mailbox. A car door slams, and Lew turns. A young man in gray slacks, a blue oxford shirt and blue blazer approaches. He walks up, smiles, and extends his hand.

"Hello, sir, are you Lew Harra?" Lew grasps his hand.

"Yes. And you are?"

"John Smith," he says reaching inside his jacket and pulling out an envelope. "And you, Mr. Harra, have been served." He turns and runs back to his car, jumps in and zooms away. Lew looks down at the envelope. Better open this one. It's a subpoena, to appear in St. Louis District Court in two weeks, in the case of Jane A. Henderson and the Henderson Family versus Lewellyn J. Harra.

So much good news and bad news in one trip to the mailbox. He's excited to tell Amy the good news; the other is irrelevant. He walks in the house and sees her at the living room table. Several of the logs they found in the secret room are spread out on the table.

"There's something kind of interesting here. Come and have look," she says.

Lew marvels at how obsessed his daughter has become with the secret room and all the Underground Railroad paraphernalia. "What is it, sweetheart? Let me see."

"Just look at the inside cover of this log – the one that looks like the oldest. It's hard to make out, but it may be something."

> Fredom is the kee as God intinds,
> Yea the kee to Fredom and spirits toole,
> Keaping faith, keaping tru til journey ends,
> Truss then ye hart to a place saf and koole.

"It's cryptic," Lew says. "It's kind of like many of the words are spelled phonetically by someone who couldn't spell very well. What do you make of it?"

"The important words seem to be 'a place safe and cool.' They could mean the ice room or the old ice box. Maybe both."

"Wow, Amy, you have an amazing talent for this. Let's go."

In the undercroft, Lew goes first to the old ice box and starts feeling around the inside. Then he turns to the ice room with the flashlight. "I don't see any place on the old ice box where a key could be hidden effectively," he says. "Wait a minute, I'm not sure they even had ice boxes like this back when that verse was written. It must be the ice room." He steps through the small doorway and shines the light around the small, dark space. The back wall is all foundation stones, and none appear to be loose.

"There was some mention of a tool in the verse, wasn't there?" Lew asks.

"Yes, there was. Up there, is that some kind of tool?" Holding Purry firmly in her arms, Amy nods at an old pair of ice tongs hanging from a hook extending from a small round wooden shive next to the door.

"Yep, ice tongs definitely qualify as a tool." Lew lifts the ice tongs off the hook and sets them outside the doorway. He reaches back up and fidgets with the wooden shive. It moves to the left, and out falls a key.

Lew picks it up and looks at Amy. "Three for three, sweetie." He steps out of the ice closet and toward the locked door. He inserts the key, and it fits. Much like the first door, there is resistance. He jiggles the handle and keeps applying pressure and feels some give, then a click. He pulls the door open and they are met with a rush of cool, damp, earthy air.

Amy leans against her dad. "Holy Harry Potter! What is this!?"

Lew shines the flashlight around the opening. "I know exactly what this is. It's the Freedom Tunnel, the route that runaway slaves took to get to the river and escape. Let's check it out."

TAP, TAP. KNOCK, KNOCK, KNOCK.

"Get that, Ernest," Owen Ducker grumbles. Ernest opens the door of the tanning shed turned guest house and Province headquarters behind Owen Ducker's house. "You're late, Davis. Goddammit, I told you to be here half hour ago."

Davis Oakes steps into the room. "Sorry, Owen, I was held up at the courthouse. County business still comes first."

Owen's boys, Jerry Lloyd and Ernest, are both standing as usual, Jerry Lloyd by one door, Ernest the other. They always seem to be standing guard. Peter Umanoff is sitting at the table with Owen and June Eastman. There are two other guys Davis has never seen before sitting against the wall, no doubt "colleagues" of Peter's from Brooklyn.

"We're discussing the O'Hara place and what we're going to do about this pain-in-the-ass nephew of Sheldon's. I guess you've heard the latest, Mr. Presiding Commissioner?"

"You mean the landmark deal that's pending? Yeah, we got a notice from the National Registry at the courthouse that an application has been filed and is being processed."

June leans forward. "Is there any way to accelerate the eminent domain process on that property before the landmark status is granted?"

Davis shakes his head. "We can try, but it takes longer to push one of those through than this kind of landmark status.

Besides Lew O'Hara will likely file for an injunction to prevent any action until status is determined. That's what they did at the history museum when they filed for their landmark status and stopped the demolition of that building."

"Yeah, and you know it's that same uppity Black whore at the museum who's at the center of this," Owen says. "The boys tell me Lew O'Hara is fucking her. Probably fucking her dog too knowing what we now know about those turncoat O'Haras. Hell, they had one of them runaway slave operations from the beginning. And always pretending to be one of us, betraying everything they claimed to believe in. I still can't believe that of Sheldon O'Hara. I hope he's rotting in hell . . ."

Davis interrupts. "You know, Owen, Sheldon might not have known about that whole Underground Railroad operation. Lotta years between the war and Sheldon's time. I suspect that Lew O'Hara has gotten a lot of his information from Jewel Bennett. And he's pretty tight with Evie Anderson at the paper, too. He's an investigative writer, you know."

Owen holds his hands out. "By the way, I'm assuming this young O'Hara belongs to Dillard, but Dill died a long time ago and I don't remember him having a kid. This guy shows up out of nowhere. Are we sure he's a legit nephew and not some grifter?"

"I never knew Dillard O'Hara," says Davis, "but I'm pretty sure he belongs to one of the O'Hara girls."

Owen sits up, eyes widening. "Well hell, Davis, there's only one O'Hara sister. Her name was Christy. I know her from our high school days. Yeah, I remember her well."

Peter Umanoff has been sitting quietly, listening. "This is fascinating trivia, Owen, but none of it solves the problem. That property by the river is the only place that makes sense if we're going to proceed with our plans. We don't get it, we're out of here. We'll find another Province and you can find another source. You know, this kind of cock-wringing over one guy standing in the way wouldn't last long in Brooklyn. We have quick ways of dealing with people like Lew O'Hara."

"Yeah, well, we have our own ways, Peter. But this ain't no fucking Brooklyn. Everybody knows everybody. You and your guys can help, but we have to approach this with a strategy." Owen turns to Davis. "Do whatever you can to push the eminent domain process along at the commission level. June, you need to pay the O'Hara bastard another visit and get him to thinking about how much he really wants to sell. Be forceful without being too obvious."

June nods. "I've had one conversation like that with him. I'll pay him another visit tomorrow."

"Good. Then we need to get my boys and Peter's team working on some added incentives."

LEW CARRIES THE FLASHLIGHT INTO THE TUNNEL, Amy at his side clutching Purry close. The tunnel is dark and narrow for about twenty yards. Then Lew turns a corner and the man-made tunnel opens into a natural cave room. It's large, at least forty feet in diameter with a ceiling that looks twenty feet high. Lew shines the light on the far wall.

"Ha! As I suspected, there's Uncle Sheldon's still."

There are several empty jars in a wooden case next to the still. As they approach the still, they can see a natural cave tunnel jutting off from the room.

"Fresh air is coming from someplace," he says. "There must be an opening on the other end." He points his light into the cave tunnel. "Let's follow this."

It's a much more winding tunnel and he can tell they are walking uphill. After about fifty yards, the incline gets sharper. Thirty more yards and there's an opening with sunlight shining in. The tunnel gets narrower the more they climb. They're able to bend over and continue walking until they emerge into the light and air.

Winded, they exit and find themselves in a clump of large rocks about thirty yards below Luna's Leap. Lew remembers being up here that summer years ago and standing at the high point, a vertiginous 200 feet above the riverbed below. It's a breathtaking view of the Saoirse River and the rocky riverbed. To the left of the tunnel's opening there's a small graveyard. There's one large natural stone about six feet tall and four feet wide with the name *O'Hara* carved in it.

"Amy, look, over here. It's the family cemetery. I don't remember this being here. But over in the corner is your Uncle Sheldon's grave." In the near corner is a small stone bearing the names:

LUNA

Baby Dawn

"And here is the Luna of Luna's Leap. She's buried here with her baby daughter Dawn. I have to tell you that story."

As they continue climbing up closer to a narrow point, Lew slips on the path. "Careful here," he says. "The dirt is loose. But isn't this an amazing view?"

"It's amazing, Daddy. It's beautiful. Is this still our land, though?"

It strikes Lew that this is the first reference Amy has made to *our land*. Something about the cellar, the secret room and the Underground Railroad has captured her attention like nothing else. It has brought her out of herself more than anything he has done.

"This is most definitely part of Free Haven. And an important part of the Underground Railroad, because from here, the runaways could go down a path to the river where your great- great-grandfather O'Hara's boat would take them up the river to a safer area to escape."

"I wish Momma could be here to see this."

Lew hugs Amy to his side, Purry between them. "I know, sweetheart. I'm just glad that we're here to share this together."

FIFTEEN

UNDAY MORNINGS WITH JEWEL ARE THE BEST. It's the only time of the week that Lew isn't stressed over something. It's so easy with her. Whether making love in the river, on a blanket on the riverbank, or talking about canning pickles, she is so in the moment, in the same place as Lew. Their intimate moments are truly intimate, sensual, giving and receiving. It was never like this with Nora. The more time he spends with Jewel, the more he realizes that his relationship with Nora was far from what he thought it to be – what he idealized it to be.

Watching a shimmering surface bubble float down the river, he wonders, *Had Nora lived, how long would we have stayed together? How long before that bubble would have burst?* Nora's taking control of Sheldon's estate and of Free Haven may have been part of an exit plan to take Amy and everything she could. It's not pleasant, but for the first time, Lew can't help thinking maybe things turned out for the best with Nora. But these are thoughts he keeps to himself.

He also can't help thinking about making more of a relationship with Jewel. This could be a real relationship, a legal marriage. They could actually be a family. Being married would also help support his claim to keep Amy. Of course, he still has to find a way to get Amy to accept Jewel. But before anything else, he has to deal with the subpoena. The damned subpoena. He can ignore mail from the court, and the Hendersons' threatening letters, but he can't ignore a subpoena.

"You're doing some pretty hard thinking there, Lew."

"Oh, yeah, sorry. Just lots of thoughts swirling in my head. Among them some questions I've been meaning to ask you about your mom."

"Well, in general, Momma's pretty locked down when it comes to information. When it comes to personal information, she's Fort Knox. She's quick to let you know when there's something that she feels you don't need to be asking or need to know."

"Oh, I definitely get that. I can see why she's like that with outsiders. But you are family. I would think she'd be a little more generous with what she shares with you."

"She is, to a degree. And there are some things I know only because my sister has shared with me."

Lew flips a couple stones into the river. "I didn't recognize Mabel when I saw her at the food bank that first day. I'd never say this to her, but between us, I don't remember her appearing so much older than us when we were kids."

"Ha! You're right, she would not appreciate hearing that. A lot of the difference is that she got her gray hair early like our momma did. She's six years older than me and it never seemed like that much when we were kids. But then she started graying right after high school."

"I hope it's not too sensitive, but can I ask about your and Mabel's father? You've said nothing about him."

"It's not sensitive, Lew, at least as far as I'm concerned. But it's not something you want to go asking Momma about if you don't want something thrown at you. All I know is that Mabel's father and Momma got married right out of high school. Mabel told me a little about him. She remembers him from when she was really young. Apparently, he had a serious drinking problem. And a bad temper. When Mabel was around three or four years old, Momma sent him packing. I never knew him."

"So, you and Mabel have different fathers?"

Jewel smiles sheepishly. "Seems so. And that's the part you'll *definitely* not ask Momma about. That's just a little too sensitive and off-limits."

"Gotcha. Do you have any theories?"

"Trust me, she has said nothing, and I know to not bring the subject up. Of course, I can't help but have theories. When I was a kid, I fantasized that my father was an African prince. And once he became king, he would send for me, Momma and Mabel to go live in his palace. And when older I fantasized that it was Andrew Young because I was enthralled by his looks and intelligence. But older now, knowing my momma as I do, I can't imagine her having a fling with someone and winding up pregnant. More than likely, and it's painful to think about much less say, but it may not have been her choice."

Lew sits back, tosses another couple of stones. "You mean, you think she might have been raped?" They sit quietly for a moment. "Well, maybe it's best not knowing. This is something that must be very painful for your momma. What about her eyesight? When did she lose her eyesight?"

Jewel slaps him gently on the arm. "You sure are nosy about my family for a guy who knows so little about his own." Lew turns his head and smiles. "Well, that was one thing Momma did talk about. It happened over a period of time, but it started when her husband, Mabel's daddy, threw gasoline in her eyes. I don't know the details, just that he was a drunkard and a cruel man. Apparently, they had a fight over something and he threw gasoline in her eyes. That's really painful, you know."

Lew shakes his head. "I can't even imagine."

"She wasn't able to rinse the gas out of her eyes right away. By the time she did, she had sustained damage to her corneas. It took many years, but she slowly lost her sight until she was completely blind. That's when I moved back to take care of her."

"Whatever happened to the husband?"

"We're not exactly sure about that. Mabel said that her husband Lucas heard from one of the old man's drinking buddies that he was living over in Christian County somewhere. He found another woman who took him in apparently. But at least he stayed out of our lives."

"Which means you grew up like I did, with a single mom and no men in your life."

"With a single mom, yes. But as you know, Uncle Shel was a constant presence when we needed help."

"Uncle Shel? Is that what you called him?"

"As children Momma wouldn't allow us to address a grown-up by their first name. But with grown-ups who were friends, it was too formal to call them Mr. or Mrs. Those folks became Aunt and Uncle. So yes, your Uncle Sheldon was my Uncle Shel."

"Fascinating," Lew says, more to himself than to Jewel. "I don't believe there were any adults around that I can think of that weren't a Mr. or Mrs. when I was a kid. My mom's friends were work friends, when she was able to work. I grew up addressing every adult quite formally."

"I'm sorry for you, Lew. Mabel and I had many, many aunts and uncles, Black and White, old and young. My momma had a way of attracting a village."

"One last thing about your mom. When Mabel's dad left, how did she make a living?"

"She did what she did before he left because I don't know if he ever held a steady job. Momma had a job in the high school cafeteria. She was there a lot of years." Jewel lies back on the blanket. "But you know something, Lew, it's awfully soon after some delicious riverside lovemaking to be doing so much questioning and answering. By that I mean *talk, talk, talking.*"

"Yeah, sorry, Weegy. I guess I'm not accustomed to letting go as I should and just staying in a quiet moment." He squeezes her breast and leans down to kiss her. "Mmm, oh yes, okay, I'm feeling back in the moment now."

Jewel pushes him onto his back and climbs on top. "And I know exactly how to deepen the moment."

LEW CAREFULLY CALCULATES THE NUMBER OF SILVER coins that he needs to sell to cover the taxes on Free Haven, the legal fees for filing the injunction to block the county commission's efforts, and some living expenses. He explains his thinking to Doreen Leach to make sure he's got the value exchange right. She confirms his assumptions and math and goes to work finding coin collectors for Lew's treasure.

It only takes her two days and a half dozen calls to broker a deal to sell the exact number of coins that Lew needs to sell. She was hoping to get a small bidding competition going among several collectors, especially given the kind of excitement the prospect of the coins engendered. She settles on a collector in Louisville, Kentucky, who agrees to a price that gives Lew about ten percent greater value than Mr. Durand's assessment and Doreen's commission to boot. The collector also asked to buy more as they may come available. Knowing Lew's need for cash, Doreen arranges for the collector to immediately transfer a money draft for the coins to Lew's bank account.

Once the money hits his bank account, Lew is eager to go to the *Cloch County Times* office to repay Evie Anderson for the lifesaving loan. On the way, he stops by the museum. During their Sunday swim date, he was so caught up in the time with Jewel that he didn't tell her about Amy finding the key to the locked door. He breathlessly tells her about opening and discovering the tunnel leading up to Luna's Leap. And about the path down to the river, which confirms what Berta told him about their ancestor Lewellyn Harra's 'Freedom Flotilla.'

Jewel's happy, although not nearly as excited as Lew about the find. Instead, she presses Lew about following up on the landmark status and working with the museum's attorney she put him in touch with a week ago. "For Christ's sake, Lew, you've got to get on top of filing that injunction to keep the county commission from steamrolling eminent domain before landmark status is granted. I told you before, that's exactly what they tried and nearly succeeded doing with this museum."

"Relax, Weegy." Jewel's eyes get round and she nods over at a couple in the museum. Lew lowers his voice. "Sorry, Jewel, I forgot where I was. But you can relax. I talked to the attorney this morning and he assured me he was filing the injunction today. He said he would call as soon as he got it done."

"Okay, okay. It's just that you can't overlook any detail or underestimate what can go wrong. You and Amy will have a lot of time to chase around looking for clues and keys once you make sure the property doesn't get taken away. But right now, you have to excuse me, because that group over in the corner is waiting for their tour guide – me."

Chase around looking for clues and keys? That was terse. It seems that Jewel gets a little slanty anytime he talks about something he and Amy do together. It appears that he has two women in his life who are not thrilled about sharing him.

USING THE COMBINATION, LEW LETS HIMSELF IN THE back door of the *Cloch County Times* and hops up the stairs. At the top of the stairs, he swings the door open and stops in his tracks. Evie is sitting at her editing table talking to Davis Oakes. She doesn't look up. They are having an intense conversation. Davis is particularly animated, bouncing in his chair and gesturing with both hands, clearly agitated. He can't really make out what Davis is saying from where he's standing. It isn't until the two stand up that Evie sees Lew. She waves and holds up her finger for Lew to wait. Then the two of them start walking toward him. Davis flashes a smile and extends his hand. "Why hello, Lew. I hope you're well. Once in a while I need to drop by and make sure that Evie gets the straight scoop about commission business and isn't getting everything filtered through her reporters."

"And I have to remind Davis that I have lots of sources and very few filters," Evie says. They both laugh, more ironically than genuinely.

"Well, there's county business to get to. Great seeing ya, Lew. See y'all around." He exits through the door and down the stairs.

Lew and Evie turn and walk back to her office. "I don't suppose Davis shared any new insights with you about how he plans to get his hands on Free Haven."

"Davis shares a lot, Lew, but nothing that clear and direct. And very little I can rely on. I was going to call you, but what brings you by?"

They sit at Evie's oak talk-table. "A couple things." He pulls several sheets of paper from his portfolio briefcase. "For one, I've started a series of articles about the Underground Railroad here in Cloch County, southern Missouri and northern Arkansas. I figure since we're suddenly revealing so much about Free Haven it might help to provide a bigger context and portray the family and the area in the most positive way. It could offset some of the negative reactions we know are coming."

"Great idea, Lew. This is going to be news to a whole lot of people hereabouts. But like you said, and we know, it's also going to get a lot of noses out of joint. Unfortunately, a lot are already out of joint, if you know what I mean."

Lew nods. "There's nothing we can do about the hardliners and those like Davis and June who have other ideas for Free Haven. But it can't hurt winning over the ones we can. This first introductory piece is about a seven-fifty wordcount. I think I can complete a series in three pieces."

"It's an excellent idea, Lew. You write really well. I think I only added a comma or two to your piece on Doreen. She loved it, you know. If you feel you need more than three editions, I'm fine with that. This is an important story for folks here to learn about no matter what their political leaning may be."

"And secondly," Lew pulls a check out of his shirt pocket. "I am happy to pay you back in full for the loan, with gratitude if not interest."

Evie takes the check and sets it down without looking at it. "That's wonderful, Lew. Thank you. But there are a couple things you really need to know. I've learned some more about Peter Umanoff and the Firebird outfit. It's true that he's based in Brooklyn. But Peter's not your run-of-the-mill businessman by any stretch. He's connected to the Russian mafia in Brooklyn. And Firebird Enterprises is international, but largely associated with several Russian oligarchs. That's the source of money behind all their developments."

"I'm hardly surprised that Peter is mafia. That's exactly the way he acted that day with June Eastman at our place. But what does the Russian mafia want with a development here? It makes no sense."

"As I've told you before, I have many sources." Evie lowers her voice as though someone could be listening. "I've learned that Umanoff is here acting on behalf of a Russian benefactor, possibly a rogue oligarch, possibly connected to Moscow, who knows. But they are smuggling military-grade rifles and armaments through the Klan to arm white supremacist militias here in the U.S."

Lew sits back in his chair. "Holy crap! That's big. But again, I don't understand how Free Haven fits in."

"We have to speculate on that. But if you think about it, Free Haven is big enough to build a sham resort which in reality is hiding and stockpiling an arsenal. It's a good site for a helicopter pad transporting goods from various airports. And the river is a good source of distribution to and through groups in the Springfield area."

"Have you talked to the police?"

"I haven't decided if I should. As we've discussed, it's really hard to know who's in the Klan and who's not and if so, what is their depth of connection. This may require a larger intervention than the local police can provide anyway."

"That makes sense. I hope your sources are safe, Evie, and keeping you safe. Knowing this is the Russian mafia means a whole different level of danger for you."

"And for you too, Lew. I can't see something like historic landmark status having much impact on the mafia or the Russians." Lew sits back taking that thought in. This is definitely a different order of things for him and Amy.

"There's something more, Lew. I've been struggling with how much to share with you, and I feel like you need to know everything. Especially now."

"Okay. But this sounds ominous."

"Well, it is and it isn't. Remember that I told you that your mom was my babysitter when I was a kid? That's true. But she was a lot more than that. My mother, Helen, was stricken early in life with multiple sclerosis. By the age of twenty-seven, she was confined to a wheelchair. My mom and dad hired your mom to take me to school and pick me up, help me with homework and spend time with me. She was more of what they call an au pair today. My mom loved Christy and they were more like best friends than employer and employee. And your mom was like a big sister to me. I would often go to Free Haven and spend time with her when Dad took Mom to Springfield for treatments.

"One evening when I was out at Christy's, Mom and Dad were having dinner at home. My dad went to his study to answer the phone and got caught up in a conversation. While he was on the phone my mom tried to reach something across the table. She fell out of her wheelchair and hit her head, really hard. She was in a coma for several days. She came to, but not really. She suffered brain damage and became unresponsive.

It's what the doctors called an awake-coma. She was never the same. My dad blamed himself for the accident. It was hard for both of us. After that, me and my dad needed even more help, so Christy came to live with us. It was close quarters in our house, with a lonely and fragile man, an attractive and sympathetic young woman. Anyway," Evie pauses, takes a breath and exhales, "anyway – the two of them had an affair . . . and your mom got pregnant."

Lew sits upright and stares straight ahead, trying to take in what Evie just told him. He sits expressionless for a full minute, then looks at Evie. "So, I think what you're saying is, your dad is my dad. And that makes you . . . my sister?"

"Half-sister, Lew. Big sister," she smiles wanly.

He turns his gaze away, then back again to Evie. "This is a lot to take in. Why didn't you tell me this before?"

"I wasn't sure what you already knew. When I mentioned my dad's name, and about the babysitting, I figured if your mom told you anything about your birth father you might already know. When you didn't seem to know, I guess I've just been trying to figure out the right time to tell you. When there was the opportunity to help you pay the taxes it seemed a good idea to wait until now." Evie picks up the check and tears it in half.

"No, no that's not necessary . . ."

"Well, maybe not necessary, Lew, but appropriate I feel. There's something more that is relevant to our earlier conversation about the Province. I implied that my father was assassinated by the Klan due to his investigative reporting work. I believe there's a Klan connection, but there was a different motive. When your mom and my dad had the affair, your mom was dating Owen Ducker. I remember a number of times when Owen would come by our place to see Christy. Or pick her up and go do something. They started dating in high school."

Lew's mouth drops and his eyes widen. "I see. You're thinking that this was a love triangle gone bad? And that Owen was the shooter."

"Deep down, yes, I believe it was Owen. I've examined my dad's work over and over and it's a stretch to think that anything he was working on at that time was so sensitive to the Klan that it warranted a hit. I believe it was an act of personal retribution and if not carried out by Owen, it was someone close to him."

Lew sits back, slowly nodding and thinking. He rubs his face with both hands. There's so much to absorb, so much to process, so much he has to think and rethink. He doesn't really know how to respond to something that so profoundly changed his mom's life and defined his own. After sitting silent for several minutes, piecing together people, places and events, he looks up at Evie, his brow furrowed and jaw set.

"You know, the only thing more remarkable than what you've just told me is how casually you said it all. I mean, when I think of my mom's life. The shame my mom experienced, rejected by her family, forced out of her home, changing her name. . . The way I grew up, always trying to explain to myself and others why I had no father. And the stinking conditions we lived in, Evie." He's getting red in the face, clenching and unclenching his jaw. "I mean, living day in and day out with the fear and dread of . . . of living. Do you have any idea?! When I was in the third grade, we lived in a car for most of a year. A fucking Oldsmobile in a Walmart parking lot. Through a St. Louis winter. My mom couldn't afford proper health care. She died penniless. Oh, oh yeah, you did know about my mom dying, didn't you? Because you read it in your newspaper, a 'small notice,' I believe you said. Well, it was one hell of a headline for me. And you think forgiving a five-thousand-dollar loan somehow makes up for a life of shame, poverty and rejection?" He stands up so quickly he knocks the chair over behind him. He turns and sets the chair back up. "Unbelievable, Evie! You, your dad – not my dad, but your dad! And this whole lousy, fucked up county are unbelievable!"

"Lew, I . . ."

"No! No more. Leave this alone. I need to go see my daughter and be with her. I've got to sit with this before any more is said. It's too much. It's too damned much."

SIXTEEN

THE DOOR SLAMS BEHIND LEW. EVIE DROPS her head on her folded hands on the table. She was afraid this is how Lew would react to the truth about his mom and her father. She should have told Lew the truth about their relationship in the beginning. She stands up and walks to the Art Deco mini bar that her dad purchased right after moving into this office. A well-stocked bar was *de rigueur* for the editor-in-chief of a daily newspaper in the days of deadlines that ignored human and mechanical frailties. Come to think of it, things haven't changed in that regard for a now-weekly newspaper. She takes out the small gold key, unlocks the cabinet, pulls out the bottle of Dewars and a scotch tumbler. The basic stuff is for pure stressing out, the good stuff for relaxing and celebrating. She pours herself a generous, high-stress, dram.

She returns to her desk chair, swirling the scotch in her glass. Swiveling around to the window, she looks out on the street, thinking, swirling and drinking. She's been living in a state of high anxiety since she learned that Lew had moved into the old O'Hara homestead. She was so prepared to dislike him. No, she was convinced that she was going to hate this bastard spawn of her dad's reckless, libidinous meanderings. But damn the luck, she liked him. From their first encounter, she liked Lew, despite setting that first meeting up to create a safe, controllable, professional distance. What she hadn't prepared herself for was how much he looks like her dad. Does he even know that he looks like her dad – his dad? He sounds like George Anderson. He even mimics some of his physical traits, like kicking his foot straight out before crossing his leg. That made the hair on her neck stand up the first time she saw him do it.

Obviously, Christy had said little – more likely, nothing – to Lew about George Anderson. She left Lew in the dark in the same way her dad intended for her to be left in the dark. As emotional as Evie feared that Lew might be in hearing this revelation, she didn't realize how emotional it would be for her. So much has come flooding back, she can easily understand how Lew is feeling hearing this information for the first time. She has been living with it tumbling it in her brain for years. Years of trying to reconcile the betrayal and anger and regret and shame. It's not her shame, but she's not oblivious to what her very proper, citizen-of-the-people, father did to Christy – and by extension, to Lew.

She notices, with some agitation, that her glass is empty. It's disturbing how quickly scotch seems to evaporate from these glasses. It's back to the cabinet and that first dram suggests the situation calls for a double. She pours generously again, returns the bottle to the cabinet and locks the door with emphasis, announcing to herself that she is officially cut off. Well, maybe and maybe not. But it helps her feel better about the generous pour. Not that she has to be so circumspect. Hell, George Anderson wouldn't think twice about his pours when he needed a drink. The liquor cabinet is there for a reason.

Glass in hand, she strolls out into the empty office area, recalling how frenetic and claustrophobic this place could feel when her dad and his team of reporters and assistants were on deadline to get the daily newspaper out. The constant chatter on the phones, the Teletype machine incessantly clicking out stories, papers rustling, doors slamming, the master printer running up and down the stairs checking on typeface and shouting deadline reminders, the reporters running down and up the stairs making corrections, additions and shouting deadline reminders. So intense, such energy, so alive, such stress. So wonderful.

George Anderson managed to assemble a remarkable team for such a small, rural news operation. His two main guys, Don Lanz and Jeffrey Ball, could do it all: reporting, feature writing, copy editing, layouts, and proofing. Each had an assistant, usually a high school senior on work-study detail. It was an intense learning experience for young aspiring journalists. The master printer, Boris Smith, kept the ancient printing press running, more than a few times making his own replacement parts when the press broke down. And his son Jon was the perfect printer's apprentice, counting on one day stepping into his dad's ink-stained shoes.

George alone handled advertising, subscriptions, and distribution. And he alone authored all opinion pieces that appeared in the *Cloch County Times*. George was the unyielding, unflappable face and presence of the free press in the county. Many thought George Anderson to be the conscience of Cloch County. Others saw him as an elitist, liberal pain in the ass who should move to a big city and stay out of their lives. He was a constant presence at county commission meetings, allowing his reporters to ask the questions while maintaining a quiet and watchful eye out for the truth.

During commission meetings he rarely did more than shift noticeably in his seat, uncrossing one leg and kicking and crossing the other, perhaps suggesting his displeasure with a comment or action. Or he would move his pipe from one side of his mouth to the other while taking notes. The commissioners could tell when George Anderson heard something coming out of their mouths that he didn't like. They could count on reading his interpretation of it in the next day's edition of the *Times*. In truth, Evie realizes, the region's only daily newspaper was another innocent victim of her father's mindless philandering.

Far from calming Evie's agitated brain, the scotch seems to be animating it. And it's not just the memories of the bygone journalistic glory days in this office that are breaking her heart. So many of the most heartbreaking memories followed her father's murder. Most especially how Helen's older sister, Evie's Aunt Martha, tried to step into the void George left at home and in the newsroom. George and Helen co-owned the *Cloch County Times*. George died without a will, leaving the newspaper in the hands of a woman in an awake-coma. Martha, who had never married, sold her house and moved in with thirteen-year-old Evie and her mom. They still had to hire almost twenty-four-hour care for Helen.

Martha, just a year older than Helen, was the first and only college graduate in the family. After graduating from the university in Jonesboro, Arkansas, she went to work in the local floral shop. Besides having a natural talent for floral arranging, she was a pretty good writer. Early on, George Anderson enlisted his sister-in-law to write a weekly information and event column that she called "Cloch County Affairs." George tried to convince Martha that the double entendre would be lost on a lot of folks and could easily offend others. But the title fit Martha's angular sense of humor perfectly.

After George's death, Martha learned quickly that writing a column and publishing a daily newspaper required considerably different talents, despite her years observing George at the helm. Still, she and George's reporters made a valiant go of it, for a while. But in less than a year, Martha had to admit that putting out a daily newspaper was more than she could handle. At a time when she should be investing in new technologies and cost-saving systems, the *Times* was hemorrhaging money. Martha had no choice but to switch to a weekly publishing schedule and reconfigure the team to match the revenue she could realistically generate.

Going weekly didn't sit well with a number of the locals, especially the older generation who had come to expect and rely on an early evening news fix. But younger folks were getting their news from cable TV or not bothering to get news at all. The paper's diminishing subscription base was an indication of this pattern, and Martha couldn't offset all the lost revenue with advertising.

It didn't take long for folks in the county to adjust to the weekly version of the *Times*. But in the process, the paper's two stalwart reporters who'd been with George Anderson from the beginning couldn't be kept on payroll. Both left to find jobs in Springfield, the closest place with a functioning newspaper. Boris and Jon stayed on and continued printing the weekly editions. Martha allowed, even encouraged, them to take on outside printing jobs to make up for their diminished wages.

In her junior year in high school, Evie started working part time with Martha. While she didn't have her father's gift for writing, she did have a talent for selling ads and making the operation more efficient. With Evie's natural management skills, Martha was able to return to writing, even revamping her old column under the title "Cloch County Living."

Evie started attending county commission meetings. She hadn't planned on following in her father's footsteps, but nonetheless found herself in that position. And she immediately understood what had drawn him into local political affairs. She also understood that she needed to develop as a writer if she were to be taken seriously asking questions and writing commentary. Consequently, Evie took an additional writing course at school, and she kept her dad's Oxford English Dictionary and his dog-eared Roget's Thesaurus close at hand.

Evie's high school senior year was shaping up well, at first. She would be able to finish her courses for graduation and work half time each day at the Times. But only ten days into the school year, Helen Anderson passed quietly in the local nursing home with Evie and Martha at her bedside. Martha had convinced Evie a year and a half prior that her mom would be better off with the full-time care the nursing home could provide. The two of them simply didn't have the wherewithal to care for Helen, keep the newspaper afloat, and get Evie through high school. Between the multiple sclerosis and the brain injury, it was amazing that Helen lived as long as she did. Evie was as prepared for her passing as a teenager could be.

What Evie wasn't prepared for was learning, just a month later, that Aunt Martha had stage four ovarian cancer. Martha was always slender and had a lot of nervous energy. But it was obvious that she had been losing weight. Her over-the-top energy had steadily dissipated, changes that are easily attributed to age and overwork. Martha had ignored the symptoms and chalked them up to the stress of running a newspaper. When she returned from Springfield after the diagnosis, she gave herself a day to comprehend what was happening to her. The prognosis was not good. She was told she had three to six months and should get her personal affairs in order. It was also clear that the pain she had been experiencing was going to steadily worsen.

Having accepted the finality of her situation, she sat down with Evie to deliver the terrible news. As stoic as Evie had been through her mom's final days, this was almost too much to bear. Even years later, it's difficult for Evie to think of all her Aunt Martha did and meant to her at the worst time in her life. She gave up her life for Evie and the *Cloch*

County Times. It takes far less than a few drams of scotch to start Evie sobbing when she recalls her Aunt Martha's life and death. Martha was Evie's hero, the kind everyone needs in their life.

Martha survived for four months. In the end, Evie was at least able to say goodbye to Martha, and thank her for her life and love in the way she never got to do with her mom and dad.

Two days after Martha's funeral, the family attorney called Evie in. Unlike her brother-in-law, Martha did have a will, and Evie was the sole heir. There wasn't much money, only a meagre $8,000 after funeral and burial costs. Martha's meticulously documented financial records revealed that over a six-year period, she had buried close to $100,000 of her own money in the newspaper to keep it afloat. Evie had no idea.

Evie also inherited a storage unit that contained an assortment of furniture and family heirlooms. To her great surprise, the unit also held Aunt Martha's fishing and gun collection. Evie was suddenly the owner of three top-of-the-line Orvis fly rods, two rifles, and three handguns. She had no idea that Aunt Martha was such an outdoorswoman who had won awards for her marksmanship. The last thing the attorney presented to Evie was a small envelope with a note on the outside in Martha's handwriting: 'G.A. keys.' Evie thought this a little strange. She'd had the key to the *Cloch County Times* building and office for a couple years. The envelope held three small gold keys on a silver keychain and Evie remembered Aunt Martha unlocking the liquor cabinet for a scotch each week after the paper had gone to press. But why three keys for one cabinet?

Her first morning back in the office, Evie pulled out the keys. It had been a couple months since Martha was in the office and able to work. The cabinet's contents are likely just as she left them. When the first key didn't work on the liquor cabinet, Evie realized that the three keys were all slightly different. She tried a second key that fit the cabinet. The lock clicked open and inside, there were three bottles of scotch: a single malt Glenlivet, Martha's favorite; a half-bottle of Dewars; and an unopened Teacher's, her father's favorite brand. It had likely been there unopened since he died. The only other bottle was a Hendricks gin, which Evie never knew her father or Aunt Martha to drink. Next to the bottles, displayed perfectly, was her father's prized set of antique Viski Admiral crystal scotch tumblers. Evie recalled her father saying, "If you can't drink scotch out of a proper glass, then you should have a beer."

Aunt Martha invited Evie to have scotch with her only once. It was when they finished the first edition of the weekly paper after Helen died. Martha and Evie teamed up to write a feature obituary on Helen, so she felt it appropriate for the two of them to drink a toast to the Evie's mom, even though Evie wasn't of drinking age. Martha was a little shocked when Evie threw the half dram of scotch back like a sailor. Recalling Martha's expression brings Evie a smile and a small chuckle.

Two keys remained, and a small mystery. That's when Evie looked up at her father's rolltop desk, which had remained untouched since he was killed. Mystery solved. Aunt Martha apparently couldn't handle sitting at George's desk, or it simply didn't suit her work style. From the beginning, she did all of her work at the round oak talk-table next to the desk where George conducted meetings. When Martha became too ill to come to work, Evie stepped fully into the dual role of publisher and editor-in-chief and took her place working at the talk-table. It didn't occur to her to use the desk. But if these were in fact the keys to the desk, it was time for Evie to confront it. That must have been what Martha had in mind.

Evie pulled her dad's swivel chair out and sat, looking squarely at the broad horizonal ridges of the rolltop. When she visited her dad in his office as a child, she never saw the actual rolltop because her dad would have it stowed away while he worked. The first time she realized it was a rolltop was her first time in the office after he was killed. But now she was going to unlock it, along with whatever secrets it held. And she was unlocking a lot more than what she expected.

Her father was shot in the back of the head as he sat at this desk, having just lowered and locked the rolltop as was his end-of-day routine. The sheriff's report indicated that the gunshot that killed George Anderson came from a high-caliber rifle fired from a second-floor window in the old Co-op Building across the street. The powerful bullet came cleanly through the window glass, creating a spider-web break without shattering the window. The bullet entered the back of George's head just above the base of his neck and exited through his left eye. Death was instantaneous. Once shot, he slumped forward on the rolltop. His chair slowly rolled back and he slid down the rolltop onto the floor, where his reporter Don Lanz found him the next morning. There are still faint dried bloodstains between some of the grooves of the rolltop that Don and Jeffrey couldn't clean out. Evie thought that the blood left on the desk was a fitting memorial to a dedicated newsman martyred on the job.

She inserted the second small gold key and heard the click unlocking the rolltop and all its drawers. Quite a sophisticated desk. With barely a nudge, the accordion-like top undulated up and into hiding, revealing her father's inner work world. The familiar aroma of his pipe tobacco greeted her. The covey slots lining the inside back of the desk were assigned to his pipes, including his three favorites. One was his Missouri Meerschaum Country Gentleman corncob pipe. He favored this pipe in public to suggest a common man's touch. He brought an expensive white quarter-bend Billiard Meerschaum to county commission meetings. This pipe exuded an air of elegance and authority. The third pipe, a Meerschaum Estate, he actually smoked while working. There was a slot dedicated to pipe cleaners and another with two pipe tools and one with a box of wooden stick matches. George believed that cigarette and pipe lighters damaged his pipes and he never used one. There were two slots with rolled packets of pipe tobacco which, even years later, accounted for the distinct smell when the rolltop opens and exhales.

The desktop is clear, except for a white reporter's pad on the right side, its cover reading *George Anderson, Editor-in-Chief*. Behind the pad were two framed photos. One was Evie's sixth-grade school photo, the other a family photo of the three taken before Evie's mom needed the wheelchair. Next to that photo was George's Man of the Year award from the Lions Club. On the left side of the desktop was an elegant, but purely decorative, pen and inkwell combination. Beneath the desktop was a horizontal drawer containing pens and pencils, some note cards, erasers and editing markers.

There are two drawers on the left side of the desk. The top one is filled with office supplies, staple guns, staple removers, paper clips and clamps, in duplicate. George Anderson always had a back-up device, supply, or system for everything. The oversized bottom drawer held George's personnel files. Those files remained as they were the day he died. On the right side, the large lower drawer held only dividers indicating that this is where George kept financial files. Most of those Martha must have relocated to the standing metal file she brought in. The upper righthand drawer was the only one that remained locked. Evie suspected this was where the third gold key fit. Hard to imagine what might be in this drawer that required more security than the others.

She was not especially eager to know the drawer's contents. As a delaying tactic, she picked up the reporter's pad on the desktop and flipped it open. It appeared that her dad was in the process of writing a letter: *My dearest darling Christy,* it began. A chill ran up Evie's spine when she read it. She dropped the pad like it was on fire and pushed back from the desk. The salutation was unmistakable. It was a love letter from her devoted, family-man father to her babysitter. Her mother's caregiver. Her father was having an affair with Christy O'Hara, even as her mother lay in a coma. And Christy's baby, she suddenly realized, may have been the result of the affair.

Evie felt sick to her stomach. She slammed the rolltop back down and locked it. Her first thought was to have the desk taken out in the parking lot and set on fire. The pain and heartbreak overwhelmed her. And the loss of not one, but three parental figures, only added a sharp, stabbing feeling of betrayal to the sense of loss.

From that day forward, Evie worked at the talk-table as Aunt Martha did, steering the *Cloch County Times* as best she could in the last years of her heroic life. Only Evie sat with her back to the desk so it didn't have to be a constant reminder. Thank God Aunt Martha didn't know about her father's betrayal. Or did she? Martha knew George better and was closer to him than anyone. They had a special kind of colleague/boss, sister-in-law/brother-in-law relationship, one that seemed to function almost intuitively. She could say things to George and tease him in ways that no one else on the *Times* team would dare to do. She was the only one who could admonish him over some inappropriate editorial or shrill commentary. And he would take her criticism to heart.

George Anderson was professionally deferential to Martha in a way he was to none other. It's possible that if anyone knew about his involvement with another woman, even a young woman like Christy, it would be Martha. Maybe that's why Martha didn't use George's desk. Maybe she opened it and found what Evie did. Of course, she did. But then, why would she leave it for Evie to find? Of course, she wouldn't. But then, Evie thought, maybe it was a way for Martha to have Evie discover something that was too painful for her to explain.

Evie was making herself crazy thinking about all the what-ifs – and she still had to figure out how to run the newspaper all by herself. She put the keys away, along with her thoughts of her dad and what Aunt Martha may or may not have known. Out of sight, out of mind.

Jon Smith had taken over the primary printing responsibilities from his dad, Boris, who still helped but was limited due to the emphysema he developed from his three-pack-a-day smoking habit. Evie enlisted one of the outstanding students from her writing class a few years before, Erin Oakes, to contribute stories while Aunt Martha was in charge. With greater need she pulled Erin in as the lead reporter, especially covering the county courthouse. Erin was working full time for the family's sod and soil company. She welcomed the opportunity to focus on reporting and writing instead. Evie also got the high school journalism teacher to assign her a couple of work-study students to support her and her growing team.

No matter how busy or distracted Evie became, every morning – indeed, every time she walked into the *Times* office – the first thing she encountered was her father's desk. The desk stuffed with secrets that she preferred not to deal with. But they still resided there.

After several weeks in charge at the *Cloch County Times*, she figured there's one tradition she really should maintain. Once the edition was put to bed, she retrieved the keys and unlocked the Art Deco liquor cabinet and pulled out the last bottle of single malt scotch that her Aunt Martha stocked. Whether single malt or blended, all was good in times of stress. Evie poured what she estimated to be a dram of Glenlivet into one of her dad's elegant crystal glasses.

She stood, leaning lightly against the bar, sipping the scotch and staring at the desk. Perhaps fortified just enough, she started thinking about the absurdity of allowing herself to be cowed by an inanimate object. Her first impulse, to burn the desk, would only destroy a piece of furniture. It wouldn't erase what happened. And why was she feeling so overburdened by something her father did years ago? She doesn't condone her father's behavior and would never attempt to justify it. But deep down she knew there was a difference between trying to understand his actions and condoning them. In matters of human relationships, especially intimate ones, things are always more complicated than they seem. There's no such thing as simple cause-and-effect when it comes to affairs of the heart – or loins.

Her mother had ceased to be a life partner before her brain injury. On that basis alone, at least in the abstract, Evie could understand her father's loneliness and needs. So why was she so angry with him for betraying her mother? The only way she was going to be able to reconcile her feelings and stop treating the desk like it was radioactive was to confront it and its secrets.

With the gold keys still in hand she sat in her dad's chair, facing the desk. She unlocked and rolled the cover up into hiding. The letter to Christy is sitting where she dropped it before. She picked the pad up, flipped the first page back. She skipped the salutation and went right to the body of the letter. To her relief, it wasn't flowery or sappy. She'd been afraid to read something that would make her dad sound like a pimply, lovestruck teenager. He obviously had just been to St. Louis to see Christy and little Lew – that must be Christy's son.

He writes about some car trouble returning home from his visit. Otherwise, the letter is about mundane topics: the weather, dreading the boring county commission meeting coming up, needing to go to the store. That's as far as he got before closing the desk to go home. Evie has had enough time to absorb the fact that her dad and Christy had an affair. Except for learning that Christy's baby was a boy named Lew, there was nothing in this letter to dread. It's hardly a love letter, and it sounds exactly like her dad, county commission meetings and all. More than enough to bring a tear to her eye.

Evie felt like she might as well go the distance and open the last locked drawer. She slipped gold key number three into the key slot. It stuck without an immediate click. She jiggled the key and the drawer handle and then heard the click. She pulled the drawer out. As expected, and feared, the drawer held Christy's letters to her dad. He must have saved them all. She took a deep breath and picked up the envelope on top. The letter was apparently from a week or more before her dad visited. It was two pages of a letter, plus a pencil sketch of baby Lew.

This letter began, "Dear George," and wasn't flowery or sappy either. Christy thanked George for a check he sent and described Lew's development. She seemed to be a really happy and proud mom and wrote excitedly about their son. And about seeing George soon. Evie opened a second, third and fourth envelope. All of them have pencil sketches of baby Lew enclosed, with a variety of expressions and poses. Christy doesn't write like a teenage girl with a crush, but a self-possessed woman who is living the life she has chosen. There's not a hint of bitterness or fawning. The letters are all signed, *Love, C & L.*

Evie felt like she was violating the privacy of two people in a serious relationship. She returned the letters to their envelopes and shoved them back into the drawer along with her dad's unfinished letter. She closed and locked the drawer and left them undisturbed – for the next three decades.

SEVENTEEN

EVIE SHAKES HER THOUGHTS BACK TO THE present, to her scotch glass, again empty – and to Lew. He was absolutely right about one thing – she doesn't know all the terrible details of his and his mom's life. She can only imagine.

Christy and Lew were victimized twice, first when Christy was exiled from her home and family, and then when her father was murdered and the money from him abruptly stopped coming. It's likely Lew doesn't even know about that.

But Evie knows exactly when that occurred along with everything that ended with George Anderson's murder. The money Christy referred to in that last letter to George was most assuredly the last she received.

Oh yeah, the letters. She hasn't opened the drawer holding Christy's letters since the day she found them. She's left them safely locked where her dad thought they would remain safely locked. Now she wonders – when Lew has had time to absorb what he's learned, should she share the letters with him? Would they provide any comfort or just make matters worse?

"Jewel," Evie says out loud. "I have to talk to Jewel." She grabs her phone and calls Jewel at the museum.

"Cloch County History Museum, Jewel Bennett speaking."

"Jewel, it's Evie. Can you talk?"

"Sure, Evie, it's quiet here. What's up?"

"No, no – I mean can I come see you? Can we talk in your parking lot?"

That sounds suspicious to Jewel. "What's wrong, Evie?"

"I'll explain when I see you. I'll be there in a few minutes," she says and hangs up.

Jewel sees Evie pull into the museum parking lot in her white Cadillac Escalade. She gives Bibi a snack to assure she'll stay put while she goes to the door and out to the parking lot. Evie pulls her car up just outside the back door. Jewel opens the passenger side door and climbs up into the formidable vehicle. Right away, she smells the scotch on Evie's breath in the enclosed car.

"Hitting the liquor cabinet a little early, Evie? And why are we meeting like this? Something's going on."

"Sorry, Jewel, I'm probably being paranoid. But I can't trust any longer that I'm not being tapped or recorded on the phone or in my office. There are sinister elements around here these days and I have to be extra careful."

"Okay, I get that. Meeting here in your Caddy is a lot nicer than most other places. So what's up? I don't have a lot of time."

Evie cuts sharp to the point and gives Jewel a massive information dump about her and Lew's convoluted relationship and the related dynamics. Including Lew's strong reaction to receiving the news of his biological father. Jewel sits stunned, looking straight ahead, much the way Lew did.

"This is incredible, Evie. I don't know what to say. Do you have any idea where Lew went?"

"He said he wanted to see his daughter. But I was hoping he might come to see you or at least called you. I can't stress enough how upset and angry he was. I wasn't prepared for that. Or how upset I would be just saying these things out loud about my father. Words I've never uttered in my life, and saying them to the person most victimized by his actions. So, yeah, after Lew stormed out, I headed straight for the liquor cabinet."

Jewel turns to Evie and puts her hand on her arm, "I don't blame you for that. I'm sorry, Evie, I didn't think of how you must feel. Or how you must have felt when Lew arrived here in the county. I feel guilty now for setting up that first meeting."

"No, Jewel, you shouldn't. I knew I was going to encounter Lew at some point. You helped arrange the meeting exactly as I wanted. The error in judgement is mine. I should have told Lew first thing, no holding back. Or not told him at all. But then I couldn't live with myself." Evie sobs, "Ye gods, what a mess I am. And what a messed-up family. And you know what else I realized, Jewel? Lew is my only family now. Everybody else is gone except for me and him. And his daughter, who refuses to meet me."

Jewel rolls her eyes. "Not just you, Evie! She won't meet me. She won't be in my presence. I don't think she's seen or been around anyone but Lew since they arrived in the county. That girl has serious problems completely separate from everything else we're talking about. And her problems make Lew's problems worse and vice versa. When it comes to Amy, Lew becomes someone I don't even know. I'm at a complete loss to know how to talk to him about her."

"There's something else, Jewel. The way I learned about my dad and Christy was going into my dad's old rolltop desk where I found a letter he was writing to Christy just before he was killed. There is also a stack of letters from Christy to my dad. I'm really torn about whether I should share the letters Christy wrote with Lew. And I can't think straight about any of this. What do you think I should do?"

Jewel sits back in the big plush Cadillac seat. "Wow, Evie, I don't know. I have to think about it. I mean, are the letters kind of steamy? You know, like a son wouldn't want to read coming from his mother?"

"I don't know. I've only read the one my dad started but never finished, and the last one Christy wrote. It was mostly about baby Lew. She sent sketches of him instead of photographs. I guess she couldn't afford a camera."

Jewel laughs. "That's possible, I guess. But she was an artist. Lew told me she sketched him all the time, especially every birthday as he was growing up. I can tell you without a doubt that Lew would love to see those sketches. But before you share the letters, you might want to take a look at a few more just to separate out any steamy ones. If you know what I mean."

"Yeah, that makes sense. At this juncture I don't think there's anything Christy would have written to shock or disturb me. Frankly what I've read so far from both of them is pretty boring. I mean, Lew was a cute baby but two pages of what they ate for lunch on top of an adorable sketch? That's a big dose of sleeping medication."

Jewel laughs. "Well, better you plow your way through those letters than offer to share something with Lew that will make him more paranoid than he already is."

"You're right. I'll do that. But I have to rely on you now as go-between. I don't know if Lew will ever talk to me again."

Jewel again puts her hand on Evie's forearm. "You know, Evie, I've learned a couple things about our boy Lew. For one, he's what they call a *high-reactive*. He responds quickly and strongly to certain things. But he's also quick to absorb information and then calm down. I've seen this behavior several times now. The other thing is that as much as I appreciate your confiding in me, I need to let Lew tell me all of this in his own time and way. He tends to get a bit paranoid if he thinks he's being talked around or if anything is being withheld. As you know, he's had a lifetime of that sort of thing. So, I'm going to pretend with Lew that you and I haven't had this conversation."

EIGHTEEN

Tap, tap, tap, "Miss Berta? Hello, Miss Berta, it's me, Lew Harra."

Berta is standing at the kitchen table pouring an iced tea. 'Why, hello Lew. Jewel's at work now. She'll be home a little later."

"I know, Miss Berta. Actually, I'm here to see you. Can I come in?"

"Of course, Lew. I'm back here in the kitchen. Have a seat. Can I get you an iced tea?"

"Thank you, that would be nice." Lew steps inside. It's strange not having Bibi to greet him, circling for a snack. He walks to the kitchen and watches Berta get a glass tumbler down from the cabinet. She knows the kitchen well and where everything is. If he didn't know better, he would think her fully sighted. She plops some ice cubes into the glass, returns to the table and pours the tea unerringly.

She pushes the glass in his direction. "This is a nice surprise, Lew. What brings you by? And I'll say nothing to Jewel. You know how jealous she gets," and she laughs.

Lew runs his hands around the tumbler. "I just came from Evie Anderson's office."

Berta senses that Lew is upset. "Nice gal, that Evie. I've always liked her. And I was so glad that you were able to do some work for the weekly. Jewel read me your story on that very interesting woman at the library. I hope you do some more stories like that one. I really liked that."

Lew takes a sip of his tea. "Thanks, Miss Berta. But I'm here to see you because of what Evie just told me about my mom and her dad, George Anderson."

"Oh? Ohhh."

"You knew, didn't you, Miss Berta? You knew all along."

She pauses, puts her hands in her lap, then looks up. "Yes, Lew, I knew. But not all along. Right about the time your mom decided to move to St. Louis, she told me. Up to then I didn't know. I don't think anybody knew, except your mom and, well, him."

"George Anderson, Miss Berta! George Anderson! You can say his name out loud. I know now!"

"Lewellyn Harra, you watch your tone! We can talk but I won't have you barking at me."

Lew sits back. "I'm sorry, Miss Berta. Please, forgive me. This is difficult information for me to digest. I'd rather know than not. But I don't understand why it has taken more than thirty years for me to know who my real father was . . . is. And I don't understand why you didn't tell me when you were telling me so many other stories about my mom. It's like I'm being shielded from something. Or maybe everyone thinks I'd be dangerous with too much information. I don't understand, and it makes me wonder about what all I still don't know."

"There's a time and a place and a way to know things, Lew. Personal information can sometimes be helpful, and sometimes hurtful. I don't blame you for being upset. I didn't tell you about your birth father because it wasn't my place to tell you. Why your mom didn't tell you I can guess, but only guess."

"Hey, a guess is better than nothing."

"Okay. Okay. I want you to be calm, though. I don't want you jumping out of your seat every time I say something. If it's going to be that way, I'd rather you come back when you're calm and in control."

Lew takes a long drink of his iced tea. "It's past time that I hear these things, Miss Berta. I'm calm now. I can handle the truth. And I promise not to raise my voice again. I want to know more, and I'd rather hear this from you than Evie or anyone else."

"Well, I'm not sure how much more Evie knows than I do. I'm sure she knows some things I don't. Now let me see, I want to remember things right." Berta sits back, tilting her head up and thinking. Then she begins recounting Christy's story from shortly after Lew was born.

"You were a big baby boy, Lew, and a breech birth. That was hard on your momma and hard for my momma delivering. It was several weeks before Christy was in good enough shape to be up and around. But we all helped. It was wonderful having a baby in the house. And you were a good baby. You took right to the nipple, you slept well. I'd

say you more than made up for coming out butt-end first."
Berta laughs and slaps his knee. "Your momma's plan from
the beginning was to take you and move to Springfield, get
a job and go to school. She had worked so hard and was
passionate about pursuing her art and her education. She
didn't want to give that up."

"But how did she plan to work, go to school, and care for
an infant? I remember when Amy was born and Nora was in
law school. It was nearly overwhelming for two of us."

"Your mom was headstrong, Lew. I know you know that.
She had some money saved from working for the Andersons.
Two of our high school friends were also going to Springfield
to school. She had talked to them about taking a room in the
house they rented. But no matter, Lew, because things never
got that far."

"What happened?"

"I'm going to tell you, in my own way, so hush. George
Anderson pressured your mom to see her and you after you
were born. Your mom resisted for a while but then gave in.
You see Lew, your mom was in love with George. And I think
he was in love with her. But they were very much aware of the
scandal it would be if it got out that Christy had had George
Anderson's baby while his wife was comatose. You know,
Lew, my momma always said that Cloch County is like a big
ripe peach. It can be mighty sweet but take too big a bite and
that stone at the center will make you pay."

"I sure get that image, Miss Berta. So, did they see each
other?"

"George arranged to meet Christy at his sister-in-law
Martha's house, which was on the outskirts of town not far

from here. Your mom would carry you and walk out to the road. George would pick her up and drive to Martha's house while Martha was at work. After several visits like that, she confided in me that she was meeting George. I remember her talking about how George looked at you. It was love at first sight, she said. He loved his daughter Evelyn, but he always wanted a son. After those several visits at Martha's, George proposed to Christy that he divorce his wife and they get married."

"Mom obviously turned him down. Or did she?"

"George's proposal put your mom in a terrible position. Besides the scandal and the cloud that Christy would have to live under after doing such a thing, your mom felt a certain loyalty to Helen Anderson. Before Helen's accident, they got really close. Helen was almost like a big sister to Christy."

"Yeah, Evie told me that my mom and hers were pretty tight before the accident. But Helen had been in a coma for quite a while at that time. Would it have been such a terrible thing for George to divorce a wife who couldn't really be a wife and marry again?"

"Ah-ha-ha, spoken like a true outsider. Yes, Lew, it would have been terrible. Maybe not so much for George, of course, but nearly impossible for Christy. Helen was fourth or fifth generation Cloch County. And the O'Haras and Andersons weren't exactly friendly. Your grandfather was never happy about your mom working for George Anderson in the first place. To a degree he could handle thinking your mom's situation was the fault of one of her high school beaus. But for your mom to marry George Anderson under those circumstances, that would have been unthinkable."

"One of her high school beaus – do you mean Owen Ducker? According to Evie, that was her high school boyfriend when she got involved with Anderson."

"So, Evie knows about your mom and Owen. Well, of course, that wasn't a secret. And George and Christy's secret didn't remain a secret anyway. Who knows how it got out, but it did, and stories like that spread and explode like a barn fire. Christy felt she had no choice but to leave Cloch County right away. George begged her to stay. I remember the two of them sitting in George's car in our driveway for over an hour while he tried to convince her not to leave. When he couldn't, he promised to give her money to go to St. Louis to stay with a friend. He also committed to send her money to live on so you and she wouldn't be wanting. Say what you will about George Anderson, but he was generous like that."

Berta sips a couple times from her glass and purses her lips thinking. "It was about a month after Christy moved to St. Louis that I received a letter from her. George had just visited the first time and he got real upset about her living conditions. He insisted that she rent an apartment that he would pay for. She said he wanted it to be a month-to-month rental, because he was convinced that she would soon want to return to Cloch County. Like many, George underestimated your mom's resolve. She was determined to make a life for you and herself away from spiteful people's gossip."

"It sounds like she abandoned the idea of going to Springfield and college."

"Yes, she did. She felt it was too close to George and her family. St. Louis was a safer distance. And she liked it there, where she had a whole new set of friends who didn't judge her. I got a letter from your mom every month or so for those first couple of years. She was really happy there, having you all to herself and making new friends. She enrolled in the community college and took a couple courses in cake and pastry decorating. It suited her love of baking and her artistic talents. She got a part-time job in a bakery. And George would pay a visit every so often. In your mom's letters, she talked about how pleasant their visits were and how much George loved spending time with you. Of course, he was always after her to come home so they could be together."

"And during this whole time he was paying our living expenses?"

"Yes, he was. The rent and groceries. One trip, he bought your mom a car because she needed transportation to get to and from school. Ol' George didn't scrimp when it came to you and your mom."

"It sounds amazing, Miss Berta. You are describing a George Anderson I couldn't possibly imagine. And I think one that Evie didn't know. It sounds like he really loved my mom. But I have a feeling that things take a bad turn."

"You are determined to interrupt me, aren't you?"

"Sorry, Miss Berta, please go on."

"Okay. But only because you've been nice and calm. George came to visit you and Christy for your second birthday. Your mom wrote that he brought her a lovely gold necklace, and he gave you a stuffed cat for your birthday."

"Yeah, that stuffed cat is now my daughter's constant companion."

"That's so sweet, Lew. George also gave your mom a copy of the book he had just finished on the history of the

Klan in Cloch County. He worked on that book a long time. They had a real nice visit, and for the first time it sounded like George Anderson was weakening Christy's resolve. She wrote to me the day after he was there that she was thinking it would really be good for you to have a full-time mom and dad. She wrote about how you would light up when he visited. But, only a few days after that, George was shot and killed in his office."

Elbows on his knees and head in his hands, Lew mutters, "My God, it had to be devastating for Mom. She really loved him. And he loved her . . . us."

"Yes, Lew, he loved you both. And it was devastating. The story gets sketchy for me here. I know that it was George's sister-in-law Martha who called and told your mom about George. Martha made a special trip here to let me and Momma know that she advised Christy against coming to the funeral. And that we should do the same. She was a spiteful woman, I tell you. But I know of no other details. That was the last I saw or heard from your mom until she came down to pick you up that summer. I wrote letter after letter, and eventually my letters came back marked *addressee unknown*."

"Well, it's obvious that the money from George stopped coming and Mom was adrift trying to support the two of us on her own. The apartment would have been the first expense to go. The story of my life as I've known it begins sometime after that." Lew sits back and stares straight ahead, thinking and saying nothing.

And then, "Miss Berta, who do you think killed George Anderson? Evie's theory is that Owen Ducker was behind it because he was in love with Mom."

"Well, I have my own theory which I've not shared with anyone. But I'll share it with you. After our dimwitted county sheriff, Ruben Burliss, took a month to rule out suicide in George Anderson's obvious murder, there wasn't much of an effort to figure out who did it. That more or less supports the theory that it was a Klan hit, since George had just published his book about Klan history hereabouts. That's still the best official theory, I guess. Yes, there's a case to be made that it could have been Owen Ducker. He was more than capable. But I never believed that he and Christy were that involved. I mean, they dated in high school. She was a cheerleader and he was a big football star – they almost had to date, didn't they? But at least in my presence, and we were pretty close, Christy never acted like Owen was all that special.

"Fact is, Lew, a lot of people in the county had issues with George Anderson. At one time or another he wrote or published something that rubbed up against the angry side of a lot of people. But who felt strongly enough, angry enough, hurt enough to do such a thing? I'd have to say Martha Lynch."

"What? You mean George's sister-in-law? You think she may have killed him?"

"George and Martha were high school sweethearts. A lot of people might have thought they'd get married. But after high school, they split up, and shortly after that George and Martha's younger sister Helen got together. But there were no hard feelings between sisters, at least outwardly. Martha even became one of George's writers over at the paper. She wrote a weekly column while working at the floral shop. Some of us believe that when Helen got real bad with her health, a spark reignited between George and Martha. Some even believe that Helen may have encouraged it. That's gossip that I'll leave right there. But I do know that Martha learned about George and Christy – and Martha hated Christy."

"So where's Martha now? I've heard no mention of her from anyone until you brought her up. She seems pretty central."

"Martha died less than a year after Helen did. A whole different set of health issues, cancer of some kind. But there was a lot of anger and spite in that woman. She was just as capable of pulling a trigger as Owen Ducker was. And she had the means to do it. She was women's sharpshooting champion for three or four years running at the Cloch County Rod and Gun Club."

"I'm guessing that Evie doesn't share your suspicion of Martha. Especially since she hasn't mentioned her to me at all."

"Martha swooped in after George was gone and became the matriarch of the family and the newspaper. There's a few of us who felt that if Martha couldn't be with George, by gum, she would just become George."

Lew sits back and rubs his face with his hands. "Dear God. There's almost too much to take in. Miss Berta, you've been able to shed light on a lot. I think I judged George Anderson a little too quickly. Obviously, I was too young to remember anything about him. I still don't understand why Mom kept so much from me, though. Why she was so, so over-protective."

"Come on, of course you understand. For heaven's sake, boy, you're doing the same thing with your daughter that your momma did with you. The only difference is that she ran away from Cloch County to protect you and you've run to Cloch County to protect your daughter. Your momma felt if you didn't get too close to this place, to certain people, certain truths, you couldn't be hurt like she was. You're doing the same. In this case, though, it's your daughter who is determined not to get close to people. And she'll keep doing that as long as you keep helping her do it out of your own fear."

"It's different, Miss Berta. I understand your point. And you are very wise. Maybe the wisest person I know. But there's also a lot you don't know."

"None of us ever know everything, certainly not enough. We each have to do what we think is right based on what we do know. I hope what I told you is more helpful than not. Because around here, it pays to know enough, but not too much."

"Yes, Miss Berta, it seems like I've heard that somewhere before."

NINETEEN

LEW LEAVES BERTA AND DRIVES TO THE PIGGLY Wiggly. He hasn't shopped for days and they need everything. Shopping The Pig is one of Lew's favorite places to be alone in his head to sort things out. And there's a lot to sort out given all the information of the day. His thoughts and feelings keep ricocheting off people, time and events. At the same time, the insidious evil that is still determined to wrest Free Haven from him weighs on his mind just as much as before. It's good to win a battle against the Klan, but this is a war and it's far from over.

Meandering the cereal aisle he's finally as calm as he's been all day, largely thanks to Berta and the perspective she brings to Evie's jarring revelations. Berta has a way of balancing Lew's mindset and moods. With that balance Lew begins rewinding his emotional response to Evie while scanning the top shelf for Cheerios.

I really exploded on Evie. But dammit, she could've told me sooner – she should have told me sooner. She didn't deserve that from me though. I've got to apologize to her. I hate this feeling of guilt and beating myself up after I fly off the handle at someone. Bottom line, there was nothing spiteful about what she told me. In fact, it had to be hard for her, spilling all that crap about her dad . . . and my mom. It had to be just as hard for her learning about them having an affair. Not to mention having a child. And she's been generous in so many ways. That money she loaned for the taxes – she didn't have to do that. I have to go see her tomorrow, first thing, and apologize. I really need to apologize, if for no other reason than I still need her help. She knows things I can't possibly know. Maybe after all this gets settled we can get to know each other better – differently. Like a brother and sister. Holy crap, that's just weird – a sister. He smiles to himself, pulling a box of Cheerios off the shelf.

Driving back to Free Haven, Lew is rolling over and over in his mind what he's going to say to Amy about what he's learned. There's no question in his mind about telling her. He won't do to Amy what was done to him by withholding information. Enough with the secrets.

He's coming up to the turnoff when a black SUV with tinted glass pulls quickly out of their drive, skidding sideways then speeding by him. And then, he sees smoke in the vicinity of the house. Turning into the driveway, he sees flames jumping. "Amy!" he screams as panic shoots through him. He floors the gas pedal, throwing gravel out behind him.

Skidding to a stop in front of the house, he jumps out of the car. *Thank God – it's not the house but the tobacco shed in flames.* He runs to the side of the house and grabs the hose. As he turns the spigot he looks up. Amy is at the kitchen window, Purry clutched at her chest. She's gazing transfixed at the flames leaping high above the shed. Lew turns and pulls the hose out and directs as much water on the inferno as he can.

The shed is completely consumed in flames and the heat is intense. The thin stream of water from the hose has little effect. All he can think of is keeping the fire from jumping to the house or barn. Fortunately, it's rained quite a bit lately and there's not a lot of dead grass and ground fuel for the fire to spread. But the shed is a lost cause. As the flames begin to wane, he keeps the hose aimed at the charred structure, trying to cool it. The superheated wood is sending up more steam than smoke now. When the fire seems sufficiently out, Lew turns off the water and goes inside the house.

In the kitchen, he gets a wet cloth and a glass of water for each of them and sits down at the table. His face is hot and smudged with ash from being so close to the fire. Wiping his forehead, he looks up at Amy, still at the window. "Are you okay?"

She nods. "It was these men, Daddy. I looked out from the living room window and saw them drive up in a big black car. One had a big can. They went to the back. The man poured something from the can inside the shed. He threw the can inside and then they both lit matches and started the fire. They got back in the car and drove away."

Lew nods, as she's confirming what he suspected from the strong gasoline smell he picked up hosing the fire and the charred gas can in the rubble. "Was it the two guys who came that day in the pickup truck?"

"No. These were other men. I've never seen them before." Lew nods. *It could be some of Peter Umanoff's thugs from Brooklyn.*

"Sit still and have some water, sweetie, I need to call someone." He goes to the living room and calls the police. Then he calls Evie. She answers.

"It's Lew, Evie. It's started. They burned down our shed."

"Oh, Lew. Are you okay? Is your daughter okay? Was she there?"

"She's okay. But I can't talk. The police are on their way. I'll call you back when I can. We need to talk – about a lot."

The deputy sheriff pulls up in front of the house about a half hour after Lew calls. He goes outside to meet him as the deputy gets out of the patrol car. He walks him around to the charred remains of the shed describing what he saw and explaining what Amy described. The deputy stops, and staring at the charred heap, he gets a pad out to take notes.

"So, Mr. O'Hara, how old was this shed? Anything of value in it? Who do you think did this and why did they do it?" But before Lew can answer any of his rapid-fire questions, he asks, "Does your daughter like to play with matches? Can I talk to her about the incident?"

Lew stops and stares at the deputy, his face gets red. "What? What the hell?! Are you suggesting somehow that my daughter set this fire? That's outrageous! And no, you can't talk to my daughter, she's been traumatized by this nightmare! And why the fuck can't anyone get my name right around here? It's Harra, Lew Harra, Goddammit!"

The deputy steps back. "Okay, okay, Mr. Harra, I have to ask about every possibility. I'm sorry if the questions are sensitive, but I have to ask."

"Okay, I get that. But there are characters here in the county and from elsewhere trying to intimidate me into selling this property, which I don't intend to do. I suggest that you find this guy, Peter Umanoff, from New York, from Brooklyn, New York, and talk to him. I have a feeling you'll find the guys who did this hanging out with him."

"I'll file a report, Mr. Harra, and report to the sheriff. If we learn anything, we'll be in touch." He hands Lew a card, "If you have any questions, just call this number. It's the sheriff's office. Someone will respond immediately."

As the deputy drives away, Lew returns to the kitchen and starts wandering around, trying to focus on preparing dinner. Amy is in her room. He collapses at the kitchen table, emotionally drained.

Resting his head in his hands, and for the first time thinking, *Coming here was a mistake. A big mistake. But now what? Where do we go? What are we supposed to do? If it were just me . . . but it's not. It's no longer a legal chess game. It's gotten dangerous, really dangerous. What if those thugs had known Amy was here alone? What if they had set fire to the house instead of the shed? Or if the fire had jumped to the house? The 'what-if's' are going to drive me fucking crazy. Maybe the best thing, the saftest thing, is just sell this damned place and get the hell out.*

After dinner, Lew sets the dishes aside at the sink. "Sweetie, let's take a walk down to the river while there's still daylight."

THIS SECOND WEEK OF AUGUST IT'S GETTING DARKER A little earlier each day. The autumnal equinox is still a month away, but mid-August always feels like the beginning of the end of summer. The river is a little higher because of all the rain, but it's flowing calmly. There are damselflies buzzing the top of the water. Periodically, one lands on the surface and instantly becomes a sumptuous dinner for a fish. The early summer tadpoles have all morphed fully into frogs and are now in league with the cicadas in creating a near deafening backdrop of twilight sound. As they walk, surrounded by the late summer symphony, Lew pulls Amy close as she clings to Purry between them. She leans into him as he hugs her, and they walk together.

"Sweetie, I may need to make a trip to St. Louis for a couple days. I would really like to have you stay with someone while I'm away."

Amy pulls away and looks up. "No, I don't want to stay with anyone. I can go with you."

"It's not that kind of trip, sweetheart. I have to go take care of some business and then I'll come right back. It's best if you can stay with someone here. And given this fire, I don't want you staying here if I'm not here."

Amy hugs Lew and starts fitfully crying. "Please don't make me stay somewhere else. I want to be with you. I don't care where we go, Daddy, please don't leave me, please, please! Promise me you won't leave me!"

Lew turns and drops to his knees and hugs Amy tight. He sobs with her, "It's okay, it's okay, baby. Please don't cry. I promise, sweetie, I promise I won't leave you. I'm here, I'll protect you. I love you so much. I'll never let you go."

EVIE IS DRIVING BACK TO HER OFFICE WHEN LEW calls to tell her about the fire. She pulls into the Hardee's so she can talk. It's a bad sign that the Klan and mob is striking so close and so violently. The only good thing is that Lew actually called to tell her about it. He hasn't shut her out entirely. But this situation with the Province and the mob is deteriorating fast. Lew is in danger, and perhaps others are too.

Since she's at Hardee's, she drives through and gets a roast beef sandwich, fries and a large Coke. This will be dinner in the office, where she's determined to stay until she reads the letters. She has to know what's in those letters before she talks to Lew again. And she can't do it on an empty stomach and the tempting comfort of the liquor cabinet so close at hand.

Jon Smith is still downstairs preparing to run the weekly edition of the *Cloch County Times* tomorrow. Evie sticks her head in to let him know that Erin will be bringing her final edits by first thing in the morning. She tells Jon to exit the side door and lock it when he leaves, because she double bolts the back entrance while she's upstairs working. This is hardly an unusual thing for Evie to be doing the night before print day.

In the office she sits at her desk. She never puts the rolltop down anymore. Doing that reminds her that it was her dad's desk. She's replaced the pipes and pipe paraphernalia in the coveys with hairbrushes, make up, scissors, pens and rolled up notes. Like her dad, she does all her editing on the oak talk-table and keeps the desktop mostly clear. She unlocks the drawer containing the letters, pulls them out and sorts the envelopes by postmark date. She places a numbered sticky on each and plans to read them from the first to the last, in proper sequence, checking off each as she opens and reads it. Once organized, she sets up her sandwich, fries and Coke and begins.

Christy has beautiful handwriting, but her writing is stilted, with a just-the-facts tone. It suddenly occurs to Evie that Lew must have inherited his writing talent from her dad . . . their dad. Something she didn't inherit. But while the letters are mundane, each envelope includes a darling pencil likeness of Lew. The sixth sketch she unfolds makes her catch her breath. It's her dad holding baby Lew.

In the letters following Lew's first birthday, there's a distinct shift in tone and content. Christy appears to be responding to George's requests for her to return to Cloch County. He must be urging her to move back and marry him. Christy makes distinct references to moving back, getting married, and all the complications it would cause with their families and friends. The letter that really gets Evie's attention refers to Christy's encounters with Aunt Martha.

I wish you would take Martha's threats as seriously as I do. Because she made those threats to me. And Lew. That day she came to Berta's house and confronted me she was a crazy person. She scared me George. She's angry about us. And she blames me for everything. I can't think of returning unless I know she won't harm me or Lew.

Evie puts down the letter and sits back. Okay, it's clear now, Aunt Martha knew about George and Christy and confronted Christy about the relationship. There's no question that Martha knew what Evie would find in the desk when she left her the keys. She intended for Evie to find the evidence of her father's indiscretions. But to what end? What were her intentions? Evie leans forward and continues reading the letters. There's not another mention of returning to Cloch County or Martha again until the next to last letter.

It was great talking to you. I think Lew was confused hearing your voice over the phone. I want to thank you for telling me about you and Martha. It explains a lot. And honestly I'm not surprised. She's still in love with you, George. I appreciate your optimism, but I question if she'll ever accept me. I mean accept us. Thanks for saying you'll talk to Martha. You're the only one who can make her accept us being together. I can't wait to see you and to hear how your talk with Martha goes. And yes, George, I really am excited about our future. I just can't help thinking about the problems.

Evie sits back in her chair, stunned. She didn't think anything could shock her anymore – except learning that Aunt Martha and her dad had been romantically involved. In one way, it explains the close bond they had, far from even the closest brother- and sister-in-law relationship she had imagined. But when did the affair begin? Evie thinks back, trying to piece together some of the sequences and signs that she must have missed and place them in some kind of timeline. Some kind of order.

Did Christy and George's involvement end her dad's affair with Martha? That seems to be what Christy is suggesting in the letter. And maybe, just maybe, this is the letter that Martha really wanted Evie to find. This was the secret that she couldn't share while alive but wanted Evie to know. Evie's mind is reeling, thinking about Martha and her dad, Christy and her dad, her mom and her dad. She's having the hardest time remembering her mom and dad as a couple, a loving married couple. None of it makes sense and yet, it does.

She drops the letters and pushes back from the desk. As if on autopilot, she fumbles for the liquor cabinet key on the small chain of three gold keys and slips in into the lock. Then she stops. Another scotch is not going to help. And she needs a clear head right now. She can't be deadened by dwelling on the past or too much booze. She has to focus on what's happening now. Lew – her brother, Lew; his daughter Amy, her niece; and their home are all in danger. And they are likely in greater danger than even Lew understands.

Burning the shed down was a warning to Lew. Evie wonders if Lew has told Jewel about this, and whether Jewel understands the full dimensions of what is happening. She needs to be looped in, because Lew trusts her. They are dealing with something bigger and more dangerous than Evie has ever known in this county. This is not just their local dime-store racist losers running amok. This is Russian mafia, perhaps even Russian government intrusion into the U.S. Their interference thus far has been digital in nature, social media and election-related meddling. But this is another order of things. This is about arming militant, anti-democratic fringe group militias hellbent on bringing the country down. This may put Cloch County at the epicenter of the greatest threat to the country since the Civil War.

Evie knows that she can't trust the county sheriff or any of the police. Most of them are either directly involved with the Province or uninclined to challenge it, because they are sympathetic, or fearful, or both. The dimensions of all this requires the resources and reliability of outsiders, of federal officials. Perhaps the FBI or the Bureau of Alcohol, Tobacco, Firearms and Explosives. She also knows that she has to be very careful in making contact with these agencies to avoid making a target of herself or any of her sources. She decides to call the FBI's regional office in Tulsa.

TWENTY

JEWEL HAS BEEN ON GARDEN DUTY EVERY MORNING for a week now monitoring the ripe and the ready. The banana peppers are close. There's about a twenty-four-hour window of ripeness when the peppers are just right to pickle and put up. Hitting that sweet window is the difference between a year of blissful rice and beans with sweet, pickled banana peppers, and bland beans without any zing. Along with the peppers, the corn is ready for picking and eating. One of her momma's favorite meals in the summertime is fried catfish, fresh picked corn on the cob and vine-ripened tomatoes. It's a meal that is only possible during that short and sweet period when everything is at peak flavor, so it can't be missed.

Her focus this morning has been diverted from the garden to the charred remains of the tobacco shed. Some of the wood is still giving off heat from the intense fire. Something is terribly wrong. Hopefully she'll see Lew and find out before having to leave for work. She's barely started aerating the cabbage row with the hoe when Lew steps out of the house. His hands are in his pockets and he's looking down. No coffee for Jewel and no treat for Bibi although the optimistic pup keeps dancing around expecting him to remember how this morning ritual works. Jewel looks at Lew, whose eyes are red from lack of sleep. *Holy crap, this situation could be as bad as it looks.* As he approaches, she steps out of the garden furrow and they hug.

"Okay, Lew, talk to me. What's with that pile of smoldering rubble that used to be your shed? When did that happen? And why didn't you call me?"

Lew turns to look at the remains of the shed. "It's complicated. I didn't call because I remembered that last night was your weekly study group at the museum. Besides, there was nothing you could do. Except worry, and I do enough of that for both of us. There's a lot I need to tell you." He fills her in on what he learned from Evie about the unholy alliance between the Province and the Russian mob.

"It appears they decided that burning the shed is the best way to convince me to sell Free Haven. I mean, why mess with legalities when arson and threatening someone's life and family is so much easier?" He doesn't go into Evie's disclosures related to their family. There's a time and place for that, and it's not here and now.

"This has become a much more dangerous situation, Jewel. It starts with torching the shed. Next, maybe it's the barn, but it could be the house. Every threat gets closer and more dangerous to Amy and me. And to people we care about, like you."

"Hell, Lew, don't worry about me. My family and our people have spent a lot of years dealing with cross burnings, house burnings, all kinds of intimidation. Lynching's are not a thing of the past, you know. I'm not inviting anything, but I'm not running either."

"I feel the same way, for myself. But I have to think of Amy. She saw them set the fire. She was here by herself. Thank God the guys who did this didn't know she was here. All things considered, this time we were lucky. I don't know how far I can push my luck. I'm supposed to respond to a district court subpoena in St. Louis next week, but I can't take Amy with me and I can't possibly leave her here alone."

"But you can't ignore a subpoena, Lew. Hell, they'll come and arrest you! What's the subpoena for, anyway?"

"It's Nora's family. They're suing for custody of Amy. That's one of the reasons I had to get her out of St. Louis in the first place. They want everything. They want to destroy me."

"Ease up, Lew. I don't see how they can they get custody of Amy. You are her father. That doesn't make sense."

"It's just one of a number of ways I have stupidly dropped the ball. Nora and I never officially married. I wanted to, but she had a thing about not needing a marriage license to legitimize things. Anyway, suffice it to say I was too trusting and failed to watch out for my own best interests, which with Nora's death became Amy's best interests. Nora's family hated me from the start. I was never good enough. They are determined to take Amy away. But what I failed to do before I won't again. I'm not letting Amy go."

"I'm sorry, Lew. I'm no lawyer, but it seems to me that ignoring a subpoena is only going to make things worse for you. Why can't you just take Amy with you?"

Lew looks down and kicks the dirt, "Because Jewel! Because I can't be sure that once she's in St. Louis and she's offered the opportunity, she won't want to stay and live with them. It's too damned risky!"

"Okay, Lew, calm down, I get it. I can't believe she would do that, but I understand, you can't take her to St. Louis with you. So, you can leave her with me and Momma. Or I can stay at the house while you're gone. It will be good for her. It's a good time and way for me and Amy to finally get acquainted."

Lew shakes his head. "No. I'm sorry, Jewel. As much as I appreciate your offer, Amy refuses to stay with anyone. She broke down crying when I mentioned it last night. She begged me not to leave her."

"Oh, come on, give *yourself* a break," she says. "Don't you think you've coddled her long enough? The longer she isolates herself, the worse it gets, and you're aiding and abetting her isolation and bad behavior. It's time for that girl to get her head on straight and help you. It's time she stopped playing you, Lew. You're the parent here."

Suddenly red in the face, Lew turns. "So, you're saying my twelve-year old daughter, who has lost her mother and then was jerked out of the only home she's known is playing me?"

"Like a one-string country banjo. News flash – young girls know how to play daddy for what they want. And frankly,

I think you've been confusing grief and displacement with textbook teenage manipulation and rebellion long enough."

Lew looks away, then turns back, visibly agitated. "Well, thanks for that, Miss Know-It-All on parenting and psychology. But *no* thanks! Just . . . just . . . You know something, Jewel, I'm damned tired of people keeping things from me like I'm the village idiot. And then telling me what's good for me, what's good for my daughter and how I should be raising her. If you want to help me with this, then just butt out."

Jewel steps back, raises her eyebrows and purses her lips in her own slow burn. She drops the hoe. "C'mon, Bibi, let's us butt the hell out." She stomps away to her van, follows Bibi inside, slams the door and spins her wheels, throwing gravel as she bolts out of the drive. Lew watches Jewel speed away, then turns and heads down to the river to walk off some of his anger.

So, Amy's playing me, huh. Really, Jewel?! What the hell is this? It's like everything and everybody has turned on me. From the time we arrived here, nothing has been what it appears to be. Everybody has a secret, another side, another face. Even Nora. Even Mom. But no, that's not true. That's Mom according to what they say. No wonder she left. Like she always said, she escaped. I get it now. Well screw them. Screw them all!

No one can tell him about his mom. Christy was the one person he could count on. Her love was fierce and unconditional. Just like her determination to protect him and keep him close. Lew understands a lot better now why she left this place. It wasn't about shame or rejection at all. She left to protect herself, to protect him, and to keep the two of them together. It's exactly what he's been trying to do for himself and Amy. Standing alone with only the background sounds of the morning, Lew can hear his mom, "Lew. . . son . . . I told you so. You've got to protect yourself. Protect Amy. Don't trust anyone. Free yourself from this place. Nothing good ever comes from here."

LEW WALKS BACK INTO THE HOUSE AND SEES AMY AT the kitchen table, Purry on her lap. She's having her morning root beer, which Lew had put out for her. Straight, no milk. "Good morning sweetie. You're up early."

"Yeah, there was all this noise outside. I thought something else might be getting set on fire."

Lew sits across from her, absorbing one of her tuned-out stares where she's looking at him but not seeing him. "Sorry we disturbed you. Jewel and I had a small disagreement about the garden. It's no big deal." As always, he wonders what Amy actually heard of that exchange.

"I've made a decision," he says. "After our conversation last night, I want you to get your things together and go with me to St. Louis."

Amy suddenly breaks out of the stare and looks at Lew with a big smile. "Really, Daddy?" She's up instantly and hugging Lew, Purry snuggled tight between them.

"Thank you, Daddy. Thank you, thank you. I'll go pack right now." She turns to go into her middle room bedroom.

"Wait. Stop right there, young lady." She stops in her tracks and return to the table, suddenly quite the obedient daughter. "First," he says, "I want you to have your breakfast. And then I want you to pack all that you will need for a while. I'm not sure right now how long we'll be gone. Now then, what do you want for breakfast?" She's smiling and almost jumping in her seat, which makes him smile too.

"Cheerios! I want Cheerios," she says.

"Great, me too."

JEWEL HAS BEEN ROLLING THE MORNING DUST-UP with Lew over and over in her mind. She swings back and forth. *Damn, damn, damn, I just had to open my big mouth. Whyyyyy, do I do that? But damned if it wasn't overdue. I should have spoken up long ago. He is so naïve about that girl. Isn't he? But who am I to say anything? Not like I've raised a kid like Amy. Hell, I haven't raised any kid. Maybe I'm the naïve one here?* No matter how much she justifies and rationalizes, more than anything she just wants to make things right with Lew. But how does she do that now?

It's like she has been in love with Lew forever. From that summer as pre-teens when he kissed her by the river and slipped his hand under her shirt, to their current lovemaking at the river, there's never really been another serious love interest in her life. By comparison, that short delusional detour with Kwaku meant nothing. Yet she has to admit, she knows so little about Lew himself. She knows about his family, his mom, and that they were both born under the same roof. She knows about the dead wife and her hideous family trying to take his daughter. She's getting agitated just thinking about it all. *How the hell can I know so much about someone and yet so little. It's like, every time I think there's a breakthrough, it's just another breakdown. This Jekyll/Hyde thing that happens to him when he's threatened or angry is bewildering, and so maddening. He becomes a completely different person. If only I knew how to help him make things right. Geez, if only I could get him to trust me.*

She's putting some books back on the shelf in the geography section of the small museum library when she hears Bibi whining. Her phone is vibrating in her desk drawer. Bibi alerts her whenever someone is calling. She answers. It's Evie Anderson.

"Hi Jewel, have you talked to Lew this morning. Do you know about Lew's shed burning?"

"Yeah, I was over there this morning. I couldn't believe that charred pile of ash used to be the shed. But making matters worse, Lew and I got into a tiff over his daughter. I should have kept my mouth shut, but I've never been any good at that."

"Sorry, Jewel. Any chance you can swing by here when you're off work? You and I need to put our heads together about Lew's situation and the danger he and Amy are in."

"Yeah, we need to work on this together. Lew needs help and frankly, so do I. I mean, I have no idea how to help him. Are you okay about meeting in your office?"

"Yes, I am now," Evie says. "I'll explain when I see you.'

"Okay, I'll close up for lunchtime and come right over."

JEWEL PULLS UP IN THE SMALL PARKING LOT BEHIND the *Cloch County Times*. She cracks the windows open so she can leave Bibi in the van while she goes up to talk to Evie. Evie is finishing what sounds like a very official call when Jewel arrives and she motions her in. Jewel stops in the office doorway while Evie finishes the call. "Yes, yes, I understand . . . yes. No, I won't . . . yes of course. I'll wait to hear from you . . . I assure you, nothing in the paper until I get the okay from you." She sets her phone down.

"Ah, Jewel, come in, come in, sit. I'll explain that call to you in a minute. Where's the pooch?"

"She's been whining and fussy all day, so I just left her in the car. She can be such a pain some days. Can we talk about Lew, Evie? I'm really at a loss for what to do."

Evie tells Jewel about reading Christy's letters and how much more of the story there is about her father and the women in his life, including her aunt Martha. Jewel sits transfixed, then shakes her head.

"You know, Evie, this fills out a lot of the story that my momma told Lew, about when Christy was rejected by her family and taken in by my grandmother. Lew and I both learned that he was born in our house, actually in my bedroom. There's always so much more to these stories. I understand better now why my momma is so careful about the things she knows and shares."

Evie nods. "All of this had to be closely guarded information. Back then, but even now, a scandal of this order could destroy lives. It could definitely devastate a news operation in a small community. While I know that a scandal would have badly tarnished my father's career, in the end, it's always the woman who bears the brunt of consequences of an affair. Of course, in this instance, my father paid a dear price for his indiscretion. I always believed that it was Owen Ducker who killed my dad. Not because of what he wrote about the Klan but out of jealousy. But now, after reading Christy's letters about Aunt Martha and my dad and all her threats, I have to wonder if she was the one who pulled the trigger."

Jewel leans forward, "I hear you, Evie. But at this point, the ill-pursued passions of those no longer with us are less important than some very much alive and threatened people we care about. These Russian mafia characters have to be our biggest worry right now. I only know about half of what's going on with them. Lew told me a little, but then we got way off track when I opened my stupid mouth about Amy."

Evie begins filling Jewel in on all that she has learned about the Russian mafia and the larger conspiracy around the efforts to acquire Free Haven. And about their intentions of running military grade armaments to hate groups. "That call I was on when you came in was with Agent Barrow from the Bureau of Alcohol, Tobacco, Firearms and Explosives. I contacted the FBI in Tulsa, who put me in touch with the ATFE because this situation is within their jurisdiction. Within two hours of the call, Agent Barrow was sitting where you are. To my relief, he informed me that the ATFE has been monitoring the movement and actions of Peter Umanoff and the Brooklyn mafia for a while. I connected him with a source of mine who has been able to give them the direct evidence they've been needing to close in on Umanoff and his thugs."

Jewel shakes her head. "I'm trying to wrap my brain around the idea of Cloch County being at the center of an international incident. It's like we're the Ukraine of the West."

"There's a reason why the most sinister elements in the world choose the most unlikely places. When you think about it, there is a certain logic, given the number and variety of hate groups in Missouri and Arkansas. The Klan has come to seem like a genteel civic organization compared to some of the others. But the lid is off now, and things are going to start happening fast. The situation is volatile, and Lew is in the greatest danger right now. Agent Barrow assured me he would get some of his agents out to protect Lew and his daughter right away. Hopefully he's done that or is in the process. In the meantime, we have to make sure Lew knows that help is on the way, if he doesn't already know. I was hoping you could communicate all this to Lew discreetly, but soon. I need to stay here and coordinate as needed with Agent Barrow. I also have to be careful about who I'm seen with and where, at least for a while."

"Don't worry, Evie, I'll talk to Lew. This a good reason for me to smooth things over from this morning. I'll go see him right now."

"Thanks, Jewel. And please keep the family information to yourself for a while."

As Jewel is leaving, she's startled to see Davis Oakes walk in. She looks at Evie, then back at Davis. "Hi, Davis. Sorry, but I have to run."

"That's fine, Jewel. Lovely seeing you," he says.

Going down the stairs, Jewel thinks it's odd that Davis Oakes would have the combination to Evie's back door lock. She walks to her van and opens the door. Bibi's not there. She calls, "Bibi! Bibi! Where are you? Come here, girl." Someone must have opened the door and let her out. Or, knowing that dog, she's figured out how to let herself out. Jewel pulls her phone out of her purse and calls upstairs to Evie. Her voice mail comes on.

"Sorry to bother you Evie, but Bibi's not in the car. And she hasn't responded to my calling. I'm going to drive around and see if I can find her. If she's scared, she may be trying to find her way home. As soon as I find Bibi, I'll go see Lew."

Upstairs, Evie pours a couple glasses of scotch and hands one to Davis. "Well, old friend, it's a little early in the day for a scotch, but I think a toast to the good ol' ATFE is in order." They clink glasses. "Do you feel that Agent Barrow will be able to protect your identity? I'd hate to see you go into witness protection."

Davis laughs. "Better witness protection than concrete slippers at the bottom of Tablerock Lake. But I think we were as discreet as possible, and the Feds are pros. They know when one of their informants needs protection. They've spent a lot of years dealing with the Klan."

"Do you think Owen will suspect you? I mean besides him and those two idiot sons of his, only you and June were in the know about the arms deal with the Russian mob."

"Hard to say. Frankly, I think he'll suspect June before me. But there are as many possible informants on Peter's side as ours. Owen most likely would assume it's one of them. I'm not worried . . . yet. The way things have turned out, I'm glad Lew refused to sell Free Haven to me. Knowing what we know now it would have been impossible for me to keep the mafia out without exposing myself. Don't know how I would have dealt with that."

"Well, fortunately, you don't have to figure it out. It's unlikely that you would have uncovered the treasure that the old place has turned out to be. I'm still amazed that there was an Underground Railroad operation here in Cloch County."

"I know. It's historic, isn't it? Oh yeah – I ran into a woman by the name of Jane Henderson in the courthouse before coming over here. She was there checking some records and said she needed to see Lew about some family business. Nice lady, very elegant. I offered to take her out to Free Haven. Agent Barrow told me that he was setting up a security detail out there. I'm kinda curious to see if he's done that. Right now, Lew and his daughter are the most at risk. Burning that shed rattled me big time. That wasn't part of any plan that I knew about. Those Brooklyn characters operate on a whole different level."

"Right you are, Davis. And it's all the more reason you have to be careful. I want you to call and let me know what you see when you get out there. Jewel was going directly to see Lew and bring him up to date on everything. So at least he won't be alarmed seeing those big black unmarked ATFE cars coming up his driveway."

Davis nods and gently twirls the scotch in his glass. "Well, Evie, when we get through this ordeal, I mean safely through, I want out. It's time. Nope, it's past time."

Evie turns to Davis, "Excuse me, you want out? What exactly are you saying?"

"Oh no, Evie," he smiles sheepishly. "I'm not talking about us. I mean the Klan. I don't want to do it anymore. I can't do it anymore. Fact is, I would have shed that snakeskin a while ago if Sheldon hadn't died. But if these ATFE boys clean this mess out, then I can walk away in good conscience."

Evie nods, "I understand. You've done your duty, above and beyond. Fact is, I want to see you out of that cesspool. I'd feel a lot better about being seen with you in public," she laughs.

Davis puts his glass down and turns to her, "And that's exactly what I'm talking about Evie. I want us to be seen together, to be open. I want to have a real relationship. I'd like for us to talk about, I don't know, maybe even getting married."

Evie puts her glass down, "Well you romantic old dog you. I hope you don't think that qualifies as a proposal. But yeah, I think we're both ready for a change." She reaches over and takes his hand. "For now, dear heart, please get out to Lew's and make sure my brother and niece are going to be alright. We'll pick this conversation up later." She lifts her glass, he picks his up, they clink glasses and then lean in and kiss.

TWENTY-ONE

J EWEL HAS DRIVEN AROUND EVERY BLOCK IN THE area a couple times and there's no sign of Bibi. It's likely that she is on her way home. One other time when she got loose from the museum, Jewel eventually found her at home. Right now, she's concerned about alerting Lew to what's happening as she promised Evie. She decides to brave a call and hope he'll answer.

LEW HAS PACKED HIS THINGS AND IS IN THE KITCHEN making sandwiches. He goes out the back door to pick some fresh lettuce for their sandwiches and some other vegetables for snacking. Enough of the season's lettuces are hanging on. Radishes are getting bitter but are still good. The tomatoes and bell peppers are at their best. He scans the garden for the best – there's still plenty left for the animals. Amy's bag is packed and on her bed. So are the books and journals she pores over most of the time. Lew's phone rings on the kitchen counter while he's stalking tomatoes in the garden. He strides up the back steps and into the kitchen and starts washing the vegetables in the sink. His phone dings – he missed a call. He dries his hands and picks up the phone. It's Jewel, and there's a message:

"Hi Lew, it's me. Listen, I'm really sorry about this morning. I was way off base sticking my nose where it doesn't belong. We need to talk, but Bibi got loose from my car and I have to find her. I'm sure she's on her way home. As soon as I find her, I'll come over. And if you see her let me know. She loves your treats, and she really loves you, Lew."

Lew tucks his phone in his shirt pocket, shaking his head. *A little late Jewel.* He turns back to washing the lettuce and vegetables, then dabs them with a towel to dry.

"Amy," he says loudly, "Are you about ready? As soon as I get lunch packed up, we're out of here." Suddenly, there's a loud bang on the front door. Stepping into the living room, he sees a black SUV speeding out of the driveway. He opens the front door, takes one step out and looking down catches his breath. It's Bibi's bloodied and lifeless body. Her throat has been slashed, and her fur is soaked and matted with blood. He falls back against the doorframe, horrified by the sight of the mutilated pup. His phone dings and vibrates in his shirt pocket. It's a text.

STRIKE 2 LEW
DON'T BE A FOOL

Davis Oakes returns to the recording office in the courthouse where Jane Henderson has been studying Free Haven records and filling a notepad with dates, names, and other details. The recording secretary, Pat O'Neill, has been helping her locate a number of other files and records. Davis taps on the side of the door to get her attention.

"I'm back, Ms. Henderson. Anytime you're ready, I can run you out to Free Haven. I'm pretty sure Lew Harra is out there now."

"Thank you, Mr. Oakes. I've one more thing to check here and then I'll be ready to go."

On the way to his Jeep Cherokee, Davis turns. "If you don't mind my asking, Ms. Henderson, what is your interest in Free Haven? Is it related to the historic landmark status?"

"Uh, no. I'm here on family business. Nora Henderson's family. You may know, she was legal counsel to Lew Harra's uncle, Sheldon O'Hara. She was killed in an automobile accident a while ago and I'm here just trying to tie up a number of loose ends."

"I see, I'm sorry for your family's loss. I sure didn't know that ol' Sheldon had legal counsel. But then there's a lot I didn't know about him."

"You know, Mr. Oakes, I've never been in this part of the state. It's really beautiful. As a county commissioner, you must know a lot about the area. Can you tell me a little about it?"

"Well, that just happens to be my favorite subject . . ."

Four more of Agent Barrow's ATFE officers have arrived from Memphis, which will allow his on-the-ground team to both close in on the Brooklyn mobsters and provide protection to Lew Harra, Davis Oakes, and others who have been cooperating. They are coordinating their movements with the combined ATFE and FBI teams in Brooklyn, who are preparing to raid the Russian mob's headquarters there. The feds are hoping to collar two Russian agents who have been negotiating the arms deal for the mysterious oligarch. This has been a long time in the making and a lot can go wrong.

Agent Barrow is moving more carefully and slowly than he normally would, but he also understands that a lot is at stake. He calls Evie to let her know his team is full strength and he can now provide security to Lew and to Davis. She tells him that his men will likely find Davis out at Free Haven with Lew. He immediately dispatches two units of two officers each to Free Haven to secure that location and provide Davis Oakes with security once he arrives there.

Lew looks again at Bibi's bloodied and twisted body. He's practically paralyzed with shock. He can't let Amy see this. And Jewel – what about Jewel? Dear God, how she adores this dog. He's to blame, because this warning is aimed directly at him. And they've upped the ante of violence. The Klan and the mob are getting closer and more threatening. He doesn't want to think about what a strike three might mean. But he doesn't plan to wait around for it. He puts his phone down on the small table by the door and runs to the back bedroom. He fumbles through the closet and finds one of Sheldon's heavy denim work shirts. Emerging from the bedroom, he sees Amy sitting on her bed. Her suitcase is all packed and on the floor next to the bed. As always, Purry is tucked under her arm.

"I'm ready," she says. "What's with all the running?"

He stops. "Stay right where you are. I'm locking the front door. We'll go out the back. Stay right here and don't move until I come back."

Lew wraps Bibi's body in the shirt and is about to carry the bundle off the porch when he looks up and sees Davis Oakes' Jeep Cherokee turn onto the drive. He quickly steps back inside the door, closes it and watches as Davis pulls up and stops in front of the house. Someone else is in the car, on the passenger side next to Davis. Lew immediately recognizes Jane Henderson.

Of course. That wretched Henderson family is in league with the Klan and the mafia. Anything to destroy me and take Amy. He looks up again as two black SUVs pull on to the drive. *Dear God, they're back. The mobsters are back. I've got to get Amy out of here, and fast.* He closes and locks the door, then runs into the middle room where Amy is resting on the bed clutching Purry. "We're leaving, right now!" he says reaching out for her. "Leave everything. We have to get out, right now! Down to the cellar." Amy holds Purry tight as Lew leads the way down the stairs to the cellar.

Lew is so panicked that the irony of using the runaway slaves' path to freedom doesn't hit him. What matters now is that this is the only safe escape route. At the bottom of the cellar stairs, he grabs the three keys hanging together by the stairs and darts into the secret room. He closes and locks the door behind. Then he opens the tunnel door and grabs the flashlight to lead the way through. He locks that door behind, putting a second barrier between them and their pursuers. His mind is reeling, but he focuses only on getting out as fast as possible. Shining the light in front, he follows the path out, into the big cave room, past Uncle Sheldon's still and into the natural tunnel. It finally dawns on Lew how similar what he is doing replicates the runaway slaves' dash for freedom more than a century before. Fear, anger, and a passion to be free from oppressors, however incarnate, commingle and blur. *Get away, whatever it takes. Just get away. Get free.*

DAVIS STEPS UP TO THE FRONT DOOR AS THE TWO ATFE cars pull up and stop in front of the house. He knocks, then looks down to see the bloodied bundle near his feet. There's no answer at the door. He bends over to examine the bundle and grimaces.

"Oh dear God, it's Jewel Bennett's dog," he says aloud to himself. He wraps the shirt back over Bibi's body. "Uh, stay down there, Ms. Henderson," he says. "Just give me a minute." He peers through the glass door into the living room and middle room. He knocks on the door. Lew is nowhere in sight and the door is locked. He goes back down the front steps to talk to the ATFE officers who have emerged from their SUV's. He fears that they've all arrived too late. At that moment, Jewel's van comes speeding up the drive. She skids to a stop and quickly jumps out.

"Davis, where's Lew? Who are these people? I have to talk to Lew!" She turns to run up the front stairs.

Davis stops her. "Jewel, wait! No one appears to be in the house. And Jewel, you don't want to see what's on the porch. Let me . . . "

"Oh my God, what, Davis? What have they done to Lew?"

"No, not Lew. I'm afraid it's your dog," he says. Jewel's face distorts in anguish. She runs up the stairs and kneels beside the bloodied shirt. She opens it and sees Bibi's lifeless body. She lets out an agonizing cry, "Bibi! Bibi! My sweet baby! My God, my God, what have they done?! What have they done?!" She bends over, rocking and sobbing.

Jane ascends the stairs and kneels next to Jewel, trying to comfort her. Davis talks to the officers, explaining the burned shed and now the mutilated dog. He's afraid that the Brooklyn thugs have Lew and Amy. One of the officers turns and goes to his car to radio Agent Barrow about what they've found.

Jewel sits back, tears streaming down her face. She looks in the house, then at Jane and down at Davis. "Lew didn't answer? He's not here?" Davis shakes his head. Jewel takes out her phone and dials Lew. She can hear his phone ringing inside on the table next to the door.

"I hate to say it, Jewel," Davis says. "I'm afraid the mobsters may have them."

"Unless . . ." Jewel says. "I think I know where they could be."

Jane looks confused. "They? Who's with Lew?"

"Lew and Amy," Jewel says. "I believe I know where they've run to."

"You don't mean Lew and Nora's daughter Amy?"

"Yes, of course. Lew's daughter Amy."

"But Amy died in the car accident with her mother."

Jewel's mouth falls open. "What? Amy's . . . dead!?"

"Yes," Jane says emphatically. "I don't know what Lew has told you, but Amy and Nora were both killed instantly in that car crash. I think . . . "

Jewel interrupts. "I have to find Lew!" She stands and runs down the steps and around to the outside bulkhead, where she pulls open the door to the cellar. In the cellar she tries the door to the secret room. It's locked and the three keys are gone confirming her suspicion. Lew has escaped through the secret room and tunnel. He locked it behind him.

She returns to the front of the house, "Davis, keep everyone here. I think I know where to find Lew, but he'll panic if he sees all of you." Jewel knows that the tunnel leads to Luna's Leap and the path down to the river. If Lew got away, that's where she'll find him.

She runs down to a path alongside the river. About thirty yards downstream, it forks. One path continues following the river, and the other winds its way up to Luna's Leap. These are both paths that Jewel knows well and has walked many times in her life – but never with such a sense of urgency and fear. The path up to Luna's Leap along this way is steep and rocky. It's a challenge to traverse in the best of conditions, but much harder in her work clothes and beige pumps.

As Jewel nears the last thirty feet of the steep path, she sees Lew standing at the point of Luna's Leap. She climbs another ten feet and stops so she won't startle him.

"Lew, it's me. It's Jewel," she says, winded from the climb. "Thank God I've found you. I was so worried." Lew turns toward her. She can see tracks of tears down his cheeks. He's clutching Purry, the stuffed kitten, to his chest.

"Jewel. You look nice. I'm so sorry about Bibi. So sorry," he sobs. "I'm not going back, Jewel. I'm not giving up. I'm not letting them take Amy. They can't have my baby."

"Nobody wants to take you, or Amy, Lew. They want to help. I want to help. And Lew, you need help. We all need help. I hope you still need me. I love you, Lew."

Lew smiles. "I love you too, Jewel. You've been the only bright spot in our lives for quite a while. Amy and I both love you. But . . . it's too late. Too much has happened. Too much is lost. I can't start over. Not again. My baby wants to go home." He turns and looks out over the river below.

"Lew! No, not that! Please don't. Please! Lew!"

Clutching Purry to his chest with both hands, Lew looks up at the sky, closes his eyes – and falls forward.

TWENTY-TWO

T HE DAY AFTER LEW'S DEATH, ATFE AGENTS arrest Peter Umanoff and two of his henchmen while they are having lunch at O'Byrne's Irish Diner with Owen Ducker and June Eastman. They charge all five with multiple counts of conspiracy. Simultaneously, four of Agent Barrow's officers arrest Jerry Lloyd and Ernest Ducker at their father's compound headquarters and secure all the computers and files for evidence. In Brooklyn, federal agents move on the Russian mafia headquarters in Little Odessa and arrest a dozen mob members and one of the two Russian agents. That raid also yields a significant amount of evidence.

A MONTH LATER JANE HENDERSON RETURNS TO Cloch County from St. Louis. She has asked Jewel, Berta, Evie and Davis to meet with her at Free Haven. They all gather in the living room. On the table where Lew set up the record logs from the secret room, Jane has placed an urn with Lew's ashes and Purry, the stuffed cat, next to it. She stands beside the table, facing the small group. Evie and Davis are on the couch, Berta and Jewel are side by side in two dining chairs. Jane is in her official attorney attire, dark gray pant suit, peach blouse, pearl necklace and earrings. With her dark gray suede heels, she stands about six feet tall. She is quite attractive with her short-cropped, prematurely silver hair and thin, black wire-rimmed glasses. As Davis noted at first meeting, she is an elegant woman, likely late thirties. She seems to maintain a constant unrevealing smile.

"Thank you all for coming here today. There are several things that I want to share with you – some legal, some purely informational. Primarily I am here as the legal representative of the late Nora Henderson and the Henderson family. I am also the wife of Nora Henderson, or I guess I should say that I am the widow."

That information engenders startled looks in the room. Berta leans into Jewel. "What does she mean? Isn't she a *she*?"

Jewel pats her mom's shoulder. "Shh, I'll explain it later, Momma. It's complicated." Jewel herself didn't think anything could surprise her anymore, and yet . . .

Jane continues. "I think some information would be helpful in putting the legal matters into proper context. I know that you already know some, perhaps a lot, of what I'm going to relate. Just bear with me because it's all relevant and necessary to cover.

"First of all, I want you to know that I am not a homewrecker. Lew and Nora got together as undergraduates in college. They had one child, Amy. But they never married. Nora was ambivalent about her sexuality early on and was leery of a marital commitment that she might not be able to keep. She also had doubts about her and Lew's relationship from the start. Lew was extremely insecure and possessive of Nora's attentions. He actually admitted to her that he deliberately sabotaged their birth control, resulting in an unplanned pregnancy. When Amy was born, he doted excessively on her, to such a degree at one point he quit a good job so he could spend more time with her.

"When the two split about three years ago, Nora took Amy to live with her. Nora and Lew agreed on shared custody, but Lew consistently failed to observe the agreed-upon terms. When his mom died just over two years ago, he took it really hard, and his behaviors grew increasingly erratic. Nora became concerned about Amy's welfare with Lew and revoked the custody arrangement. Then Lew's outbursts and threatening calls forced her to get a restraining order. Suffice it to say, it was a far less ideal relationship than Lew may have related to you.

"Nora and I met shortly after the two of them split up. I was a rookie and she a senior officer in the public defender's office in St. Louis. I was assigned to her as legal assistant and, well, it was love at first sight. We quietly dated for a year and then, when it became legal, we got married. Amy and I hit it off from the very beginning. Marrying the woman I loved, taking her name and making a home for us was a dream come true for me. And to instantly have such a sweet and wonderful daughter like Amy? Well, I never wanted more.

"But what was a dream for me proved to be a nightmare for Lew. Nora came out to him about our relationship and marriage. Given his still shaky mental state after losing his mom and the conflicts with Nora, Lew began having psychotic episodes. And that led to a complete breakdown. Nora and I got him into a treatment facility where he received counseling, medication, and close monitoring. It was a good program and Lew made rapid progress. Nora took Amy to visit him every week.

"Lew completed the program and Nora and I got him a small apartment not far from where we lived. She and I took turns taking Amy to visit him. We assured him we'd pay for the apartment until he got a job and on his feet. And then . . . and then, the accident. Nora and Amy were killed. It was the worst day of my life. The same for Lew. Except with him, I believe it threw him back into a psychotic cycle. His therapist at the treatment center theorizes the same.

"Lew was extremely angry that I ordered the bodies cremated. He screamed and threatened me at the funeral facility. But both Nora and Amy were burned beyond recognition in the accident. He was so overwrought the funeral director brought in special security. Then, Lew offered a compromise. If he were allowed a private sitting and meditation with Nora and Amy, he would not attend the funeral and allow me and Nora's family a peaceful ceremony and interment without his presence. I gladly agreed, considering how on edge everybody would be with Lew there."

"Jane," Jewel interrupts. "I know you're trying to bring some balance to this discussion since all of us had a relationship with Lew and not with you or Nora. To be honest, on the one hand you're doing a lousy job with the balance and on the other hand you're pissing me off."

Berta turns. "Jewel. Your language."

"Sorry, Momma, but Jane needs to hear me out. Granted, there are things none of us knew or understood about Lew. But there's very little in your description of Lew's nature and personality that rings true. Yes, he had us all convinced that Amy was alive. But in retrospect, I would say it was more delusional than psychotic. Lew talked about how horribly Nora's family treated him. Maybe they did, maybe they didn't, but that was his experience. And while Nora may have struggled with her sexual identity, it was Lew who was strung along, wanting to marry her and to be a family and not getting an honest answer until the two of you . . . well, blew him out of the water with your relationship. I can't refute any of what you're saying. Lew had a quick temper, but I never felt threatened by him. He might erupt over something, but then he would quickly calm down and respond thoughtfully to kindness and honesty. Seems to me those were two things sorely missing in Lew's life with Nora and her family."

Evie chimes in. "I agree with Jewel, Jane. Lew was smart and insightful. He was a terrific writer. He was intuitive and empathetic. And yes, he was very sensitive and wore his feelings close to the surface, but he was open and honest about those feelings. I never had to wonder or guess what Lew was thinking. There was a lot in his life that could have easily made him a very different person than he was."

Jane nods, "I hear you. I hear you both. You got to know

a very different Lew than I did. I'm sorry I didn't get to know that Lew. So, I'll get right to the point of all this. Lew was given an hour alone in the funeral chapel with Nora and Amy's remains. Only the funeral staff were in the building and they were very respectful of his time and privacy. It wasn't until late the next day, following the funeral ceremony, that it was discovered – while alone, Lew swapped out the stuffing in Purry with Amy's ashes. By that time, Lew was long gone. It wasn't until I called the county records secretary that I learned Lew was here."

Davis raises his hand. "Excuse me, Ms. Henderson, but I'm trying to understand. Did Lew break the law by taking those ashes? I've never heard of anything quite like this."

"No, Mr. Oakes, he didn't strictly break the law. He did violate Nora's family's wishes to inter Amy with her mother. And please keep in mind, Nora and Lew weren't legally married and he didn't enjoy full parental privileges. Had he broken the law, then yes, he might have been arrested. We petitioned the court in St. Louis to order Lew to return the ashes, but he chose to ignore the court's orders. Please, all of you. I want you to know that neither I nor the Henderson family felt any ill will toward Lew. At most, we wanted peace and closure having lost a beloved daughter, granddaughter and wife."

Davis follows up. "Then the reason you made the trip here was to convince Lew to return Amy's ashes?"

"No, that was not the purpose of my trip, although I was hoping to talk to Lew about that. The purpose of my trip was, and is, to implement provisions put forth in Nora's Last Will and Testament, for which I am personal representative.

"To that end, several years ago, Nora assisted Sheldon O'Hara with a number of legal issues related to Free Haven, his possessions, and relationships. He brought her into his confidence about matters that could not be disclosed until his death. At that time, Mr. O'Hara made a specific request to Nora, as his personal legal representative and as far as he knew a family member, that she transfer the property and certain assets from his name to hers. He confided to her that he was having health issues, and in the event of his death he wanted his wishes to be carried out legally, without question and without reprisal. He didn't feel that he could trust any legal counsel in the area to the same degree as Nora, the wife of his only sister's son."

"So, Jane," Jewell interrupts. "Did Nora happen to mention to Sheldon that she and Lew weren't actually married? Seems like an important detail for a lawyer to mention if that was the basis of being brought into Sheldon's confidence."

"I really don't know, Jewel," Jane says, slightly exasperated. "It may have been an assumption Mr. O'Hara made that didn't even come up. Or if she did mention it, it may not have been as important to him as Nora's legal expertise at the time."

"Seems like a mighty important detail to me," Jewel says under her breath.

Jane quickly turns to Evie. "Ms. Anderson, you are here in part because Mr. O'Hara asked Nora to give you this cassette tape and transcription. On this tape you will find a recording of a private conversation that Mr. O'Hara had with Owen Ducker a few years ago in which Owen confesses to shooting and killing your father. According to Nora's notes,

Mr. O'Hara was deeply troubled that he couldn't give this to you before, but he couldn't do that without compromising his role within the Province."

Evie takes the large envelope from Jane. "I understand. Sheldon walked a tightrope inside the Province. There was a lot at stake for him. But I'm grateful to have my long-held suspicions confirmed . . . for more reasons than I ever imagined." Evie glances at Jewel. "Maybe this along, with federal conspiracy charges, will keep that asshole Owen Ducker out of our lives for a good long while."

Jane turns to Davis. "Mr. Oakes, Mr. O'Hara instructed Nora to transfer his loaned artwork in front of the fire station and the sculpture at the county courthouse to the ownership and specific care, protection, and preservation of the county commission. And I have here a check to the commission in the amount of $10,000 toward a fund for proper upkeep of the artwork." She hands Davis an envelope with certificates of ownership of the two works being transferred and the check.

"That's wonderful, Ms. Henderson. The commissioners and I have already had several conversations about how to care for Sheldon's work. This is a very welcome and appreciated gift to the county."

Jane steps back to her briefcase and plucking two manilla folders from it she continues.

"There are several generations worth of family records, documents, photos and the like, that Mr. O'Hara directed in his Will to go to his nephew Lew. Those records are boxed up in the next room. He also included a check to Lew of ten thousand dollars, that he hoped might be applied toward

Amy's education. But the money is not restricted in any way. In light of current circumstances and new information, the family records and money now transfer to Lew's closest living relative, Evelyn Anderson."

Evie's brow furrows as Jane hands her one of the two files. She opens the file and holds up the check. Her face reddens and lips purse. "Wow, unbelievable! Do you have any idea what this money would have meant to Lew if he'd had it . . ."

"I understand," Jane interrupts, visibly agitated. "But listen, all of you – for months I tried to communicate with Lew. I couldn't call him because he changed his phone number. And when I found out where he was, I wrote letter after letter. And all of my letters went unanswered."

"Of course they went unanswered," Jewel says. "Lew was convinced that you and Nora's family were trying to take Amy from him. You'll find some if not all of your unopened letters in a shoe box underneath the table where Lew stashed them, out of sight, out of mind. He had no reason to trust or believe you were trying to contact him for anything but to take, not give."

Regaining her professional composure, Jane pivots to Jewel holding the remaining folder in both hands. "The most important directive that Sheldon O'Hara entrusted to Nora was this: That upon his death, Free Haven – the house, the property, all of its treasures and all of his remaining worldly possessions therein – is bequeathed to his beloved daughter, Jewel Bennett."

Jewel sits up stunned. "What? Wait. I'm his . . . Uncle Shel is . . . " Jewel looks back and forth from Jane to her mom then pushes her chair away from Berta to face her. "Uncle Shel . .

. is my father?! Momma is this true?! All this time, all my life and you never told me? You kept this from me? How could you do that?! Momma, for God's sake, say something!!"

Berta reaches out toward her daughter. "No, no, Jewel baby. You don't understand. It's complicated, don't you know? And this is private. This is family. We should talk about this at home. People don't need to hear this."

Jewel stands up, turns away, then turns back, her hands clenched at her side and jaw set. "Yes Momma, people do need to hear this. People need to hear the truth. Secrets, Momma! Damned secrets!" she shrieks. She turns to Evie and Jane with her arms out, "Goddamned secrets! Secrets and lies! Lies to hide the secrets! Lies about the lies! Don't you get it? Damned secrets and lies killed Lew! When is it enough!?'

She turns back to Berta, still clenching her fists. "I don't care who knows, Momma. I just don't care. What difference does it make? And how dare you torment me all these years about being dishonest about my life – when you've been so dishonest about yours?" She sits down in her chair, sobbing.

Berta drops her hands to her lap and looks down, "Jewel baby, I'm sorry. Don't you know, Shel and I had to be careful? So very careful. There are people here who can't abide Black and White folks stirring paint in bed. You're right, poor Lew suffered unfairly. But you have to know, the truth gets people killed too. We feared for you and your safety. You know how much Shel loved you. He was proud of you, Jewel baby. He would have loved being a real father to you. But not here. Not in Cloch County."

Jane interjects. "Jewel, I'm sorry you had to learn about Sheldon in this way. I didn't know. It seems that he was a man of conscience but also great caution and concern when it came to loved ones. Mr. O'Hara further bequeathed the amount of ten thousand dollars to Berta Bennett, who was, according to him, the only woman he ever loved. He dictated the following to Nora to read to you:

> *My dearest Berta. You brought light and joy to my life. Every second I spent with you was better than a year without you. I am sorry we were not allowed to live in a kinder and more accepting place. I will always love you. Your Shel.*

Jane places the note in an envelope with a check and hands it to Berta. Jewel moves her chair back closer to her mom, and with a tissue she dabs the tears running down her momma's cheeks.

Jane continues. "Among the things Nora did for Mr. O'Hara was to set up a Trust to hold and handle his art and art sales transactions. She set it up in the name of Mr. O'Hara's artistic persona, Ward Sheldon. Nora agreed to serve as director and de facto artist representative, brokering a number of significant sales. As Nora's personal representative, the director and trusteeship role has been passed to me. Knowing the relationships as I now do, I would like to propose to you, Jewel, that you assume principal trusteeship of the Ward Sheldon Trust and manage and direct the entire estate as you believe your father, Sheldon O'Hara, would want. I will be happy to continue serving as legal counsel as long as you'd like or provide for a transfer to another counsel as you direct."

Jewel nods. "Thanks, Jane. I feel certain that Evie, as the lone surviving family member of Lew's, would be willing to share this responsibility with me." Evie sadly smiles and nods assent.

"Wonderful," Jane says. "The one last thing I want you all to know is that I have had Amy's ashes removed from the stuffed kitten and returned Purry's rightful stuffing. I divided Amy's ashes. Half have been interred with Nora in St. Louis. The other half are commingled in the urn with Lew's. Those remains and Purry will be interred in the O'Hara family cemetery here at Free Haven. I have also authorized and paid to have Christy Harra's remains moved here to be interred next to Lew and Amy.

"With that, be it known to all present that the last Wills and Testaments of Nora Henderson and Sheldon O'Hara are fulfilled and complete." Without another word, Jane places Jewel's folder on the table, closes her large briefcase, turns and exits through the front door.

The room remains silent, everyone deep in their own thoughts. Jewel stands up, tears tracking down her cheeks, and steps over to the doorway. She watches as Jane pulls her bright red Mercedes around the circle drive and heads up the gravel road, stopping briefly before turning left on County Road toward the highway going north.

"Yeah, complete," Jewel says still staring out on the gravel road as the dust settles. "Complete and done. And why not? There's nothing left to hide . . . or hide from," she laughs ironically. "What a strange, strange, twisted place this is. I mean, just think of it. Just think of what we got here today –

property . . . money . . . the truth. But dear God, at what cost? So much lost." She turns back to the others, shaking her head, "I don't understand. I swear, I will never understand." Tears again stream down her cheeks. She wipes them away with the palms of her hands. "Well, I guess if anything good has come out of all this meanness. . . all this sick, twisted meanness . . . it's that Lew, sweet Lew, is finally at peace."

"And Luna," Berta adds. "Luna and Lew, and their babies. They're all at peace."

"Yeah, Momma. Luna and Lew. . . yeah. Damn!"

Berta whispers, "It's amen, baby girl. Amen."

EPILOGUE

Cloch County, Missouri, May 2019

EXCUSE ME, ERIN, I NEED A MINUTE." ERIN Oakes nods and turns off her recorder. Jewel stands.

"Attention, please. Those of you with tickets for the 2:30 tour of Free Haven Underground Railroad Way Station and Library, please follow Jeff through the door on the right outside to the van." She sits back down. "Thanks. Now, where were we?"

Erin smiles and turns her recorder back on. "You were going to tell me about the new Sheldon O'Hara Sculpture Park."

IT TOOK JEWEL, EVIE, AND JANE LESS THAN A YEAR to change the name of the Ward Sheldon Trust to the Sheldon O'Hara Trust and officially affix Sheldon's name to all of his artwork. Soon thereafter, Jewel transferred the ownership of the Free Haven house, Sheldon's workshop barn and property to the Trust. At that time, the Cloch County Historic Museum and the Sheldon O'Hara Trust entered into an affiliate agreement, making the Free Haven Underground Railroad Way Station and Library an official museum annex. With the assistance of several National Underground Railroad scholars and curators, the annex opened to visitors and tour groups in the fall of 2018. The curators trained four docents, including Jewel's nephew Jeff, to conduct guided tours and oversee the site and collection at Free Haven. Upon graduation from Cloch County High School this spring, Jeff received a scholarship to attend the University of Missouri, Columbia, and study art history and museum management under Dr. Janet Field.

That same fall, the county commissioners, led by presiding commissioner Davis Oakes, renamed Founder's Park in the Cloch Village Center, "O'Hara Freedom Park." The park's new name was inaugurated with the unveiling of a Sheldon O'Hara sculpture donated to the County by Lowell and Janet Field. The Fields donated their two Sheldon O'Hara sculptures, *River Life* and *Cloch Children,* to the permanent collection of the New Visionary Museum in North Carolina.

The sculpture in the park, entitled *Beings Move, Spirits Merge,* stands ten feet tall and is made of two six-inch metal pipes–one black, the other white–intertwining halfway up, then becoming a single twelve-inch gray pipe atop. And at the top the pipe splays open like a large, ever-blooming flower. Davis made a point of placing a small plaque with the name of the work and artist attribution at all of the O'Hara sculptures now owned by the county.

"I'm pleased to give you a scoop, Erin. We are holding the grand opening of the Sheldon O'Hara Sculpture Park on the fifty acres surrounding the Free Haven Underground Railroad Way Station and Library next Saturday. The park features trails leading to twenty of Sheldon's works, several never before seen. Most of the work has been stored in the workshop barn or was donated or loaned by local folks who have sculptures that Sheldon made for them. And – *annnnd,* we have established a fund with a seed contribution from Dr. Lowell and Dr. Janet Field to acquire and commission artwork by visionary artists of diverse backgrounds, especially women and Black artists."

"That is so exciting, Jewel," Erin says. As she places her hand on Jewel's forearm, the small gray mutt at Jewel's feet raises up. *Rrrrruff, ruff.*

Jewel places her hand on the pup's head. "Hush, DeeDee, you know better than that." The small dog looks up at Jewel and quietly sits. Then she perks up her ears at a gleeful sound and stands. "Mommy, Mommy!" Jewel picks up the little girl and puts her on her lap. "Baby girl, shhh, use your inside voice."

"Mommy, I had stasho iscream. Pretty green."

"You had what?"

Evie and Davis step up. "She had *pistachio ice cream,*"

Evie says. "We just had to have some ice cream after all our exploring."

Erin stands to leave. "Thanks, Jewel, I have plenty for my story. I have a sudden craving for some stasho iscream."

"Thanks, Erin. I appreciate your time and helping us get the word out about the grand opening of the sculpture park." She turns to the toddler on her lap. "So, baby girl, besides eating and wearing some pretty green ice cream, what else did you do with Aunt Evie and Uncle Davis?"

Evie holds her hands up and shrugs with a *guilty as charged* look. "We took Lewella up to Luna's Leap to see the new headstone marker for Gramma Christy next to Daddy Lew and Sister Amy's marker. And that little marker you put up there for Bibi is really sweet."

Lewella looks up at her momma and smiles from dimple to dimple, evoking Jewel's own whole-face smile. That sweet smile, her olive skin, and electric blue eyes are constant reminders to Jewel of time and places too soon lost. Lewella points to Evie's bag. "I show Daddy and Sister Purr-Kitty."

Evie pulls a small stuffed cat out of her bag and hands it to Lewella. "Yes, you did. But I had to put Purr-Kitty in my bag so she wouldn't eat Lewella's ice cream."

"Thanks, Evie. This is now her favorite stuffed animal. I still can't believe you found a stuffed cat that looks so much like you-know-who."

Davis interjects, "Lew's and his mom's markers match up really good, Jewel. Nice job. In fact, the whole cemetery looks really beautiful now, especially with the sculpture of Luna and Baby Dawn that you found in the barn. People are putting lots of flowers around it."

"That's wonderful. I'm so glad to hear that," Jewel says. "Are you ready to go see Gramma Berta, baby girl?" Jewel looks up at Evie. "Are you good to close up?"

"Yep, we'll wait until Jeff's last tour group checks back in, then shoo everyone out and lock the shop down. Not to worry."

"Thanks, both of you, for everything. And when you get everybody out of here, don't do anything I wouldn't do," Jewel says, smiling at Lewella.

From the Author

The Three Keys is a work of fiction. Free Haven, the river Saoirse and the county setting are all inspired by my maternal grandmother's family homestead in Stone County, Missouri. And while a number of the characters in the story are likewise inspired by family and friends, all in this story are fictional characters and relationships.

There are many to thank for helping me bring this story to life. First, my love and gratitude to my wife Mary, who refused to let me quit this project. Her encouragement and critical eye shines on every page. Thanks to my good friend Danny Miles, whose gentle prodding and non-judgmental criticism nudged me through a number of writing blocks.

My love and thanks to a great circle of incredibly helpful readers, including Karen Witherspoon, Cathie Thomas, Susan Cartwright, Kathy Scaletty, Karen Jernigan Fischer, Nancy Trovillion, Jim Wallace, Matthew Lombardy and Suzanne Fetscher. A special thank you to PJ Casey, for your timely butt-kick to "get 'er done."

My sincere thanks to: Emily Colin for your generosity and expertise regarding the various dimensions of publishing; Catherine Holecko, for your many insightful content suggestions and thoughtful editing; Greg Rupel and your Enchanted Ink Publishing team, for your outstanding formatting designs and patience; and, Krystal Tibbs, my resourceful and resilient illustrator for the splendid cover art.

Nello McDaniel

Nello McDaniel and his wife Mary live in Downtown Brooklyn, New York. He is the founder and director of ARTS Action Research, an arts management consulting business, serving performing, exhibiting and literary arts organizations in the U.S. and internationally. He has worked at Western States Arts Federation, Denver, Colorado, and the National Endowment for the Arts, Washington, D.C. Nello is a Fulbright International Scholar and has authored and published more than a dozen books and special report publications related to the arts and artist-led organizations. Originally from Springfield in the Missouri Ozarks, Nello and his wife met as dance students at Stephens College in Columbia, Missouri. He loves to cook, read, write and dance. He and his wife attend many theater and dance events and love to travel.

WWW.NELLOMCDANIEL.COM